Dying Art

Joe Kilgore

Dying Art

A Brig Ellis Saga

Addison & Highsmith

Addison & Highsmith Publishers
Las Vegas ◊ Oxford ◊ Palm Beach

Published in the United States of America by
Histria Books, a division of Histria LLC
7181 N. Hualapai Way, Ste. 130-86
Las Vegas, NV 89166 USA
HistriaBooks.com

Addison & Highsmith is an imprint of Histria Books. Titles published under the imprints of Histria Books are distributed worldwide.

Library of Congress Control Number: 2021931440

ISBN 978-1-59211-091-9 (hardcover)

To old friends, and good memories.

They say when you're dead, you're gone.
Seems that's something else they got wrong.

Prologue

Monroe Greenberg was once a living, breathing, functioning human being. Now, he is quite literally a rather large saguaro cactus. The fluted columnar stem that centers him is a mixture of what Monroe used to refer to as his prominent belly and love handles. The branches that curve skyward in that iconographic Southwestern pose are various bits of Monroe's internal organs plus his pelvis and metatarsals. The creamy white flowers with bright yellow centers that bloom at the tops of Monroe's ribbed appendages are concentrated elements of his skull, ankles, fingers and toes.

Unlike the saguaros that dot the Sonoran Desert in southeastern California, southern Arizona, and northwestern Mexico, Monroe's flowers do not close by midday. They bloom continually and serve as both home and permanent detention center for the Whitewing Dove, Gila Woodpecker, and gilded Flicker that forever sit astride them. Which, by the way, are also constructed from the rudimentary physical makeup of Monroe himself.

The reason Monroe's blossoms never close and his indigenous pollinators never fly away is because they are all held fast to a sixty by sixty by sixty inch triangular canvas stretched tight, stapled in place and framed in tasteful blonde maple. Monroe is more than content to be this way. He is long past boredom, irritation, wanderlust, or any other tiresome human emotion. He simply exists within his confines as might any other landscape, portrait, or still life.

You see Monroe is awaiting a buyer, or exhibitor, or curator, who will one day see the splendor in his transformation from mere mortal to object de art. It is not implausible that Monroe might wind up gracing the wall of a famous museum, the lobby of a grand hotel, or perhaps the entryway of an eccentric collector.

But for now, Monroe Greenberg is simply a dead human being spending eternity as part of a surrealistic depiction of the great American southwest.

Chapter 1

United Airlines flight 467 languidly slid beneath the cloudbank like a pearl descending in a bottle of shampoo. Outside, the weather was sunny and gave no indication of changing its status. Inside, the forecast had already turned ominous.

Seconds before, the striking flight attendant with cocoa skin, bright red lips, and gleaming white teeth, had methodically recited her mantra; *"We've begun our final descent into Houston's George H.W. Bush Intercontinental Airport. Please return to your seats and make sure your seat belts are fastened and your tray tables are returned to their upright and locked positions. We'll be coming through the cabin to pick up any remaining cups or trash you might wish to get rid of before landing."*

But, in reality, they wouldn't be coming through the cabin. The stunner who had just made the announcement was unaware her fellow flight attendant lay in a heap at the back of the plane; her neck obscenely cantilevered to one side where it had been silently snapped by the man walking briskly up the aisle toward the front of the aircraft. He was small in stature and dressed in blue jeans and a black pullover with the sleeves pushed up to his elbows. His hair was platinum, combed straight back, and his eyes were cobalt blue and frighteningly lifeless. As he neared row sixteen, he focused on a mother sitting between her toddler by the window and her adolescent daughter on the aisle. Adrift in the tedium of frequent flyer monotony, almost all the passengers failed to notice the swift blow the white-haired man struck to the jaw of the hapless woman. She violently careened over and onto the younger child as her assailant quickly depressed the button unfastening the seat belt of the older girl on the aisle. In one motion he scooped her up then spun around and continued walking backwards up the aisle. With his right arm tucked under her throat and his palm wrapped around the back of her head, she dangled helplessly in front of him.

"Come close and I'll break her neck," shouted the stocky thug as he continued toward the nose of the airplane.

Events sometimes happen too fast for people to later piece the actual sequence together. And so it was with the flight attendant who made a move to run down the aisle as the words "break her neck" rang in her ears. She had gone no more than a step when a man in the bulkhead aisle-seat sprang up and clotheslined her. She was knocked back into the galley she had just attempted to leave. Then the co-conspirator quickly constrained her with the same hold the first man was employing on the young girl.

While the majority of passengers were still unaware that mayhem had begun and potential catastrophe was looming, virtually all of those in eye line of the struggles were frozen in their seats with fear. Virtually. But not all. Seat 11C was occupied by Brig Ellis; up to this point, an unassuming traveler with an Elmore Leonard novel that appeared to hold more interest than anything else on the aircraft. Anything previously, that is.

Ellis's head had come up quickly when the first man shouted. He immediately focused on the events surrounding him without moving the book still held in his hands. At first, he thought his eyes must be deceiving him. It looked as if the man dragging the frightened child up the aisle was indeed the same man using a chokehold to pull the flight attendant to her feet near the pilot's cabin door. But reality quickly set in. The two assailants were, if not twins by birth, certainly twins by design. And their intent became readily apparent as well.

Screaming into the microphone that the flight attendant had previously used, the forward-based double shouted, "Open the cabin door or we'll kill the black bitch and the kid!"

Fear does different things to people. Some are immobilized. Some seek immediate compromise or negotiation. Others however, trained to respond to aggression with superior aggression, have neither the luxury of paralysis or the restraint of logic. They are programmed to evaluate and execute in seconds. Which is exactly what Ellis did.

He quickly weighed three questions. How determined were these aggressors? Was one hostage more expendable than the other? And with two potential confrontation points, did one provide any greater likelihood of success?

Knowing hesitation would limit opportunity, Ellis moved his right hand from the book to his seat belt and used his thumb to release his restraint. Then, looking straight into the eyes of the scared little girl being dragged up the aisle, he brought his arm up to his mouth and clamped his teeth around it. The girl had no time to contemplate the consequences of her actions. She only knew she was being pulled farther and farther from her mother and sister. So when she saw the man in the aisle seat bite his forearm, she sunk her buckteeth into the sleeveless, meaty part of the hairy arm that was keeping her in check.

In milliseconds the platinum-haired abductor's nerve ends sent a message to his brain that his skin was being gnawed and torn. An involuntary response followed immediately as his head reeled back and he shouted, "Fuck!" in pain. The length of that shout was all it took for Ellis to spring from his seat. When the mugger's gaze switched from the girl to some sort of movement his peripheral vision was picking up, he lost the moment needed to focus on Ellis's hand rushing toward the middle of his face. The hard bottom of Ellis's palm struck the bridge of the man's nose driving it upward and into his brain. He was dead before his body slumped back into the aisle with the girl still in his grasp.

The flight attendant, witnessing what had just occurred, took her own course of action. She let her legs collapse and fell totally limp as if she had fainted. Her abductor struggled to adjust his grip and support her weight. In doing so, he lost valuable seconds.

Ellis had never slowed down and the second captor looked up just in time to see a blurry mass slam into him and his prey, crashing all three against the cabin door. Once down, Ellis managed to wedge himself between the startled hijacker and the battered attendant, who was now struggling with all her might to flee the collision of entangled bodies.

Before Ellis could pull himself away from the man, he felt a mass of weight piling on both of them. Passengers' weight. They pushed Ellis aside and held down the assailant's arms and legs. Managing to get to his feet quickly, Ellis unbuckled his belt, pulled it from his trouser loops and said to the trio who had come to his aid, "Flip him over, I'll tie his hands behind his back."

Then turning to the flight attendant, whose crisply starched blouse had pulled loose from the confines of her skirt, and whose hair was now hanging awkwardly askew, Ellis asked, "Do we have time to get him into a seat?"

"No," she replied, "just squat on the son-of-a-bitch and grab hold as we get ready to land."

"You heard her," Ellis said to the three male passengers who had helped him.

"Oh yeah," the flight attendant interjected, "just one more thing." Then she pulled the coffee pot from the galley counter top and swung it like a hammer across the forehead of the man who had pinned her down minutes before. Not once, but three times. No one did anything to stop her.

Once the plane landed and started to taxi to its assigned gate, the flight attendant's mind seemed to refocus and she realized she hadn't seen or heard from her coworker during any of the mayhem that had recently transpired. She strode quickly toward the back of the plane and upon reaching the aft galley found Ellis standing between her and two feet in uniform flats protruding from beneath an airline blanket that had been used to cover her.

"Trudy?" the attendant began, in a mixture of shock and recognition.

Ellis put one hand on her shoulder and the other near her mouth and said, "She's gone. No need to get more folks worked up than we have to. Are you going to be okay?"

The young black woman who had spent the majority of her twenty-six years developing her own particular style of grace under fire, found the inner resolve to simply answer, "Yes."

"Why don't you go back up front and do what you need to do there," Ellis suggested. "I'll make sure no one comes back here."

She didn't answer, just pivoted sharply and headed back toward the front of the plane.

Shortly after touchdown the pilot made an announcement that all must stay in their seats. Local police, plus federal officers, as well as the company's security contingent, would be boarding the aircraft as soon as the plane arrived at the gate. A few minutes later when armed personnel entered the cabin, relieved the brave volunteers of their prisoner, and began to do a seat-by-seat check of every passenger, all were resigned to the fact that it was going to be a while before they deplaned. The surviving flight attendant told the officers boarding the plane of the murder of her coworker and walked them back to the rear of the aircraft where Ellis was still standing between the last row of seats and the body in the galley.

"It was lucky for us," the now exhausted attendant said to the stern-faced security team who accompanied her aft, "that this Air Marshall was on board and was able to react as quickly as he did."

Ellis, who had remained silent as she spoke, looked at the flight attendant and the professionals standing behind her and said, "Uh, sorry if you got the wrong idea. I'm not an Air Marshall. I'm just a passenger on this flight."

"What? You're a passenger," the flummoxed attendant exclaimed. "Then mister, believe me... after what you did today... well, you can push my call button any time."

Chapter 2

Waiting at airports isn't what it used to be. Once, there were observation decks where you could stand and watch the planes beginning or ending their journeys. You could arrive early, go to the gate, and press your face against the glass in hopes that the one you were waiting for had a window seat so she could see you trying to see her. There were Hallmark moments carried out right in front of God and everyone – joyously inconsiderate shows of affection that frequently annoyed the momentarily stalled departing passengers who had no one there to hug or squeeze or celebrate their arrival.

But that was all before 9/11. Before airports became fortresses – antiseptic imitations of the very human places they were at one time. Now of course, no one goes to the gate that doesn't have a boarding pass. Loved ones, business associates, limo drivers, and lonely onlookers whose only experience with heartfelt hugs and kisses is as observers, are all herded down to baggage claim, which often possesses the dubious charm of a warehouse loading-platform, complete with conveyor belts.

It was in such a place that Lela Mangas stood waiting for Brig Ellis, though *stood* is actually inaccurate. In point of fact, she stood very little. *Paced* is the more appropriate term. In the United Airlines baggage claim basement, terminal C, George (the father) Bush Intercontinental Airport, Lela Mangas paced continually as she waited for Brig Ellis.

A beautiful woman, some might call exotic, Lela had a face that seemed more oval than most. Perhaps because her hair started farther back on her head than other women's. A feature she made no attempt to hide. So the circular curve of her forehead had a rounded, almost moonlike effect. Her eyes were chestnut brown and far apart. A straight nose with small nostrils pointed down to a thin upper lip with a full one beneath it. Her hair sprung from her head in toffee colored ringlets that caressed her bare shoulders. The ruby peasant blouse she wore flared at the cuffs helping accent her long fingers and French manicured nails. A semicircle of red roses and bluebonnets ended midway between the center of the blouse and the top of her jeans. Jeans that were also adorned with roses and green clinging vines that ran up the side of her leg, highlighting her rail thin frame. All of the aforementioned rode on high-heeled, red leather, pointed-toe shoes. She was unabashedly in full Texas attire.

Looking at the monitor for the umpteenth time, she knew something must be wrong. For over forty-five minutes it had been indicating that flight 467 had already arrived. Yet there were no passengers from the flight coming to pick up their bags. And there were no bags to pick up yet. It was all taking much too long, even for Houston. Then her cell phone, which she carried in the outside pocket of her red Coach bag, began to ring.

She pulled it out and said, "Hello."

"Lela?"

"Yes."

"This is Brig. Brig Ellis."

"Brig, where are you? Is the plane here?"

"Yes, we arrived some time ago. There's a problem that I can't get into over the phone. But we should be getting to baggage claim in the next half hour."

"Well, that's where I am. So I'll just stay here."

"Okay, listen... I'm sorry... I'll explain about the delay when I get there, okay?"

"Sure, fine. I'll see you here. Oh, by the way, what are you wearing... in case I don't recognize you. It's been almost twenty years, you know?"

"Uh... brown suit, white shirt, no tie. What about you?"

"Red shirt, blue jeans, red handbag, red shoes.

"Well, that shouldn't be hard to spot... of course, you never were."

"I'll be here, Brig. See you in a bit."

Funny how a voice can slice through the years. After just a few words you start to remember how someone used to say things. The cadence, the intonations, even the way the eyes smiled as the mouth followed suit. *"God,"* she said to herself, *"high school. Has it really been that long?"* And it had been. Eighteen years actually, since she said good-bye to the boy she had dated for over a year. The boy who left to join the army. The boy who was man enough to understand that when she said no, she meant she simply wasn't ready yet. An odd thing for her to have said, she mused, especially considering everything that had happened since then.

She had looked Ellis up on the Internet. Out of boredom she told herself. Something to do on that particular night at that particular time. Was there anyone you couldn't find on Google in one form or another? Probably not. And what a surprise when she found the listing that said, *Brig Ellis, Investigations, Security, Confidential Matters.* She wondered if it could be the same person. But how could it not be? How many Ellis men could there be in the world with a first name like Brig? She e-mailed. He e-mailed back. And somehow, even within the generally impersonal world of the Internet, she felt his quiet strength once again. So she asked him to help, and she wasn't surprised when he said he would.

"Lela?"

She turned and saw his face. A face she didn't recognize at first. Then it started to emerge. There were lines beneath the eyes, but they were still the kind, green eyes she remembered. The hair was short, close cropped. Perhaps the hairline didn't start where it once did, but it was still atop a broad strong forehead that was as tan as she recalled. A straight nose lead to a friendly smile, just above a dimpled chin. He was older, sure. But he was still Brig.

"Brig," she said warmly as she stepped forward and gave him a cautious hug. "I would have known you anywhere."

"Lela, you look fabulous. Believe me, even if I hadn't recognized you, I probably would have tried to hit on you anyway."

"Flattery, my friend, is always welcome. And look at you... you're not bald, or paunchy or anything. My God, if anything, you're even better looking than in high school. There ought to be a law."

"Well, if there were, you would have certainly broken it. It's really good to see you."

The banter continued for a few more seconds, but there is only so long a conversation can sustain itself with gratuitous small talk before it becomes patently obvious what's going on. So after a few more compliments, Brig began to explain why his departure from the plane took so long. He omitted the specifics of what had happened, particularly his involvement in bringing about a resolution. From his days in covert opts, he had gotten into the habit of only reporting the success or failure of a mission. His superiors would grill him for details when something went wrong, but success was another story. If the objective was achieved, the last thing those in charge wanted was specifics. Knowledge of details had a way of playing hell with plausible deniability. So, Brig let Lela know that some sort of catastrophe had been averted by heroic passengers. He just didn't make a point of telling her that he led the charge. And he certainly didn't get into what he had to do to start the resistance. If it came out later, he'd deal with it then. But in all likelihood it wouldn't. The authorities would do what they could to help him maintain his anonymity. They were more than happy to say that a number of passengers overwhelmed the would-be hijackers. It was more motivational for people on future flights, and it was one less hero they'd have to keep out of harm's way should the perpetrators have cohorts with revenge on their minds.

By the time his bag had been retrieved and they had walked to the parking lot, Brig had shared everything he wanted to share about his flight. So as she steered toward the exit, he steered the conversation to why he had flown from San Diego to Houston in the first place.

"I think it's time we talked about why you asked me to come down," Brig began. "In case there's anything more you want to get into before I meet your husband."

Lela kept her gaze on the access road and her hands on the mahogany steering wheel of the black Lexus as she thought for a moment before she answered. Over the phone, she had told him she was worried. Her husband, Tilton, was an artist. A controversial artist. As his stature had grown, so had the controversy. She asked Brig if he had ever acted as a bodyguard. And she remembered he answered affirmatively, but haltingly, explaining that it was his least favorite form of making money these days. But the more they talked, and the more he could tell Lela was really concerned and looking for help she wasn't even sure she needed, Brig made the decision to come to Houston, if only to give her an outside opinion.

They entered the freeway and started passing huge billboards advertising divorce lawyers and gentlemen's clubs. Ellis noticed them and wondered if their proximity to one another was intentional or just a quirk of fate.

"Well, as I said on the phone, I'm not even sure he really needs personal security, but if anything were to happen, and I hadn't done something, I never would forgive myself," Lela began.

"Hey, look... that's why I'm here. To help you decide. And the more you can tell me about *why* you think you might need help, well… the easier it will be to make a decision."

"You're right," she replied. "Okay, here's the thing. I mentioned to you that Tilton's work is controversial."

"You did, but you didn't say why. What's the deal? Does he paint a lot of naked people? I thought all artists did that. Of course, as I mentioned over the phone, what I know about art you could fit in your cup holder here."

"It's not what he paints, Brig. It's what he paints with. Tilton paints with ashes. People's ashes. You know, human remains."

Ellis paused before replying. In fact, he wasn't quite sure what to say. So he opened his mouth and simply went with a question. "Really... how exactly does he do that?"

"Tilton's an oil painter. He mixes the ashes with his oils. The texture on canvas can be really amazing."

"No doubt," Ellis replied, still at a bit of a loss for words.

"The more Tilton's work has gotten recognized," Lela continued, "the stranger the individuals have been who are turning up at his shows and events. It's probably silly of me to be worried. But I just have this odd feeling, you know?"

"Woman's intuition?" Ellis asked.

"Don't know. I'm just glad you're here."

"That makes two of us," Ellis said as he smiled at the girl he had once left behind. The girl who was definitely all woman now.

Traffic on the freeway was relatively crowded for mid-afternoon, but Lela was a lane switcher and they kept a good pace heading toward the city. Interstate Highway 45 was flanked on both sides with mile after mile of shopping centers, office parks, and row upon row of automobile dealerships. There were also furniture barns, service stations, and more fast food franchises than you could shake a chicken nugget at. Urban sprawl in full glory. Showing absolutely no signs of letting up any time soon.

"Is it far?" Ellis questioned.

"No," Lela replied. "We're on the north side of the city now, and our place is north of downtown, in the Heights. Shouldn't take longer than twenty-five minutes or so." Then without missing a beat, she added, "You never wrote, did you? Not once. Why was that?"

Ellis hesitated before he spoke. "Well, we were both so young, you know. And I've never been one to look back. Guess I'm more the moving forward type. Plus, the military has a way of keeping you busy."

"Yeah... excuses, excuses. You were just glad to be rid of me, weren't you?"

"Oh," Ellis began, rubbing his hand over his forehead and through his short hair, "I wasn't rid of you for some time. But that's all water under the bridge now," he added, in a hurry to change the subject. "Tell me what you've been up to for the last couple of decades."

As the Lexus wove its way in, out and around slower moving cars, eighteen wheelers, pickup trucks, and every make of SUV known to man, Lela condensed the story of her life to just the highlight reel. It included the regretful loss of her virginity to a law student in college. The loss wasn't the regrettable part, the would-be lawyer was. She followed with, in her words, the predictable attraction to and liaisons with a university professor and the manager of the public relations office she worked in for a short period of time. Both were far older than she and both, she recounted with a noticeable lack of nostalgia, were married. She spent little time on any particular accomplishment, either in recent or ancient history and seemed to focus more on the things that had gone wrong in her life than the things that had gone right. Until she came to her husband.

Lela involuntarily smiled more as she talked about Tilton Mangas. To hear her tell it, Tilton was a certified, card-carrying, perennially loquacious Lone Star legend-to-be. Not only did the lilt and speed of her conversation increase, she also drove faster as she spoke, almost without taking a breath, about the man who put that big yellow diamond on the third finger of her left hand.

"Tilton said, here's a yellow rose of Texas for a yellow rose of Texas." Then her entire demeanor seemed to race up the energy scale as she told Ellis about the first time they met. It was a business lunch in the Petroleum Club downtown. She said she had never realized how mind-numbingly dull the majority of men were until she sat there, trying to pay attention to her boss and his client's billing inequity concerns, while at the next table, Tilton waxed profound about the need for more penis art in corporate conference rooms. Later the two exchanged pleasantries over the desert buffet. A week later they were lovers. A month later they were newlyweds.

"I still do some occasional freelance P.R. writing," Lela added, "but Tilton's sold enough work up to now so that we're a little ahead of the game. If this new work catches on, things could be really great for us."

"So this... this kind of painting he's doing now is a relatively new thing for him?"

"Yes. He's only been into it for about the last couple of years. Nothing happens fast in the art business, regardless of what you might read or hear," Lela explained.

"I see. What kind of painting did he do before this?"

"Oh, you know, still life's of steer carcasses... portraits of serial killers, modern day Lautrec-like cafe society engaged in dwarf tossing competitions... the usual sort of thing."

Ellis waited for her to say, "just kidding." But she never did.

As they got closer to their destination, the downtown skyline came into view. There was not as much of it as Ellis thought there might be. Though he did like some of the architecture.

"I assumed it was bigger... more buildings, you know. I mean, didn't I read somewhere that Houston is the country's fourth largest city? Just behind Chicago, I think it said."

"That's right," Lela replied. "But it's really spread out. Over nine hundred square miles. Houston's more than twice the size of Rhode Island. Didn't you notice when you were landing how far the city stretches?"

"No," Ellis answered. "I guess I was a little preoccupied."

They swung off the freeway and onto the access road. Then at the stop light Lela turned left and drove under the overpass into a residential area.

"This is the Heights," Lela said.

Curious name, Ellis thought. Particularly since it appeared to be one of the flattest cities on the planet. But he gave it little thought as the drive down Heights Boulevard took them past an eclectic combination of redone Victorian Bed & Breakfasts, nondescript two story apartment complexes, postwar wood frame cottages, antique stores, a bar, a Mexican restaurant, and a school. Turning off the boulevard, Ellis noticed that there were a lot more of the older, pre-World War II homes. He assumed they had made up the bulk of the neighborhood for years. But gentrification was noticeably under way. While some of the old single-family dwellings and duplexes had been preserved, and many brought back to their original modest, yet honest design, some had been replaced by new brick and stucco structures that seemed too large for the lots they were stuck on. This diverse display of the past and present intermingled in a rather ad hoc sort of way that was jolting but not without an odd appeal. A lot like people, Ellis thought to himself. The good, the bad, and the ugly all sort of making do with one another in whatever space they found themselves inhabiting.

"We're just around the corner," Lela said, turning the steering wheel to the left. Fifty feet down the pavement she turned left again and said, "Here we are."

They sat facing a steel-gray cyclone fence. Set behind it about thirty feet was a structure that put Ellis in mind of an industrial building far more than a home. On the right, a doublewide carport jutted out from a wall of glass. Lela reached up with her right hand and pushed the button on the rearview mirror to open the electronic gate. It swung inward as they drove through. Under the carport she parked about three feet from the glass.

"I guess you have to constantly make sure your brakes are in good shape," Ellis quipped.

"It's not the equipment, it's the driver you really have to worry about," Lela replied with a smile.

Ellis pulled his travel bag from the back seat and followed Lela to the main entrance, which was just to the left of where they had parked. Opening the sliding glass door and stepping in, she said to her old boyfriend and potential employee, "Have to run to the bathroom. Too much coffee waiting for you at the airport. Make yourself at home. I'll be back in a minute."

Ellis, still standing near the door, tried to take it all in. But it wasn't easy. Setting his bag down beside him, he noticed that the floor was dark gray concrete. And it ran, unencumbered by tiles, parquet, carpet, or oriental rugs, from one end of the building to the other. Estimating the math quickly in his head, he guessed that the place was around seventy-five feet wide and at least a hundred feet deep. The ceiling looked like it was at least three stories tall. To his left, the wall that extended from the front to the back of the structure was floor to ceiling plywood. A row of paintings each spaced about two feet apart, also traveled the length of the wall. A curator would have a hard time categorizing these, Ellis guessed. They were big, small, tiny, huge, and every other size in between. While most were either rectangular or square, there were a couple of rather large triangular pieces and even a circular one or two along the way. And if the shapes lacked any particular commonality, the subject matter and styles were even more foreign to one another.

There was a gold, ogre-like face on black that seemed to grow from one canvas like some disturbingly malevolent Shroud of Turin. A nude, black and white pinup struck the classic Betty Grable pose from the nineteen forties, except the perspective was from well below her skyscraper legs leading to an outlandishly prodigious derriere. A blond-haired adolescent with horn-rimmed glasses stared outward from one painting while behind him soldiers in fatigues peered around corners and up hallways. In another, two cows were kissing. Next to that, the frame held what appeared to be the giant head of the Venus de Milo with Japanese Koi swimming around it. There were several abstract pieces full of colliding colors, as well as scenes filled with various forms of domestic chaos, like the one with two women fighting on the couch while a youngster sits on the floor watching TV and cradling a beer bottle in his lap as an elderly man sticks his head in the oven. There was a tree atop a transparent mound of earth, the roots branching out below the earth's surface then quickly contracting into a human arm. On first glance, a still life seemed to bring some repose to the lineup. It featured a bottle of wine beside an open book with eyeglasses sitting atop it. Then it became apparent that the eyes were still in the glasses. Mounted on the wall was a long, thin painting of a sophisticated older man in a dark tunic playing the violin. Next to it was a seascape with bodies washing ashore still strapped in their airline seats as Mere Cats stood erect on their back feet and watched. There was a bear in a tutu, plus other paintings stretching back into what Ellis assumed was the bedroom. The bed being a dead giveaway.

The other long wall was bare of any covering save for the interior metal. A dozen or so four-foot, rust-colored I-beams protruded inward. Naked wood and glass panels sat atop them and served as shelves that held books, compact discs, DVD's, framed photographs, and a decidedly plump black and white cat who appeared to be less than interested in Ellis's presence.

The right side of the front of the building also contained Tilton's working studio. Two large triangle canvases sat atop two sturdy wood-framed easels. Works in progress, Ellis assumed. One was a simple and beautiful flower in a cabbage patch. He had to look at it a couple of times before he saw that one of the cabbages in the back row was a human head. The other painting was of a forest. Or what had once been a forest. Now it seemed merely a collection of trees rising from a mud-colored lake. The trees were baron and the branches scraggly like the fingers of a dying man.

Immediately inside the front door was the living area. Modern furniture, as uniquely shaped as much of the art, surrounded a glass-top table framed with reinforced steel bars welded in the center. Below the top, was a diamond shaped steel plate that served as home for magazines, newspapers, and assorted junk mail.

Located directly in the geographic center of the building was the kitchen. A concrete countertop sat astride a stainless-steel elongated island that housed the stove and sink. Behind it was a larger working sink, dishwasher, and refrigerator flanked by a cocoon of cabinets, also stainless steel. *Great place to cook a meal or do a hell of an autopsy,* Ellis thought to himself.

Behind the kitchen, a stairway led up to what appeared to be a collection of open topped rooms. From his vantage point at the bottom of the stairs, he couldn't really be sure what was up there. And judging from what he'd seen up to that point, he assumed it could be just about anything.

Hands in pockets, Ellis strode over toward the pot roast of a cat he had seen earlier. He was just about to attempt to make contact when he heard Lela say, "Well, what do you think?"

"Definitely unique."

"Yeah, that's what we love about it. It's as bizarre as we are. Get your bag and I'll show you where you'll be bunking."

She led Ellis up the flight of stairs. At the top, to the left, was an open office area. It looked down on the back half of the building including the master bedroom. To the right was a small bedroom nook with a bathroom next to it. It overlooked the living area and Tilton's studio.

"Interesting," Ellis said. "This whole area could serve as sort of a combination sleeping quarters and sentry stand."

"Are sentry stands something you think about a lot?"

"Yeah. Sorry. Force of habit I guess."

"Really? Come to think of it, I was doing so much talking in the car, we never did get around to all those years you spent in the army. What were you doing, anyway? And where were you doing it?"

"Oh, this and that. Here and there. You know, various postings."

"Yes, well, that's certainly enlightening. But I can take a hint. If you don't want to talk about it, you don't want to talk about it. You weren't one of those clandestine types, were you? Dropped behind enemy lines for... what do they call it... covert ops?"

"Na," Ellis lied. "Just another grunt taking orders and putting in my time. Pretty boring stuff, really."

"Okay, I won't press. Not now anyway. I'm going to start getting ready. Feel free to freshen up. Use whatever you need. *Mi casa es su casa.*"

"Gracias," Ellis replied.

"Hey, don't get carried away. I've just used my entire Spanish vocabulary."

"Good. I'd be hard pressed to take it much further myself."

Lela went downstairs as Ellis hoisted his bag on the bed. He hadn't been wearing his suit coat during the altercation on the plane, so he didn't have to worry about it looking less than presentable. His shirt was pretty much a mess but he had a couple more in his bag. A bag that also held a tool of his trade. Ellis had called the airline ahead of the flight to find out about their firearms restrictions. It was his experience that different airlines often had somewhat different regulations. He was instructed to let the airport personnel know when he checked his luggage that he had a gun in his bag. The weapon had to be unloaded and it had to be locked in a hard-sided container. Ammunition could be locked inside with it. Ellis had no problem abiding by their rules. He really had no idea whether or not he'd even need his piece, but he liked having it with him just in case. That's why his concealed-carry permit occupied a prominent place in his wallet at all times. It tended to make things a lot easier if it became necessary to discuss with local authorities the Glock 19 frequently cradled in the shoulder holster hidden by his jacket.

Barefoot now and stripped to the waist, he entered the guest bathroom. As he looked in the mirror, preparing to remove his five o'clock shadow, he saw a face looking back at him that had its share of wear and tear. He wondered how much different Lela found it than the one she used to look into years ago. Hers looked different, he had to admit. Still lovely, but now alluring in the way that an attractive woman is different from a pretty girl. He remembered how taken he had been with her. And though her face had changed, he had to admit his attraction hadn't. But that was all long ago, he reminded himself. So Ellis decided to follow his shave with a quick shower. Then he'd be ready for what Lela had referred to as an art happening. Whatever the hell that was.

Chapter 3

The Lexus looked as out of place among the abandoned warehouses and gravel streets as a debutante in a soup kitchen. Meticulously negotiating the potholes and railroad tracks, Lela slithered the slick sedan past various impediments that time and neglect had put in her path. Every town seems to have a section like this, Ellis thought to himself. Long past its glory, or even its usefulness, it falls into something resembling a ghost world. Once populated by foremen with short sleeves and clipboards and laborers who piloted forklifts past row after row of crate after crate, the population had been slowly yet inexorably replaced by winos and gang bangers drawn to the shadows. Human cockroaches seeking habitats far from the glare of society's light bulb. And then came the art crowd.

They always seemed to find places like this. Which is understandable, Ellis mused. Space in these buildings is cheap. Dirt-cheap. And aren't most artists poverty stricken and afflicted with ill health that hygienically challenged environments often breed? Well, reasoned Ellis, certainly not all artists. Lela's husband seemed to be doing okay. The plush leather seat and the cool air conditioning that enveloped him made that obvious enough. No, he suspected, there was more to tonight's venue that simple economics. There was the irresistible lure of the seedy. An enticing opportunity for the straight-laced, the upwardly mobile and the well-heeled to do some safe slumming in the name of culture. It was a chance perhaps for the perfumed set to mingle, albeit antiseptically, with sculptors and painters and practitioners of what Lela had described, somewhat derisively, as performance art. The car's headlamps illuminated a long line of luxury vehicles stretched almost the length of a two-story warehouse that was dead ahead. They had arrived.

"We're here," Lela said. "It's show time." She had changed for the occasion. Now she was attired in white heels and white jeans with a similarly white form fitting body suit underneath. Lela had topped it off with an extra-long light blue denim blazer. It was festooned with silver studs along the generous lapels. Matching silver hoop earrings and a broad link silver bracelet set it all off.

Ellis had changed his shirt.

The sun had been replaced in the sky by a fat, round, yellow moon presiding over a typically humid Houston night. As they approached the concrete steps leading to the platform that was serving as the main entrance to the building, both their heads rose in unison to gaze at the gaudy blue, orange, and red neon sign spelling out *Flashpoint* above the door.

"Supposed to mean anything?" Ellis questioned.

"I think it means Entrance," Lela quipped.

The music came out to greet them before they actually stepped inside via a waft of piercing unpleasantness that seemed to be looking for any escape hatch it could find.

"What would you call this music?" Ellis asked.

"Loud." Lela answered.

They made their way down a narrow passage flanked on both sides by whitewashed walls that occasionally opened into artist's nooks. These were little cells furnished with easels, canvases, brushes, rags, cans of turpentine, plaster casts, books, magazines, and other items the eye could scan but not identify in a passing glance. Beneath their feet was a wooden floor blackened by time and use that magnified the sound of their clopping heels. After about forty feet the walls that formed the banks of the hall ended, and Lela and Ellis stepped into a sprawling open area filled with gawking, chattering, drinking, laughing, patrons of the arts.

With both her hands, Lela grabbed Ellis's arm just above the elbow and said, "Stick with me, good sir, while I navigate." She then began to weave through the clamorous crowd with Ellis in tow. Smiling, nodding and doing her best to avoid being buttonholed, she finally reached the bar. The two were about to order when a tall, thin, hawk-like man stepped in their path and said, "Lela, I hoped you would come."

"Alejandro, how are you? Let me introduce Brig Ellis."

As they exchanged pleasantries, Ellis noticed that even as the young man gave him his name, he kept his gaze on Lela. Alejandro Reyes was at least four inches beyond Ellis's six-foot height. His hair was black and thick and pulled back in a ponytail that reached to the middle of his back. He wore silver, wire-rimmed glasses over a prominent nose that turned down at the end. Sculptured cheekbones added to the somewhat predatory look of this odd young man in the beige linen suit and brown shirt.

"Alejandro is a painter," Lela said to Ellis, still holding his arm. "He has some work in the show tonight."

Ellis had planned to respond by saying he'd like to see it, but the young Mexican didn't give him a chance. Avoiding Lela's compliment completely, he continued to stare at her as he said, "I must speak to you alone for a moment. It is very important. Let's just step over —"

Lela interrupted him by linking her arm completely around Ellis and saying, "Perhaps later. We've just arrived and I have to make sure Brig meets Tilton and the rest of the heavyweights."

A flash of self-recognition came over Reyes's face that perhaps his interest was a bit too intensely focused on Lela. He responded quickly, saying, "Of course, of course. I understand. Forgive my rudeness, Mr. Ellis." But then, just as quickly, he turned to Lela and said, "But later, yes? Later we will talk?"

"Absolutely," Lela said, smiling and already turning on her heel and guiding Ellis around a couple that was the last obstacle before reaching the bar that had been set up to serve from three different sides. Ellis was waiting to see if Lela was going to make a comment about the Mexican's desire to speak to her in private. When she said, "What would you like to drink?" He assumed she wasn't.

"What are you having?"

"I'd like a Jack Daniels on the rocks," Lela said to both Ellis and the bartender.

"Make that two," Ellis added.

After clinking their glasses and taking a sip, Lela said, "Let's go. I'm sure Tilton's around here somewhere holding court and telling lies."

As they made their way past the gazers and the talkers and the hangers-on, those more concerned with the poses they struck while looking at the paintings, rather than the paintings themselves, Ellis kept wondering which ones were Tilton's. Which of the many giant canvases that adorned the walls were painted with the granular bits and pieces of actual people? The whole idea seemed rather macabre to him, but then again he had never thought of himself as particularly cosmopolitan. He was more a meat and potatoes guy and he knew it. Not totally without sophistication mind you, but certainly not one frequently referred to as edgy. Oh well, live and learn, he thought.

A few moments later, Ellis actually heard Tilton's voice before he saw him.

"Toro bravo. They're an ancient race of bulls almost extinct today, except of course on the continent, in Spain."

"What did I tell you?" Lela asked rhetorically. "Holding court."

The voice was coming from a man who had garnered the rapt attention of at least six or seven people. They had formed a casual semicircle in front of him. The closer Lela and Ellis got to the group, the louder the singular voice became.

"Their primitive ancestors were called urus. They were spread all over the world. Civilizations held them in positions of honor. On the Greek island of Crete, they were sometimes sacrificed in flamboyant rituals honoring divine justice."

Finally they were close enough for Ellis to get a look at the object of the group's and obviously Lela's affection, Tilton Mangas. He was dressed in black slacks and a black long sleeve shirt, open at the neck. Brown ostrich skin cowboy boots made him seem a little taller than those around him, though Ellis judged him to be just about his own height. There was a belt around his waist that looked similar to the boots except for the big silver buckle in the middle of it. On his head was what appeared to Ellis to be one of those gray hats that western men used to wear with suits in the fifties and sixties. It put him in mind of the hat he had seen in grainy black and white television replays of a famous day in 1963. Yes, it definitely looked similar to the hat the policeman was wearing. The tall Texan who was escorting Lee Harvey Oswald when Jack Ruby fired a thirty-eight slug into the reviled assassin at point blank range. Tilton would later tell Ellis his own hat was a Stetson Open Road Silver Belly with a two and three quarter inch brim. But for now, it just looked like that hat Ellis had always remembered.

Tilton smiled a lot when he talked. His teeth were straight and his nose pointed. A full but trimmed beard, streaked brown and gray, covered a lean face that was easy to look at. He waved his hands around like a traffic cop as he spoke. Ellis guessed he was a few years older than Lela. But he could understand the attraction. The guy obviously kept himself in good shape. And he kept those around him hanging on his every word.

"No, no, there won't be any picadors on horseback. No banderillas driven into the mighty beast to weaken his shoulders and neck. No swords. No death. No ears lopped off. We're all much too civilized for that sort of thing. This will be a bloodless bullfight. Just the matador and his capote and the ballet of bravado. This is art, for Christ's sake."

The last line sent a chuckle rippling through the onlookers that Lela used as an opening to step forward with Ellis by her side. "Whatever are you going on about?" Lela asked loudly enough for all to hear.

"Alas, my lovely wife. You look striking tonight," Tilton said, pulling her forward to give her a kiss on the cheek.

The listeners used this as an opportunity to smile and go their separate ways. Tilton didn't seem concerned that his audience had just dissolved.

"And who is this fine... though perhaps too rugged looking fellow?"

"This is Brig Ellis, the man I told you about. He's here to help keep an eye on things. Or to help us decide if we need to keep an eye on things."

"A pleasure to meet you, Mr. Mangas," Ellis said extending his hand.

"Please call me Tilton," Mangas replied, shaking Ellis's hand with a strong, firm grip. "I'm afraid Lela gets these ideas in her head from time to time that I just can't seem to dislodge. I've tried to tell her that we don't really need any... what do you call it... security? But she was not to be dissuaded."

"I'm really here just to observe," Ellis came back, "and help you two make some decisions. If it turns out that I'm not needed, well, the trip will have been worth it just to see Lela again and meet the man who won her heart."

"Oh yes, that's right," Tilton said, "Lela tells me you two were once high-school sweethearts."

"That's not exactly what I said," Lela interjected.

"No," Tilton countered, "but I could tell that's what you meant."

"Well, that, as they say, is ancient history," Ellis volunteered. "I think Lela just felt more comfortable speaking to someone she had known. About her concerns, I mean."

"Don't want to worry about concerns tonight. This is a happening. A Flashpoint. At least that's what it says on the sign. Let's enjoy ourselves. I'm off to the bar. Can I freshen that drink for you?"

"No, I'll just nurse this one. I'm kind of working you see. In fact, don't think anything about it if you keep seeing me hovering near you this evening. I'll stay out of your hair, but that's sort of what I'm here for."

"Hover as near as you like. But for God's sake, don't tell anyone you're my bodyguard or anything like that. They'll think I'm taking myself much too seriously."

"He can just be a friend of the family," Lela interjected, taking Tilton by the arm. "Because that's what he is."

"Well, come along friend. Let's get me a drink and take a look at what they're trying to pass off as art tonight."

As they headed toward the bar, Lela asked, "Tilton, what was all that bullfighting bilge you were spouting off about earlier?"

"Preparation my love. I was just priming the crowd. Later tonight, we're having an actual bullfight. Well, sort of an actual bullfight."

"You can't be serious," Lela said, with a tone as surprised as her look.

"Serious as a somnambulist on the freeway, dear. Remember, this is an art happening. A veritable Flashpoint!"

"Oh God," she replied, "I definitely need another drink."

At the bar, Tilton had a vodka martini while Lela repeated her Jack Daniel's. True to his word, Ellis stood pat. He even asked the bartender to throw in a couple of extra ice cubes so it wouldn't be obvious that he was carrying around a glass for no apparent reason.

The next hour turned into a round of imaginative introductions, clipped conversations and Tilton giving Ellis color commentary on various paintings that adorned the walls. Lela stuck with them as they walked and talked but would occasionally get pulled into other klatches that took her away for a while. Her absence had no perceivable effect on Tilton's glad-handing.

"Hey, Brig. Let me introduce you to the power behind the paint. The Cardinal Richelieu of the art world. One of the impresarios of tonight's event, Mr. Ernie Beeker."

Ellis stepped forward and shook the hand of a slight, middle-aged fellow in a Hibiscus-splashed Hawaiian shirt. He had tortoise shell glasses and a bad comb-over and was obviously used to Tilton's hyperbolic preambles.

"Sorry, I didn't get your last name," Beeker said, leaning forward to better hear amid the chatter of the crowd and the continuing irritation of the heavy metal music threatening to shake the speakers off their hastily constructed wall mounts.

"Ellis. Brig Ellis. I'm a friend of Tilton and Lela."

"Well, if you're a friend of Tilton, then I don't have to warn you to take what he says about anyone here with a jumbo size grain of salt."

"Come on," Tilton cut in, "don't be modest, Ernie. You're one of the movers and shakers, man. If it weren't for you, most of the impostors around here calling themselves artists wouldn't be hanging in this or any other hall. Including me."

Beeker continued to deflect Tilton's compliments as the trio chatted about the size of the crowd, which had now grown to something around two hundred or so, Ellis judged. They also discussed the distinction of the work, which Ellis made no attempt to gauge. Plus, each man's estimation of the babe quotient, which Ellis agreed was quite high. After a few minutes they left Beeker with an elderly couple and continued milling. Ellis happened to catch sight of Lela across the room. She seemed to be in a rather animated conversation with the tall artist they had met earlier. Reyes towered above her as they spoke. Then he reached out and put his hand on Lela's shoulder. A hand she quickly jerked away as she turned and strode off. Reyes stood impassive for a moment, then as if a light bulb had been turned on, reminding him that he was in the middle of a crowded room, he glanced quickly around his immediate vicinity to see if anyone had noticed the rebuff. When he saw Ellis looking his way, he quickly downed what was left of the drink in his hand and headed off in the opposite direction that Lela had taken.

"This is Motif," Tilton began, "and his adoring scribe, Alison Wayne."

Ellis found himself looking into the brown, round face of a thick, curly-haired cherubic-like Creole wearing a multicolored dashiki tied in a double knot at his waist. Olive drab pants with cuffs that ended at his calves made up most of the southern hemisphere of his wardrobe. High top, red Converse All Stars, sans socks, anchored the ensemble and gave cover to his rather prodigious feet. He stood with his arm around a buxom redhead and his hairy claw encircled the massive mound that was her left breast. Her nipple pushed the light cotton fabric of the dress forward protruding through the space between the big Creole's index and middle finger. It appeared to be challenging the confines of the daisy dotted sundress that covered it. She slurped the raspberry slush in her glass and seemed unconcerned about the location of the artist's paw.

"Tilton, you grizzled old cunt," Motif bellowed. "Who's this butch, boy toy with you?"

Ellis was about to respond non-verbally when Tilton interjected, "Pay him no heed, Brig, for he's as drunk as he is talented and by tomorrow he won't remember one of what I'm sure is countless insults he's hurled this evening."

"Motif is a genius," the big redhead replied. "One should never take offense at genius."

Ellis, giving the chunky curly-top and his carrot-haired partner the benefit of the doubt, simply replied, "Yeah. Nice to meet you both." The tone of which, while not overtly menacing, certainly conveyed no continuing desire for snappy repartee.

"Whoa, maybe I'm not quite drunk enough," exhaled Motif, as he quickly steered Alison away from Tilton and Ellis and back toward the bar.

"A brilliant painter but a real dumb ass when he's drinking," Tilton confided. "She writes for the trade magazine, *All Things Art* . Thanks for not overreacting. Believe me, it's not personal. He's actually a nice guy and she can be helpful to one's career. It's just that they're both shit-faced."

"I picked up on that," Ellis replied.

Turning to head toward one of the triangular shaped paintings on the wall closest to them, Tilton put his hand on the shoulder of a man standing alone with his back to the approaching pair, "Wendell, what the hell are you doing here?"

As the man turned, he brought his hand up and adjusted his glasses northward.

"Hello, Tilton," he began, "I decided to come down and see if there was anything worth seeing in this hothouse swamp." The bespectacled fellow spoke softly and smiled haltingly, volunteering sarcasm but betraying a timidity as to how it would be received.

Tilton seemed to pay it no mind and simply said, "Wendell James, meet Brig Ellis. Brig's a friend of the family."

Ellis started to extend his hand then noticed that the man he was about to extend it to was definitely keeping both of his wrapped tightly around a glass of white wine. So he merely nodded and said, "Pleasure."

Tilton, as usual, jumped in to fill the pregnant pause, "Wendell's a gallery owner in Austin. We don't see him often enough."

"Tastes are a bit different from Austin to Houston. You know that, Tilton," James inserted almost apologetically.

Turning to Brig, Tilton said, "Wendell thinks Austin's a bit more refined. Not as earthy as we are here."

"Well, it would be difficult to get much more earthy than the kind of work you're doing now, Tilton," James added, appearing a bit more at ease.

"Ooh, Wendell, a pun. Better watch it, that vino just might be getting to you."

After trading a couple more barbs, Tilton moved Ellis away from the out-of-towner and over to a huge three-sided canvas on the wall. "What do you think," he said to Brig, as he stood staring at the canvas while awaiting a reply.

"An abomination," came the answer. But it didn't come from Ellis.

It came from a distinguished looking man of middle age, dressed in a conservative gray suit, white shirt and red tie. And apparently he had more in mind than a two-word critique. "Defilement. Pure and simple. An atrocity that mocks the sanctity of human beings. How dare you, sir? How dare you?"

Tilton and Ellis had turned to face the man as he began his appraisal. They were looking into the piercing blue eyes of an earnest fellow who gave every outward appearance of being just another businessman dragged in by a wife or a date who had infinitely more interest in being there than he had. Though no wife or date was at his side.

"I get the feeling sir," Tilton began, "that you know who I am. But I don't believe I know who you are."

"I'm Pastor Barry Tompkins of the Evangeline Baptist Church and I am sickened and appalled at the very idea of using the sacred remains of God's most precious creation in such an atrocious way."

Ellis could see the color rising in the religious critic's face and he readied himself to step in front of Tilton if it became necessary.

The artist, who had just about polished off his Vodka martini, and was starting to feel the pleasant warmth of its liberating effects, couldn't help himself. He said, "What do you have the biggest problem with... the use of the flag itself, or the fact that the whole thing is pretty much the color of shit?"

Tompkins became even more flushed. "The content is indeed tasteless. But even that pales in comparison to the very idea of turning what's left of a human being into an object to be sold or displayed or exhibited. Have you no morals... no shame?"

"Listen padre," Tilton responded. "We've all done things we're ashamed of. But as far as I'm concerned, this painting is not one of them. If you'd like to have a civil conversation about my choice of materials, we can, but only if —"

The preacher cut him off. "I have no intention of listening to your ridiculous rationalizations. I only came here because one of my parishioners told me what was going to be exhibited tonight and I couldn't believe it. I had to come see for myself. Having done so, I am sick at heart and find the sight of this iniquity even more disturbing than I could have envisioned. You are an agent of evil and you will be punished for what you are doing.

In fact, I plan to personally see to it. Rest assured sir, you have not seen the last of the Reverend Barry Tompkins."

As the reverend turned on his heel and began to stride away, Tilton turned to Ellis and said, "Well, ain't that just a fucking shame." He didn't wait for an answer though as he drained the remains of his cocktail and said, "I'm definitely in need of another."

Chapter 4

As the night wore on and the introductions and conversations continued, Ellis couldn't keep from silently questioning how he himself felt about the whole idea of ex-people hanging on walls and being referred to as art. Moralistic introspection certainly wasn't something he frequently indulged in. Things had always seemed relatively clear to him. Something was either right or it was wrong. You knew right away simply by the way it made you feel. But Ellis wasn't sure how he felt about this. It was all rather new to him. He would have liked to talk to Tilton or Lela more about it but that could happen some other time he told himself. They were both busy working the crowd and as Ellis reminded himself, he was supposed to be working too.

Mercifully, at ten o'clock, the band announced they had to split for another gig. The crowd reacted to this news as they had to their music throughout the evening. They ignored it. The man whom Tilton had introduced Ellis to earlier as the patron behind many of the artists on display, Ernie Beeker, stepped to the microphone and said, "In half an hour, the bullfight will begin in the arena behind those doors to the left of the stage. But for now, please continue to enjoy yourselves and listen to the classic styling of the one and only, Benny DeMarco."

A diminutive fellow, violin and bow in hand, waddled to the stage as Beeker pulled up a stool and helped what Ellis assumed was an octogenarian, take a seat behind the microphone. He wore a black turtleneck with gray slacks and the remnants of his silver hair, which covered only the sides of his head, were combed back and tied in a small tight ponytail. His prominent nose and untrimmed eyebrows seemed to emboss themselves from a round face with the typical lines and crevices and liver spots that life imposes on those who overstay their welcome. His presence in no way hindered the milling-throng. They were far too interested in themselves and their ceaseless chatter to notice that the caterwauling they had been forced to endure earlier was now being replaced by lovely, moving, sensitive sounds emanating from the tiny man's touch of bow on strings.

"Let's go listen to Benny," Lela said. She had joined Tilton and Ellis just a few minutes before the rock band bid farewell.

"Come on, Ellis. You're going to love this guy. He's fabulous," Tilton added as the three strode to just a few feet from the ancient violinist.

The fact that only a trio of people, out of two hundred or so, paid any attention at all to the little old man alone on the stage, didn't seem to faze the mesmerizing musician. He was one with his instrument, bouncing jauntily through a Cole Porter medley of *Let's Do It, Just One Of Those Things, You're The Top* and *Let's Misbehave*. Then slipping effortlessly and flawlessly into heart rending versions of *Begin The Begun, What Is This Thing Called Love* and *In The Still Of The Night.*

With each move from one tune to the next, the three would smile broadly and applaud lightly to intimate their approval of both the maestro's selection and skill. DeMarco acknowledged them with a respectful nod each time, but never changed his blank expression or opened his closed eyelids as he played. The music was his escape as well as his profession. Each song conjuring up memories his mind found difficult to recall when his hands weren't actively engaged in recreating the soundtrack of his life.

Ellis felt honored to be in the presence of such a professional. He had always had a fondness for the popular music that had been created long before he was born. And while he had a hard time identifying with much of the art on the walls, he had no problem whatsoever being moved by the art rising from the aged elf's fiddle.

Exactly fifteen minutes after he started, Benny DeMarco stopped. As he took his foot from the rail of the stool it had been resting on, it became obvious to his three-person audience that he might need help stepping down. Both Ellis and Tilton stepped forward together to offer a hand. Benny took hold of Ellis's extended arm and let himself down slowly mumbling, "Thank you, but no autographs tonight."

"That's a joke," Tilton said to Ellis. "Benny's sense of humor is dry as an Alcoholics Anonymous poker game."

"He is so sweet," Lela said. "I just love him," she added, bending over and kissing the violin virtuoso on the cheek.

"Enough already," Benny replied. "You know that gives me a chubby."

The threesome looked at each other and couldn't keep from giggling as Ernie Beeker returned to take Benny away. "I've got a driver who'll take Benny back to his place," Beeker said. "Catch you later."

After Beeker and Benny DeMarco turned to walk away, Ellis asked Tilton, "So, what exactly is behind those doors Beeker was referring to earlier?"

"It's a stock arena. They once used it for auctions. It's not that big, but it's big enough for the kind of exhibition we've got planned. You know, dirt floor, a few rows of grandstands. That sort of thing. But I want to grab another drink before we go in."

"Now Tilton," Lela chided, "are you sure you need another?"

"I didn't say I needed another, dear. I said I wanted another. There's a big difference, you know?"

Ellis cut off escalation of the potential debate by saying, "I'm just going to run to the gents. I think I saw it back toward the front entrance.

"We shall see you at the bar upon your return lad," Tilton piped in.

"I'll keep him there until you get back," Lela said to Ellis as she took her husband's arm.

Ellis made his way back toward the long, narrow hallway where he and Lela had entered. He thought he remembered seeing a sign that said MEN just past the initial row of artists' nooks. Upon arriving there, he pushed the rectangular brass plate that was flush with the edge of the door. It balked as it moved backwards a bit, emitting a slight squeak. Ellis gave it another shove and it opened enough for him to see that it had been partially blocked by a large pair of red sneakers that he had remembered seeing earlier in the evening. Continuing past the tiled entryway, he turned the corner and quickly came to an abrupt halt. There, less than thirty feet in front of him, an animated assignation was underway. The curly topped Creole, Motif, pants lying crumpled around his ankles, was thrusting himself into the bare backside of the redhead writer Ellis and Tilton had seen the artist with an hour or so before. Her dress, which had previously clung precariously to her ample curves, was now wadded at her waist as, bent over, her breasts banged about the bowl of the sink she hung onto with both hands.

Too late to make an unnoticed exit, Ellis said simply, "Oh, don't mind me, I'm just here to take a leak," as he stepped into one of the stalls and closed the door behind him.

Unable to keep from hearing the continuing grunts and moans that echoed around the restroom while Ellis was relieving himself, he determined his surprise intrusion upon the coupling had made absolutely no difference whatsoever to them. Finishing his business, Ellis flushed, exited his enclosure, walked to the sink farthest from the sweating pair, washed his hands, dried them, and left the men's room without ever turning his head to take a second look.

After Ellis reconnected with Tilton and Lela at the bar, the trio joined the rest of the crowd making its way through the large double doors and into the arena. Ellis decided to keep what he had seen to himself. At least for the time being. As they filed in, a trumpet solo began over the speaker system. The beautiful, yet strangely mournful melody was something that sounded vaguely familiar to Ellis, but he couldn't bring to mind exactly where he'd heard it.

"What's that music from?" Ellis asked.

Tilton answered, "That's the deguelo. General Antonio Lopez de Santa Anna had it played prior to the final assault on the Alamo. It signals no mercy. No quarter. No one will be spared. Of course it's not at all traditional for a bullfight. But we thought it would be a nice touch, you know. Think of it as artistic license run amuck."

Tilton indicated that some seats along the front row of the grandstands had been reserved for them. They walked over and sat on the backless bench with only a single metal railing separating them from the dirt floor where livestock were once shown to prospective buyers. Across the twenty yards that made up that floor, and opposite the doors they had entered through, the main attraction stood behind a slatted six-foot wooden gate. Through the slats, a black, eight hundred pound fighting bull stared solemnly at the growing number of spectators that were now filling the stands.

"Tilton, are you sure this is safe?" Lela asked her husband who was sitting between her and Ellis.

"Of course," Tilton replied. "This pair... the bull and his matador... they make a living taking their show on the road. They've done their little dance of death over and over again in all sorts of places. They know what they're doing."

"Yeah, but do we," Lela replied.

Once the final stragglers had made their way to their seats, Tilton scanned the crowd. Satisfied they were all seated, he rose, stepped under the rail in front of him and walked to the center of the arena as the canned music came to a halt.

"Thanks so much for coming tonight," Tilton began to address the crowd. "Art, as I'm sure you all agree, takes many forms. We are about to witness the art of the *corrodes de toros*. An abbreviated version for an inebriated audience." A smattering of chuckles rippled through the crowd in response.

"Tonight, the bull, the matador and capote. Alone in the ring for your enjoyment. Let me just say a word about the magnificent animal you are about to see. The fighting bull is one of the most ancient of beasts. His lineage is traced to the Egyptians, the Arabs, and the Africans. Spain and Mexico have been but the latest breeding ground for what is, debatably, the most dangerous animal on earth."

Lela leaned over and said to Ellis, "Laying it on a bit thick, don't you think?"

"I think he's definitely enjoying himself," Ellis replied.

Tilton continued, "This magnificent specimen is bred for one thing and one thing only, to fight. In times past, he has been pitted against lions, tigers, even wild elephants. And in each instance the fighting bull has emerged victorious. Such is the ferocity of this great animal, that he has even been known to charge oncoming locomotives... however not more than once."

This time a bigger collective laugh emerged from the assembled onlookers. And Ellis noticed it seemed to awaken the object of Tilton's diatribe as well. The bull raised his head and looked from side to side.

"And of course," Tilton went on, "we cannot forget the similarly brave matador."

Some, though not all, would later remember hearing a low metallic sound just prior to the lights going out. But all would recall that in mid-sentence the arena was instantly plunged into darkness. Tilton's narration came to an immediate stop. The crowd assumed it was all part of the show. Tilton assumed it was a momentary technical problem. But after a number of seconds went by and the lights did not come back on, nervous chatter began to sporadically break out. Ellis reached across the darkness to touch Lela's arm saying, "Hey, is this part of the... Lela... Lela?" No response.

Tilton's voice rose from the darkness, "Please, no one panic, I'm sure it is just some sort of technical problem."

This time Tilton's voice was drowned out by earsplitting feedback from the loud speakers, followed by the resumption, even louder now of the deguelo. The piped-in music plus the rumble of multiple conversations and occasional shouted heckling almost drowned out the bellow of the black beast across the arena. But for Tilton, there was no mistaking the rattle and bang of the wooden gate being flung open as the bull left his temporary confines and muscled his way into the still black ring.

People who had been sitting relatively close to the doors had risen and began to stumble trying to find the nearest exit. The few who reached the doors however, found them locked or blocked from the other side. Claustrophobia and darkness do not go well together. The crowd soon became as loud as the music.

Tilton, because he was closer than anyone else in the arena, had already heard the bull make his untimely entrance. The drink in his hand wasn't even visible in front of his face, but he could feel his stomach starting to make its way into his mouth when he smelled something decidedly non-human wafting his way. From the opposite direction of the smell, he heard what he assumed was the excited voice of the matador getting closer and closer to him. "Be still senor, no move. Be still senor, no move. Be still senor, no ugh!" The Mexican ran headlong into Tilton, tumbling both to the dirt beneath their heels. Though neither could see, both men struggled to their feet with the matador advancing toward the aroma that now filled his nostrils too. As he rose, Tilton felt a chill against his chest and thought for an instant he had been injured. Then, still holding the martini glass in his hand, he raised it to his lips only to find it drained. "Shit", he said, now realizing he was wearing what he had hoped to drink. He didn't have time for prolonged disappointment however, because suddenly he heard an unearthly snort, followed closely by what sounded to Tilton like a knife entering a watermelon and being ripped across it. Then there was a desperate gasp as if the air had just been released from an inner tube. Silence reigned momentarily but it was quickly followed by a thud as the body that had careened into him moments ago came crashing back to earth from eight feet in the air where el toro had just sent it spiraling. Tilton began to tremble where he stood

When Lela had failed to answer Ellis, he immediately rose and reached out for the metal rail. Finding it, he bent at the waist and slid under, entering the ring as he had watched Tilton do just a few minutes earlier. He started calling Tilton's name as he moved slowly forward but the music and the swelling sound of the crowd kept him from being heard. Unable to see in the pitch-black arena, he moved cautiously and ever so slowly in the direction where he had last seen Tilton.

Those few in the crowd who were smokers began to light matches, or flick their Bics. Some in the crowd used their cell phones to create some measure of light for themselves and those who were seated next to them. The scattered flames and iridescent glows gave an eerie color to segments of the grandstands. From where Tilton stood, those flickering lights provided the direction he reasoned some degree of safety waited. Now it only required him mustering the courage to put one foot in front of the other and head that way. Just as he was about to do so though, paralysis nailed his feet to the dirt as an ominously large, horned silhouette strode between him and his destination. It was all Tilton could do to keep his pants dry as he stood looking into the outline of a monstrous form breathing heavily, slobbering and shaking his head from side to side as he raked at the earth in front of him with his massive hoof. The artist didn't know what to do. He probably would have broken and run if he had the ability, but he felt as if his feet were encased in concrete. He was simply unable to lift either of his expensive, but now dusty Lucchese's.

It was also impossible for Tilton to take his eyes from the black mass that stood between him and the stands. Then he wondered if he wasn't beginning to hallucinate. It appeared a piece of the silhouette was breaking off and beginning to form what seemed to be the shape of a man. A man moving slowly and cautiously, his hands outstretched in front of him cradling something that took the profile of a stick or a cylinder, Tilton couldn't be sure.

As he stood there transfixed, the shadow kept circling in a way that would bring it between Tilton and the enormous being that seemed to have no interest other than the quivering painter. In another three steps, the dark figure would complete the arc that would land it between Tilton and *el toro*. But the bull tired of the wait, bellowed and charged.

The only movement Tilton could muster was the involuntary release of the grip on his glass. By the time the crystal hit the dirt, the shadowy figure had pumped three rounds into the head of the night's entertainment. One exploding the great beast's eye. The powerful thrust of the animal was such that even as its legs crumpled they dug the earth up, sliding forward until it came to a stop inches from Tilton's boots. Turning its great head slowly, blood oozing from both its mouth and now gaping socket, it was allowed to suffer only a moment longer. Ellis stepped in front of Tilton, pointed the muzzle of the Glock toward the base of the bovine's skull, and discharged two more rounds. Thus sending the proud circuit performer into fighting bull legend.

Chapter 5

By the time the sun had risen, Ellis had been up for over an hour. After showering and dressing he had slipped silently downstairs to spend a little quiet time with his own thoughts. The hairy balloon of a cat he saw the day he arrived had deigned to sit in reasonable proximity to Ellis on the other end of the couch. Not to be petted or stroked or anything like that. More to let the visitor know that he was keeping an eye on things even if his masters weren't.

Ellis sat thinking about the events of the previous evening. Particularly the botched bullfight. There seemed to be a number of loose ends dangling. Oh sure, he said to himself, Ernie Beeker had done an impressive job of pulling strings at the end of the night. He had satisfied the cops smoothly enough. The boys in blue certainly seemed to be more inclined to accept Ellis's version of the shooting once Beeker corroborated his and Tilton's account of how it went down. And there was no denying that he was more than happy to get Lela and Tilton out of there and let Beeker take care of bringing in Harris County Animal Control to dispose of the massive carcass. Yes, it was obvious to Ellis that Beeker had all the right contacts in all the right places to sweep something as big as a fighting bull with five slugs in it under the rug. The outcome wasn't the thing that was causing his mental calisthenics. It was what caused the fracas in the first place, and what actually went on during the initial moments of darkness, that was the focus of Ellis's concentration this muggy Bayou City morning.

Why had the doors been locked from the other side? Beeker's explanation that they couldn't risk the possibility of the bull getting into the other part of the warehouse was plausible. Ellis didn't doubt that, to this crowd, people's safety probably took second place to making sure their art wasn't harmed. Was everything thrown into darkness because of faulty wiring? Possible. Certainly the rest of the building looked as if it wasn't exactly up to code. Did the bull decide to come through that gate on his own, or did someone help him with that decision? Did Lela immediately panic, as she said she did, and slip beneath the stands to avoid a hysterical crowd? Did that pissed-off preacher decide to do something crazy? Was there anything malevolent about any of it? Or was it all just a cascade of cockeyed events that often happens when a little danger and a lot of alcohol mix? The fat cat at the end of the couch appeared to have no interest in helping Ellis figure it out.

With her hair recently brushed and tumbling down around her shoulders, Lela strode barefoot across the smooth concrete floor. She was wearing a green satin robe, tied at the waist. From his seat on the sofa, with his back to her, the first thing that came into Ellis's view was a sculpted calf grounded by a dainty foot aflame with fire-engine red toenails.

"Cosmo doesn't say much, does he?"

"He's a quiet cat," Ellis agreed.

"That's what makes him so irresistible," Lela added, bending over and scooping the bilious feline up in her arms. "I'm going to go drop him on Tilton and watch the fur fly. There's no better way to get him out of bed."

Tilton's voice preceded his entrance into the room. "No need to carpet-bomb me, my dear. As you can see I'm vertical. And I'm even dressed. Which is more than I can say for you."

"All right, all right. I'll go get dressed. You put the coffee on. And don't forget Benny's coming by this morning. We'll all go to breakfast," she added, plopping Cosmo back on the couch then sweeping down the hall toward the bedroom.

As Tilton rummaged through the kitchen to get the coffee started, Ellis rose from the couch and walked over to join him. Their conversation quickly turned to the events of the night before. Tilton continued to express his gratitude to Ellis for dropping the marauding bull before he skewered the artist, as he had the unfortunate matador. Ellis brought up the questions he had previously been rolling over in his mind. Except the question about Lela. But Tilton was convinced that everything could be chalked up to pure dumb luck. It was their own fault really, Tilton indicated, his and the other artists, for not making sure the building was checked thoroughly. They had left too much for Ernie Beeker to oversee. And when trouble ensued, hadn't Beeker taken care of everything, Tilton added. Ellis agreed he had. Their conversation was then interrupted.

The knock on the glass front door was faint as the figure standing in front of it. Ellis recognized the pear-shaped performer he had helped from the stage. At Tilton's urging he went over and held the door open for Benny DeMarco.

"Good morning," Ellis said, as the little man walked past him without saying a word. Even though it was a typically warm Houston morning, Benny was wearing a short leather jacket and a snap-brim hat. He kept both on as he pulled back one of the dining chairs and took a seat at the table.

"Who's your butler?" Benny questioned Tilton.

"A house guest of ours," Tilton replied. "You met him last night."

By now Ellis had come back to the kitchen. Thinking the oldster's lack of response might be due to impaired hearing, Ellis said rather loudly, "I really enjoyed your music."

Benny addressed Tilton again. "He always yell like that?"

Tilton just looked at Ellis and smiled. Both men knew they were being played. "Come on, let's have some coffee," Tilton said, heading toward the table with a cup in each hand. "Brig, pour yourself one and join us."

Benny's hand shook on its way to pick up the cup Tilton had set in front of him. Once it gripped the porcelain though, and his other hand joined it, he steadily brought it to his lips and took a sip. Ellis thought to himself, what the hell, he'd keep trying. He said to Benny, "You know, I really enjoyed that Cole Porter melody last night."

Benny's head turned slowly and his eyes opened wide as he said, "A connoisseur, eh?"

"Not an expert. Just a fan. I've always liked music from the twenties, thirties, and forties."

"There was a good tune or two written in the fifties, you know," Benny replied. "After that it was all crap."

By the time Lela joined the group they were into their second cup. Ellis's initiation was over. As far as Benny was concerned he was now part of the ensemble.

On the way to Goode Company, where they were to have breakfast, the conversation continued to focus on the Flashpoint proceedings. Benny was brought up to speed on what he had missed and Ellis decided to share his sighting of Motif and Allison Wayne in the restroom-turned-tryst-parlor. Tilton and Lela didn't seem shocked or even surprised. "Outlandish behavior and Motif go together like Champaign and orange juice," Tilton said. Benny asked about the size of Allison's knockers.

Over migas and chorizo, chili and eggs, Bloody Mary's and more coffee, the talk turned from the night before to the coming evening. They told Ellis another event was scheduled.

"Decidedly different from Flashpoint," Lela said.

"Yes, tonight is a much more sophisticated soiree," Tilton added. "Remember those huge houses on Kirby Drive we passed on the way over here. Well, that my friend, is River Oaks, home of Houston society's crème de la crème. And tonight, a Tilton Mangas painting and a Benny DeMarco performance are on the menu."

Ellis remembered the section well. As they drove through the area, Lela had made a comment about it being the city's ritziest neighborhood. A comment that really wasn't necessary. The surroundings spoke for themselves. Oak and pine trees soared to the sky. Massive homes both classic and modern were surrounded by immense lawns that gave the impression they were manicured every night so not a blade of grass would have the audacity to appear uncut.

"Our hostess this evening is Gloria Preston," Tilton began, "a real patron of the arts. Of course, she can afford to be. Her husband, well, ex-husband that is... he was in real estate. Put up more apartments around this city than a Cheetah has spots. Got to give Gloria credit though, when she finally got tired of his Tomcatting she made the old boy pay off like a Spindletop gusher. Now she uses a lot of her excess cash, of which she has boatloads, to entertain her friends by showing off different artists. Not just us homegrown types. Painters and sculptors from all over. But tonight's kind of a regional thing. You'll see some of the same folks who were there last night."

"How many people are expected?" Ellis asked, trying to get a feel for how he'd need to operate later.

"Oh, a hundred, a hundred and fifty or so," Lela answered.

"All at her home?"

"Believe me, that won't be a problem," Tilton said knowingly.

"They'll have those great little meat balls," Benny added.

After breakfast, they drove back to Tilton and Lela's. Benny left and Ellis asked if there was a place he could get his suit cleaned and pressed and back to him that day. Lela knew just where to go. Tilton left to make sure the painting he was going to be showing was arriving at the Preston home in time to be hung just as the patron wanted it. Lela and Ellis took the suit by the dry cleaners and left to have a drink while it was being renewed. Alone together, Lela conveyed some of the same concerns that Ellis had voiced to himself about the Flashpoint melee. Over a glass of wine, she took his hand in hers while saying how glad she was he was there. The taste of the wine and the touch of her hand combined to remind him how he felt about her long ago. It wasn't a feeling he was completely comfortable with, so he simply said he was glad he could help and then asked for the check.

Chapter 6

It was definitely big, Ellis thought, but a lot less ostentatious than he expected. There were two great rooms on the ground floor connected by leaded crystal pocket doors. A library, sitting-area and three different powder rooms were connected to them through arched doorways. A formal dining room with its own fireplace and a table that could easily sit two football teams was a few steps away. Though he never saw it, Ellis assumed that the kitchen was relatively nearby as well, since uniformed waiters and waitresses were able to respond quickly with whatever drink a guest ordered.

The Preston party had fewer guests in a smaller venue that the previous night's Flashpoint, but Tilton and Lela's role seemed to be the same. Milling, talking, drinking, simply being sociable. Ellis tended to drift along in tow, much as he had the night before. Even to the point of running into some of the same people. Ernie Beeker was there. He had traded his flowered shirt for a suit and tie. The lust birds, Motif and Allison Wayne, were in a far corner. Both looked to be getting snockered again. Alejandro Reyes was there and one of his paintings was on display and getting lots of attention. It was mounted over the fireplace in one of the great rooms and people had been stopping to admire it since Ellis, Lela, and Tilton arrived.

Trying to explain it to himself, in case someone asked his opinion later, Ellis thought of it as a combination realistic and surrealistic representation of some sort of revolution in progress. A huge Spanish Mission bell-tower in the center anchored the painting. In the lower foreground, flames were lapping at its base. While, in the background, explosions were going off on the horizon. A young dark-haired woman was on one side of the ledge that framed the tower. The other side had a cherub floating above it. A cherub wearing an old leather flight cap and smoking a cigarette while holding a microphone. The tower itself was riddled with bullet holes. As was the poster of Emiliano Zapata that was plastered on one wall. To Ellis, it was certainly striking. Perhaps because it seemed the most familiar. A battle scene; smoke, flames, and the destruction that accompanied it. Ellis had seen enough of those to be able to identify with the fear, despair, adrenaline, and exhilaration that got jumbled together in those kinds of situations. He wasn't exactly sure what the artist wanted the two characters on either side of the tower to symbolize. Perhaps the girl represented the bystanders who always seem to get caught in such conflagrations. And maybe the cherub with the cigar and microphone was innocence being turned into propaganda for whichever side was winning.

"That's the thing about art," Alejandro Reyes, the tall creator of the piece, said, interrupting Ellis's silent interpretation. "It means something to the artist who paints it and the person who sees it. And those two meanings are frequently not the same."

"A bit like life, isn't it?" Ellis responded.

"Si. That is true. Pardon me if I was rude to you last night, Mr.—?

"Ellis. Brig Ellis."

"Yes. Mr. Ellis. I was preoccupied. I had some things I needed to discuss with Mrs. Mangas. Some things regarding last night's show and this one. I'm afraid I was not very hospitable. Do forgive me."

"Don't give it another thought. I didn't."

"Ah, good. By the way, she does look lovely tonight, doesn't she," Reyes said, referring to Lela who was standing next to Tilton and talking with an elderly couple just a few feet away.

"Yes. She does indeed," Ellis agreed.

Lela was wrapped in a salmon, formfitting dress that had been turning heads all evening. The short, lettuce-edge sleeves and low-cut, square neckline made the most of her deep brown tan. Her white open-toed sandals featured long straps that wound lovingly to just below her calves. And those toenails that had been gumball red earlier in the day now sported a French pedicure so they'd blend perfectly with her footwear. Ellis wondered if perhaps she was as much on display as the paintings.

Tilton had dressed for the occasion as well. A subdued plaid sport coat over cream-colored slacks made him look cognizant of, but not beholding to, any particular dress code. Especially since his signature short-brimmed Stetson still sat atop it all.

In addition to the Reyes work, other paintings that seemed to be attracting the most attention from the well-heeled guests ambling back and forth in front of them, were Motif's *Car Wreck* and Tilton's triangular *Five To Go.*

Ellis had looked at the Creole's abstract earlier. He listened to Tilton and Lela praising it and waxing poetic about the young man's talent and future. While he acknowledged they knew infinitely more about this stuff than he did, he silently found little appealing about the huge rectangular canvas bordered with some sort of primitive sea birds and splashed and slathered with a cacophony of colors that seemed to start and stop and splatter and drip for no apparent reason. *Eye of the beholder,* Ellis thought to himself.

Tilton's painting was almost the polar opposite. Completely geometrical in its design, the massive rectangle was separated into five different segments that stepped from the wide base of the painting to the pointed peak. Complimentary, but slightly different hues of brown, black, gray, and sand, sat atop one another in a rather formal way. There was a solemnity about it, which manifested itself even if you didn't know what constituted the colors on canvas. Once you did know, it made the piece even more imposing. At least that's how Ellis reacted to it.

Standing beside Tilton as the night went on, Ellis was sure he saw the somewhat subdued Austin gallery owner he had met the previous night. Wendell James was at the far end of the room, apparently bidding adieu to the people he had been chatting with and heading toward the door. Just as he was about to ask Tilton if the man leaving was who he thought he was, Lela excused herself to go to the ladies' room and Gloria Preston came striding over.

"Tilton," the hostess began, "is Benny here? Should we start?"

"Yes, Ernie Beeker's helping him set up in the music room now," Tilton replied.

"All right. I'll have everyone move over there."

Stopping one of the waiters who was weaving his way through the crowd, Gloria leaned in and spoke to him. He then pulled a small bell from his waistcoat and holding it above his head, jangled it about as she said loudly, "Come... come... let's all head into the next room where we have a surprise for you."

"Let's head in," Tilton said. "Lela will know where to find us."

As they trooped in with the others, Ellis could see that Benny was already seated on a tall stool in front of a single microphone that had been set up just below Tilton's painting. The guests pushed tighter together, hemming in Tilton and Ellis as Gloria Preston began to speak.

"We thought you'd enjoy a brief interlude of music this evening from a true virtuoso. Mr. DeMarco has been delighting audiences on a number of continents for more years than he cares to remember. He's graciously consented to give us a brief concert that I'm sure will help us all reflect on the never ending spiritual bond between music and art. We felt it was appropriate to conduct this mini recital beneath Tilton Mangus's stirring *Five To Go.* And now, Mr. Benjamin DeMarco."

Benny, giving no particular acknowledgment of the crowd's polite applause, brought his violin beneath his chin, raised bow to strings, closed his eyes and began the first strains of *Autumn Leaves.* But just as he began, one by one, heads began to turn away from Benny and toward the massive picture window that looked out onto the floodlit yard fronting the Preston home. Whispered twitter quickly accelerated to obvious mumbling, which swiftly rose to astonished gasps and was immediately followed by shouts for the hostess to come to the window. As bodies parted to make way, Gloria Preston took three steps toward the glass and saw the last thing any River Oaks socialite ever wants to see. A noisy group of sign-carrying zealots were shouting, marching, and marauding through her prize-winning azalea bushes.

Gloria's eyes grew wide. Her nostrils visibly flared. The sound of her voice echoed through the room as she spun on her heel and shouted, "Come on then... before they breach the ornamental kale."

Matrons with martinis, husbands with highballs, waiters, patrons, and partygoers all funneled through the main entryway to follow the hostess onto the lawn that now seemed under direct assault. Ellis and Tilton had been in the middle of the mass of bodies and were swept along like silt being washed downstream.

As the first defenders of conspicuous consumption reached the gaggle of protesters they were blinded by spotlights shining from various news-team panel vans parked at the curb. The glare was so bright, Gloria Preston and her ritzy retinue could barely make out what was written on the signs and placards being pumped up and down by the howling demonstrators. ITS NOT ART, IT'S AWFUL one read. IS NOTHING SACRED another asked. PEOPLE AREN'T PAINTINGS said still another. And the largest one screamed DEAD DESERVE DIGNITY.

Standing in front of the boisterous faithful, a three-piece-suited middle-aged man was flanked by a gaggle of reporters all trying to squeeze their logo emblazoned microphones under his nose. Ellis and Tilton, who had managed to slip around to the side of the chaos, recognized him right away. It was Tilton's nemesis from the night before, the Reverend Barry Tompkins.

"Not only should the evil perpetrator of this abominable art be vilified and publicly chastised," the reverend ranted, "but so too should be the enablers...these amoral patrons who make it possible for blasphemous atrocities like this to take shape and form."

"Well I guess that guy was serious," Ellis said to Tilton.

"Serious as a sawed-off shotgun in an elevator, son," Tilton replied. And added with glee, "Hot damn! You can't buy publicity like this."

Just then, Gloria Preston, who definitely didn't share Tilton's joy over being the subject of the ten o'clock news, stormed into the reverend's spotlight and yelled at the assembled press, "Get this trailer trash off my lawn! I know the mayor! I know the chief of police! I know the presidents of your television stations. I'll have your jobs by breakfast if you don't move these mental-defects now!"

The exchange was about to get a lot more heated, but Ellis and Tilton missed the live feed because just as Tompkins started to tar Gloria with the term, elitist heathen, Ellis's peripheral vision picked up the glare of headlights bouncing over the curb, into the yard and barreling straight for them. There was no time to ascertain whether or not Tilton was aware they were about to become hood ornaments. There was only time for Ellis to drop his shoulder and ram into Tilton sending both of them sprawling into the lantanas that lined the driveway. The careening sport utility vehicle couldn't keep coming their way without crashing headlong into a twelve foot crepe myrtle, so it swung hard to the right, cut ruts in Gloria Preston's meticulously manicured lawn and spun back over the curb, into the street, and sped away fishtailing wildly as it went.

"Are you okay," Ellis asked Tilton, who had ridden out the ruckus with his hat still sitting snugly atop his head.

"I'm okay," Tilton said, dusting himself off. "How about you?

"Seem to be in one piece," Ellis answered.

"You know the worst part?" Tilton asked.

"The fact that none of those damn cameras got the vehicle on tape?" Ellis offered.

"No," Tilton replied. "We're missing the music."

Sitting in the middle of the bushes, dirt, and debris, both men looked back through the grand convex window to see the lone figure of Benny DeMarco swaying and sawing away, eyes clamped shut, feeling the melody in his fingertips and soul. The aging virtuoso had never stopped playing.

Chapter 7

Two events, two close calls. It wasn't that Ellis found the concept of coincidence unimaginable, but it was not a phenomenon he put a lot of stock in. Neither he nor Tilton had been able to pick up the license plate number of the SUV. Leaping for your life tends to take precedence over getting the goods on your would-be assassin. But was assassin too strong a word? There was certainly a lot of confusion and emotions were running high. It was possible that some yahoo could have gotten carried away, and fueled with too much passion or too many longnecks, let his accelerator and his lack of restraint get the best of him. Sure, it was possible that it could have been an accident. But it could have been deliberate too. When a chromium-plated cowcatcher, backed up by three hundred and fifty horsepower is bearing down on you, it damn sure feels deliberate. Or at least it did to Ellis.

Tilton was willing to chalk it up to the heat of the moment. "Crazy, but not necessarily malicious, mob mentality run amuck." That's what he said to Ellis as they made their way to the Montrose neighborhood just southwest of downtown Houston. It was one of those half gentrified, half hardcore sections of town where new money mixes with old homes and you're just as likely to run into a two-income-earning couple on their way to a trendy restaurant as you are a homeless junkie on his way to the blood bank. This particular moment they didn't have to worry about either, encased as they were in the leather, steel and glass of Tilton's expensive Japanese sedan.

"Look Brig, I know you're just doing your job," Tilton intoned, "but anything could have caused that blockhead to bound over the curb. Hell, it probably scared him more than it did us."

"Well, if it did, he was one scared son of a bitch," Ellis answered, his mien devoid of the irony inherent in his tone.

They were heading south on Dunleavy street, stopping, then starting again at the frequent red lights and four-way stop signs that kept the speed of traffic to a minimum in the combined residential, commercial area that zoning steered clear of. Grocery stores, fingernail parlors, gas stations, even a small college mingled with bungalows and shared the surrounding environment with apartment buildings, and mansions that had seen the high life come and go a number of times. So Ellis was not that surprised when Tilton wheeled into a parking lot adjacent to a white, two-story, wooden framed house that had a black and yellow sign out front reading FONTANNA FUNERAL HOME.

Tilton killed the engine, but made no immediate move to open his door. He turned to Ellis and said, "You know, we never did get to discuss what you think of my work. Ordinarily I wouldn't give a damn, but you've gotten me out of a couple of close scrapes and I was just wondering if you thought doing so was worthwhile."

"I'm no art critic," Ellis said quickly. Then paused and went on. "And while I like your paintings, I guess I'm not totally sure how I feel about what you paint them with. But you seem to treat Lela well and you guys are definitely not boring."

"Life's biggest sin, you know. Being a bore. That's why I go out of my way to keep from being one. I hate to waste anyone's time. Especially my own. Time's all we really have, Brig. If we don't fill it up with fun and ferment and things that provoke thought and growth, then what the hell good are we?"

"On top of not being an art critic," Ellis answered, I'm also not a philosopher."

"Yep," Tilton agreed in his own elongated way, "you're a bona fide strong, silent, straight-shooting, lone wolf type. Not one of those who just talks to hear his head rattle. But I tell you what... if and when you do have something to say about any of my work, just spit it out. 'Cause yours is an opinion I'd care something about. Now, fuck it, let's go see a man about some dead people."

There was a curved walkway leading from the parking lot to the front of the house. Tilton led the way and Ellis followed as they climbed six steps that put them on the front porch. Dispensing with a knock, Tilton grabbed the knob on the front door, turned it and stepped inside. Ellis trailed him and closed the door behind them.

Since he had already seen the sign out front, it was impossible for Ellis to know whether the morose feeling that enveloped him as they stood in the main parlor was from the house itself or the fact that he knew death was the primary resident. Victorian in style, the architecture and decor matched the restrained times in which it was built. Heavy, dark wood covered the floors and constituted the bulk of the interior trim, window frames, and moldings. Few windows let in light. All the furniture was straight-backed and looked uncomfortable. The entire environment was definitely designed to keep things somber.

There was no time for Ellis to share his unease however, as they were immediately met by a young black man in an even blacker suit who obviously knew Tilton, referred to him as Mr. Mangas, and led them out of the parlor, up the stairs to the second floor, and down a long hallway toward the back of the house. He stopped in front of a closed door on the left and said to Tilton, "Mr. Fontana is expecting you."

Frank Fontana was sitting behind a big oak desk, head down, pen in hand, absorbed in a stack of papers. He was red-faced, white-haired, and burly as his desk. His dress shirt was starched and his striped tie was fastened with a gold clasp. He looked the part of a funeral home operator, Ellis thought, or a used car dealer.

Tilton and Ellis were already in front of him when he looked up, took his glasses off, ran a fat hand through his silver mane and said, "Why do you have someone with you? Who is he?"

Tilton took one of the high back, leather chairs in front of Fontana's desk and motioned for Ellis to do the same. "He's a friend, Fred. Just passing through town. I'd introduce you, but you'd never remember his name. So... like I told your man when I called this morning, I'm just stopping by to..."

"I know why you're here," Fontana interrupted. "But I don't have anything for you. I can't give you anymore."

"What do you mean *can't*, Fred? That sounds a bit absolute."

Ellis couldn't miss the fact that the older man behind the desk would rather be having this conversation with Tilton alone. But since the artist hadn't asked him to step outside, he simply busied himself looking around the office at the certificates and association memberships on the wall and feigning disinterest in what was being discussed.

"What's the problem, Fred? Business been that slow lately? Life expectancy suddenly skyrocketing and nobody told me about it." Tilton joked.

"Look," Fontana began, "after all that commotion on the news last night... well, I've just rethought a few things."

"Fact is, we didn't catch the news last night, Fred. What are you referring?"

"Didn't catch it. No, I guess you didn't. You were too busy making it."

"Oh, you mean that little flare at Gloria Preston's. That was nothing. Just a bunch of misfits making noise."

"Well they sure as hell made a lot of it," Fontana came back quickly. "And as for misfits, listen, Barry Tompkins has one of the biggest Baptist congregations in the city."

"You turning religious on me all of a sudden, Fred?"

Ellis could tell Fontana didn't especially want to be saying what he was saying. But he was saying it anyway.

"Look at it from my end, Tilton. If Tompkins has beau coup Baptists up in arms over this thing... well… they're going to be just as up in arms over whoever's supplying you. 'Cause he won't stop with just you. He showed that last night. Believe me, if he went after a big name socialite, he's certainly not going to hold back on a lowly funeral director. And if I start losing my Baptist business, who knows where it might end?"

Tilton's response took on a more reassuring tone. "Fred, you know I've never told anyone where my materials come from. And I never would. And anyway, like we talked about, no laws are being broken."

"No legal laws perhaps. But Tompkins can damn sure rant and rave about moral laws being bent and twisted. Whether we agree with him or not. And the last thing a funeral director needs is being in the crosshairs of any kind of moral debate. No, Tilton, I'm afraid we just can't do this anymore."

"Look, Fred," Tilton countered, "while I don't share your opinion that the rambunctious reverend is going to successfully put together a religious rebellion to smite anything that in their opinion isn't art... I'd never ask you to do anything you don't want to do. The fact is, the more my work gets exposed, the more I've had people coming to me about using them and their loved ones in future frescos. But the future's the future, you know.

I've got a couple of big shows coming up in the days ahead, and I'm running a little low. I could sure use anything you might have on hand. You know, sort of one for the road?"

Fontana's gaze left Tilton for a second and veered out the window. What had begun as a sunny day was turning gray and overcast. Perhaps in more ways than one. The man with his name on the sign out front turned back to the two men sitting in front of him and said, "This is the last time, Tilton. The very last time."

"You got it Fred. This last one and I'll darken your door no more."

His chair creaked a sigh of relief as Fontana rose and turned to the wooden filing cabinet behind his desk. Pulling out the top drawer and reaching deep into the back of it, the funeral director retrieved what appeared to Ellis to be approximately a four inch by ten inch white cardboard box that he set in front of Tilton saying, "This one's been here over two years. Like the others, no one's ever come for it."

Tilton turned the box around and read from the top of it, "Monroe Greenburg. Sounds like a Jewish gentleman."

"When we get to this state, Tilton, we're all the same religion. Via con dios, my friend," Fontana said, "I'll keep an eye out for you on the evening news... or in the scandal sheets."

Tilton reached out and shook the big man's hand saying, "Just so you don't find me in the obits, Fred. That's the main thing. Take care."

On the way back to his house, Tilton filled in the blanks for Ellis. He told him that he had met Fontana a couple of years previously. And that, like most funeral directors, he did work for the city and county as well as private business. That meant frequently, he was having to dispose of indigent or homeless types whose remains were sometimes claimed by relatives or friends, but often, were never claimed at all. After a certain period of time, when it was apparent no one was going to come forward, cremation was the most economical way to dispose of the body. Eighteen hundred degrees of heat and flame has a way of condensing the average adult into a much more manageable three to eight pounds that's infinitely more space saving. The boxes, or sometimes plastic containers of the dearly departed's remains, must eventually be disposed of in a crematory lot, a cremation garden, inured in a columbium or scattered. Fontana, having listened to Tilton's point of view regarding the symbolic immortalizing of individuals rather than the helter-skelter disposal of them, agreed to supply the artist with those who had managed to sever all ties with anyone who had the least interest in being involved in their final resting place.

"The point is, Brig, I take what's left of those the world has sluffed off, forgotten about, or simply given up on, and I give them a kind of immortality. Some degree of history that people will see and remember. They become a reminder to everyone that every individual is unique, important and shouldn't be simply swept away like yesterday's dust. I didn't know them personally, so I make no attempt to recreate what they were. Rather, I exalt them in symbolic ways to remind people that we're all part of life's incredible passing parade, in one way or another. Fred understood that. He agreed with it. So he helped me. But hell, you can't blame a guy for being afraid he's going to turn up on *60 Minutes* and have his business go down the toilet. I understand that. Let's face it, what's good for the goose is sometimes hell on the gander. Publicity will only get more people interested in my work. The more people who are interested, the more people will come to appreciate it. More and more folks will want to be immortalized themselves, or they'll know someone they want to make sure is never forgotten. That's great for me, sure. But there's no big upside in it for Fred. So I take no offense at his decision. The man's just covering his ass. A smart thing to do these days."

Chapter 8

When they got back to Tilton's and walked in, Lela was just hanging up the phone. "You'll never guess who that was," she said.

"Don't have a clue, my dear," Tilton responded as he carried the box full of Monroe Greensburg over to his easel and set him down amid the brushes, pallets, and other boxes of life's castoffs. Ellis started to walk over and say hello to Cosmo but the formidable feline just turned and sauntered away.

"Wendell James," Lela continued. "Says he putting together some kind of weekend wake for world peace at the Chinati Foundation in Marfa. One of his artists pulled out at the last minute and he wanted to know if you'd be interested in filling in and exhibiting some of your work."

"Hmm," Tilton contemplated. "Chinati doesn't usually allow temporary showings. And it's a mighty long way to Marfa."

"Well, according to Wendell, it's a special one-time only event. And he says he's got commitments for national art coverage," Lela added.

"So, I'm not quite right for Austin, but Wendell thinks I'd be just the ticket in West Texas, does he?"

Lela answered, "He's in a bind, that's why he called. But maybe you can do him a favor and help yourself at the same time. National coverage," she repeated.

Tilton turned to Ellis. "That's why I love her, Brig, the beauty's as crafty as I am."

Lela and Ellis shared some coffee while Tilton called the Austin gallery owner. He and she discussed what had happened at Fontana's while Tilton and James worked out just how many canvases the artist could bring and display. Fifteen minutes later, Tilton, with his own coffee now firmly in hand, joined the pair at the table.

"Well amigos, looks like we're going to Marfa," Tilton proclaimed.

"You'll come with us, won't you, Brig," Lela asked. "I know we were never specific about how long you'd stay, but with everything that's been going on, I'd — we'd just feel a lot better having you there. Wouldn't we, Tilton?"

"Sure thing, compadre. And as far as I'm concerned, you've been on the clock since you got here. I'm a pay-as-you-go kind of guy and you've damn sure earned your money so far. Even though I still believe bad karma's had a lot more to do with the last couple of nights than anyone's evil intent. But money's money and say... what the hell kind of freight are we paying you anyway?"

"Well," Ellis began, "we never actually got around to working that out. I always thought of it as more of a consulting thing really. A favor for an old friend," he said, looking at Lela and smiling. "What kind of timing is involved in this?"

"A couple of days getting there," Tilton replied. "No sense knocking ourselves out. Set up time, the weekend show, then... if you decide to head back to San Diego, you can always leave from El Paso. It's less than two hours from Marfa."

"Why don't we just do this," Ellis offered. "I'll pick up some additional clothes before we leave Houston. Nothing fancy. Just enough to get through the trip. You guys spring for that and cover the traveling expenses. Once this excursion is done, we can determine if there's a need for anything more. And more could be simply me helping you find someone locally who's experienced in this kind of security."

"Thanks Brig, we really appreciate it," Lela said, reaching out and touching his hand.

Tilton plopped his paw on top of both of theirs and said, "All right then. It's a good time to be putting some distance between our local detractors and ourselves anyway. And you'll get to see some of the real Texas, son. If you're like most folks, you won't forget it."

Chapter 8

A six hundred mile road trip from the clammy gulf coast to the arid Chihuahua Desert requires a modicum of planning. So the next couple of days were filled with preparations, along with a surprise or two.

Tilton concentrated on selecting the paintings for the exhibition, packing them and arranging transportation. He didn't want to ship them by air because of the cost and the fact that they'd still need to be trucked to Marfa after they arrived in El Paso. He was leery about them arriving on time and uninjured if he shipped them by truck from Houston. So he decided on a more independent course of action. "Hell, I'll just rent a U-Haul trailer and tow these babies behind my big ass Lexus."

Lela suggested that the Galleria was probably the easiest place for Ellis to find whatever additional clothing he might need. So she drove him over to the massive monument to shopping at the South Loop and Westheimer. The multiple floors and hundreds of stores was a great deal more than Ellis needed, but it seemed to be just what Lela had in mind. She suggested that they separate and meet back at the coffee shop on the west side of Neiman Marcus in a couple of hours. Women and shopping, Ellis thought to himself, some things never change. So they went their separate ways.

Inside half an hour, Ellis had scored the jeans, t-shirts, underwear and lightweight pullovers he needed. He took a turn around the enclosed, air-conditioned merchandizing Mecca, doing a degree of people watching as he walked. Stepping onto the descending escalator at the east end of the promenade, he caught sight of two men coming out of a glass-fronted shop bearing the name, *Adrian's Gallery* over the door. On first glance they seemed a comical paring. Sort of the long and short of it. One small, balding, older. The other tall, lean, gangly. Then Ellis realized they weren't just any oddly matched shopping duo, they were both acquaintances. It was Ernie Beeker and Alejandro Reyes.

Beeker was shaking his head from side to side. Whatever the Mexican artist was saying to him, and he was saying a lot, wasn't being received with any indication of agreement. At one point Reyes put his hand on Beeker's arm to press his case. The smaller man's head-turn and quick stare at the taller man's appendage was all that it took for the hand to be immediately removed.

Just as Ellis was reaching the bottom of the escalator, Beeker was pointing a finger at the stooping artist's face. Two shakes of the digit quickly followed for emphasis. Then the bespectacled man turned and walked away. Reyes watched him for a second, then stole a quick glance at his watch and headed off in the opposite direction.

Ellis had nothing but time on his hands and still harbored questions about both men. So he decided a bit of reconnaissance might be in order. But with the two men parting in opposite directions, he was forced to prioritize his curiosity. Reyes seemed to be in a bigger hurry, so Ellis fell in behind him. The Mexican's height made it easy for Ellis to keep him in view while maintaining considerable distance between them. And the growing length of the artist's stride let Ellis know the tall man was much more interested in whatever was ahead of him than anything that was behind him.

Dodging giggling girls, mothers and strollers, ambling seniors, and various other committed consumers in search of Texas-sized bargains, Ellis stayed in Reyes's wake. Past ice cream shops, lingerie stores, jewelry counters, toy kiosks, souvenir stands, and haberdasheries, the tall man made his way to the south side of the Galleria. There, the pedestrian traffic lightened, the hallways narrowed and Ellis watched Reyes turn a corner to the right that momentarily took him out of sight. Picking up the pace and rounding that same corner, the surroundings quickly made Ellis realize that their journey had lead from the shopping mall to some sort of attached hotel lobby. Twenty-five paces ahead Reyes was stepping into the elevator bank. By the time Ellis reached the elevators, the doors had closed. There was no display indicating which floors the different elevators were heading to, but neither was there much time for Ellis to fret about it. For just then another set of doors opened and a young, attractive black woman stepped off the elevator and directly into Ellis's face. "Well I'll be," she said, "if it isn't 11C."

Ellis recognized the flight attendant right away. Even though she was out of uniform, her deep brown eyes and sparkling smile were easily remembered "Oh, hello," he said, with his mind still following Reyes up the elevator shaft.

"What a surprise. Are you staying here in the hotel?" She asked.

"No, I'm just sort of... waiting for someone."

"Oh. Well, you know we never really met formally," she began, "I'm —"

"Rebecca," he interjected. "Saw it on the name tag on your uniform."

"And you remembered that? After all we went through on the plane."

"Got an eye for details," Ellis said. "Particularly when it comes to beautiful women."

The compliment widened her smile. She asked coyly, "Well, how long are you going to be waiting for that someone you mentioned?"

"A bit, I think." Then Ellis looked over and saw that the lobby bar afforded an unobstructed view of the elevator bank. And since he could tell by the tone of the question she asked just what her answer would be, he said, "Do you have a moment? Can I buy you a drink?"

"Now that's an offer I definitely won't refuse. I'm used to serving the drinks. But I much prefer to be served."

After walking a few steps to the seating area, he pulled out a chair for her that would keep her back and his sight line toward the elevators. They ordered drinks and began a conversation with Ellis sympathizing again about the loss of her fellow attendant. There was the inevitable replay of the life threatening moments they had experienced together. She told Ellis that she had learned from a friend of hers who worked in the airline's security department that the would-be hijackers were apparently terrorists who had stolen the identity of a couple of California brothers and planned to crash the plane at the Houston airport. Hundreds dead on the runway at an airport that bore the name, *Bush*, would provide worldwide headlines and secure the pair their martyrdom as well as Allah's ration of virgins in the great beyond.

"It's always the little guys who aren't getting laid enough that cause all the trouble," she said with no small measure of gallows humor.

The longer they talked, the liquid libations worked their mellowing magic as afternoon drinks often do. For an hour or more their conversation flowed freely from chitchat to mutual interest to unabashed flirtation. By the time they were well into their third round Ellis's interest in the elevator bank began to wane. Earlier in their conversation, he had given her his card, which read *Investigations, Security, Confidential Matters*. She now took it between her thumb and forefinger, held it up and said, "So just how confidential are these Confidential Matters you get involved in?" Barely keeping from slurring.

"Very confidential," Ellis replied. "I'm not one to kiss and tell. It's bad for business."

"Ah, there... see. You said kiss first. I didn't say it. You said it. Are you coming on to me, Mr.," she had to glance back at the card, "Brig Ellis?"

"Well, if you have to ask, I guess I'm not doing a very good job of it. By the way, have you, by any chance, had lunch today?"

"Nope. Didn't have lunch. Didn't have breakfast. But don't try to change the subject. We were talking about you trying to kiss me."

Jesus, Brig thought to himself, she's had three vodka tonics in the early afternoon with nothing on her stomach. No wonder she's melting. "Actually, I haven't tried to kiss you... yet," Ellis replied, bringing his Bloody Mary to his lips.

"Well that's dumb," the now sky-high flight attendant babbled bluntly. "That's like having a chocolate sundae and not nibbling' the cherry on top."

Ellis involuntarily spat vodka and tomato juice through a mouth clamped tightly in defense. As he was apologizing profusely and using his napkin to wipe away the bit that managed to escape, he heard the elevator bell ring, glanced up quickly and saw not Reyes, but Lela emerge. She turned in the direction he had taken coming in and walked away briskly.

Ellis looked at his watch. It was five minutes prior to when he had agreed to meet Lela at the appointed coffee shop. Turning swiftly back to his tablemate, he found himself peering directly into her eyelids. She was asleep sitting up.

"Rebecca. Rebecca," he repeated, reaching out and taking her hand.

She opened her eyes slowly. "Oh, I'm afraid I'm feeling a little woozy."

"You didn't drive here, did you?"

"No. No. I'm staying in the hotel," she said raising her hand to her forehead. "Would you be kind enough to help me —"?

"Sure," Ellis said, before she finished her sentence. Keeping one hand on her arm as he rose, he reached into his pocket to leave two twenty-dollar bills and one Lincoln on the table. Then he helped her up, walked her over to the elevator bank, and asked for the floor number. She mumbled something that sounded vaguely like she couldn't remember and held her purse up. Balancing her, his packages and her purse as he opened it, he looked inside and extracted the credit-card-size slipcover that held the electronic card that would open her door. Luckily, she had jotted down the room number on the outside of the card cover. Reaching her floor and keeping her firmly in his grasp, for fear she wouldn't stay vertical, he managed to open the door and guide her toward the bed.

As Ellis was setting her purse on the bedside table, Rebecca crossed her arms at the waist, grabbed each side of her sweater and prepared to pull it up over her head. With a smile as inviting as a toothpaste commercial close-up she said, "You're in for a wild ride, cowboy," and proceeded to get her sweater north of her ample chest and fully over her face when her momentum and her consciousness collided. Momentum won as she passed out and wound up sprawled across the bed, flat on her back, bare armpits and midriff broken only by the white satin bra caressing her charms.

Ellis pulled her arms down along with her sweater. Then he reached down to the floor, slipped off her shoes and swung her feet and legs onto the bed. He slipped a pillow under her head and pulled the side of the bedspread up and across her. He took a moment to look for her wallet in her purse. Finding it, he pulled a pen from his coat pocket and, on the back of one of his business cards, jotted down her full name and address that he read from her driver's license. Then he took another of his business cards, turned it over and wrote, "call my cell" on it, and placed it on the bedside table by her purse. Still sitting on the bed, with his left hand he ran the backs of his fingers against the silky softness of her cheek. Then he smiled, got up and left to go meet Lela.

As the elevator made its downward journey to the lobby, Ellis kept expecting the doors would open wide and Alejandro Reyes would join him in the mirrored enclosure. But it never happened. Well, he thought, there had been plenty of time for Reyes to make his way down while Ellis was taking the mostly comatose Rebecca up to her room. Retracing his path toward Neiman Marcus and the designated coffee shop, he kept looking for reasons other than the obvious one for why the Mexican artist and Lela were in the same hotel in the middle of the afternoon. Of course there was no way he could be positive they shared a room just because they shared the elevator bank. But random coincidence as a recurring explanation was starting to wear a bit thin. He went over his options as he walked. He could wait and see if Lela mentioned the hotel at all. If he asked her about shopping, and she said she'd spent all her time in the stores, he'd at least know she was being less than truthful. He could address it directly, point out that he saw both her and Reyes in the same elevator bank, though not in the same elevator. Of course, it would be pretty easy for her to explain her way around that. It was a public place. People come and go all the time. He could be absolutely blunt and remind her that he hadn't actually seen her during the episode with the bull or the runaway SUV. Though he knew she'd be likely to reply that she had already told him she was cowering under the grandstands that first night and sitting on the toilet the next. Or, he could just let it go and see what happened. It was absolutely possible that it all could be coincidence. Whether she was or wasn't having an affair with Reyes might or might not have anything to do with Tilton's safety. And damn it, she was the one who brought him down here in the first place. Why offend her if there was really no proof of any of the possibilities running through his mind. Best to just sit on things for a while, Ellis reasoned, and see how they play out. So that's what he did. Sort of.

"Hey, sorry I'm running a little late. Do we have time for me to grab a coffee too?"

"Sure," Lela said. "Take a load off. Pretty good place to shop, huh?"

"Yes it is," Ellis answered, taking a seat beside her. "But where are all your bags? You seem to be empty handed?"

"Yeah, Tilton will be thrilled. I wound up not spending one thin dime."

Ellis couldn't help pressing, a little. "You mean you walked all over this entire shopping center and didn't find one single thing you wanted to buy."

"There is such a thing as a discerning shopper, you know. Not every woman sprints from store to store snapping her credit card from one counter to the next. Plus, I decided to pop in on a friend here in the hotel."

"Hotel?"

"The Westin Hotel. It's attached to the Galleria here on the south side. An old friend of mine works in their P R department. I decided to say hello. Say, what's that on your collar? Right there. Looks like tomato juice."

Chapter 9

It was a decidedly odd site. The classy, black luxury sedan towing the boxy rental trailer behind it. Not the sort of thing one normally sees on Interstate 10 between Houston and San Antonio. If one were passing it on the highway, as many were doing, one saw two males in front drinking coffee and talking. Two females were in the back. Both appeared, as they actually were, to be sound asleep. Tilton had decided to get a pre-sunrise start and beat what he called the "crawling contest" that is rush hour traffic in the largest city in Texas. He had also agreed to take along the second woman in the back seat. The one who wasn't his wife. The one who sat, head back, mouth open, eyes closed, clutching the pillow that she insisted on bringing. The pillow she said she couldn't possibly sleep without. Of course, everyone assumed the pillow went beneath her head rather than bound to her midsection by freckled arms that rested atop it.

Alison Wayne had called Tilton the day before they were to leave. She was distraught. Her paramour, the volatile Motif, had left for Marfa without her. He too was exhibiting in Wendell James's west Texas weekend extravaganza and said he wanted some quiet time to meditate prior to the event. Alison immediately assumed this meant he planned to meet another woman in Marfa. She begged Tilton to take her along and offered as recompense a thirty-five hundred word, double page spread in *All Things Art.* Never one to pass up publicity, Tilton jumped at the offer. Though truthfully, he confided in Ellis, that while the article would be great, he was just as interested in seeing the furor that would likely ensue should the randy Creole actually have a separate squeeze lined up for extracurricular activities.

They had started so early, and the women seemed to be sleeping so soundly, Tilton advised Ellis that it was likely they would reach San Antonio before the slumbering duo awoke and demanded breakfast. He was almost correct. Just outside of Seguin the ladies became uncomfortable enough to wake up, want breakfast and a bladder break. Not necessarily in that order. They stopped for both at a roadside restaurant just off the interstate called LuAnn's. Linoleum floors, Formica tabletops, and paper place mats didn't mar the stomach soothing pleasure of eggs, bacon, sausage patties, and biscuits. Ellis skipped the grits. Coffee was consumed all around and Tilton even got one to go.

As they were easing out of the parking lot and back on the feeder road that would take them to the interstate, Tilton suggested that since they were making such good time, they might as well push on all the way to Marfa. Ellis felt like he was just along for the ride so he didn't venture an opinion. Lela said she was game if everyone else was. Alison said, "Damn straight. I can't wait to see the look on you-know-who's face when I come waltzing in."

To continue making good time they took the Anderson Loop around San Antonio. It would spill them out on the west side of the city, which is where they needed to be. Ellis had never been to San Antonio, though he had been extremely close. Randolph Air Force Base is just outside the city and it was a stopover for him once on a mission to Nicaragua. The kind of mission that never appears on flight plans or official documents. He thought of it as they drove past the exit sign highlighting the base. Not because he wanted to. In fact, he usually went out of his way to keep that particular mission locked deep in the farthest recesses of his mind. But every now and then, something as simple as a highway exit sign would open the lock.

Brig had been young then. Just out of airborne training. There was nothing he felt he couldn't do. And he'd done some pretty hairy things already. Sniper duty. Both spotter and shooter. Unofficial death from a distance. Neither the government nor the military ever referred to it as assassination, but that's what it was.

Ellis didn't question his assignments or let them get to him. Twenty year-olds seldom do. The morality of what he was ordered to do was the province of older, wiser, superior officers. And ultimately, the commander in chief. Surely they knew what had to be done. As far as Ellis was concerned, it just seemed like the natural order of things. You join the military. You train. You put that training to work. He had trained well and had a skill that was valuable. His marksmanship scores in both basic and advanced infantry training had gotten the attention of his commanding officers. The psychological tests they put him through convinced them he'd be far more of an asset in the field than on some high profile exhibition shooting team. And up to that point, nothing had proven them wrong.

This particular assignment actually seemed easier than most. Forward reconnaissance and clearing if need be. But that would be unlikely. This specific stretch of the Nicaraguan coast had been chosen because it was virtually uninhabited. Still, before the platoon of the U.S. trained Contra insurgents came ashore to start their hike into the interior that would link them with the larger force of freedom fighters, the brass wanted to make sure this beach was as empty as it was isolated.

Ellis remembered the moon was high but covered by passing clouds when he went over the side of the fishing trawler a mile off shore. Taking a rubber boat in alone wasn't standard operating procedure. But if something did go wrong and he was captured or killed, covert ops reasoned the Sandinistas would think he was simply an American spy or adviser coming in solo.

Dressed in a head-to-foot black wet suit, that was more for concealment than protection from cold water, Ellis brought the boat to within two hundred yards of the shore. The remainder of the distance he covered lying on his stomach paddling with his hands and arms from the front of the craft. The beach appeared deserted as the softly lapping waves drew him in. Pulling the strap over his head that had secured the submachine gun on his back, he held the weapon with one hand inside the boat and slipped over the side to make sure he was in shallow enough water to stand. Feet on the bottom, he cradled the weapon's stock in his shoulder, slid around behind the boat and pushed the craft in ahead of him. Intelligence had confirmed this was a totally deserted strip of beach, and up to this point that definitely appeared to be the case.

As the water level dropped from his chest to his waist, he brought his feet up from the bottom and floated to shore hanging on the back side of the rubber boat. It beached itself on the sand while Ellis maintained his concealed position. The infrared goggles he was wearing allowed him to scan the shore and the tree line fifty feet from the water's edge. All was quiet. No movement. Still, he decided to cover the distance from the water to the woods on his belly. He slithered across the sand and into the tall grass surrounding a palm tree. Then he braced himself with his elbows and began to peruse the thickening jungle that stretched out in front of him.

Minutes passed. And while he detected no movement, something seemed out of place amid the croaking frogs, fluttering birds, and the silent insects that surrounded him. There was something ahead that was not part of the natural ecosystem. He couldn't see it. He couldn't smell it. But he could hear the tiniest beginning of what he quickly recognized as a sigh. Then the grass began to rustle about thirty yards inland. Slowly at first. As if something was stretching, or rolling or laboriously beginning to rise. The head came first. A dark brown head with full black hair that covered each ear and stopped just below the jaw line. As the form continued its upward motion, it quickly became clear that the head was atop the naked body of an adolescent. A young boy, no more than sixteen or seventeen Ellis judged from his hidden position. The boy bent at the waist and extended his hand toward the ground. The grass moved again as a thinner, more delicate arm and hand reached up to clasp the boy's. As she was pulled upright, a girl, bare as her lover, folded herself into his embrace.

Ellis's mind was racing. His finger wrapped around the submachine gun's trigger and held its position. Were they alone? Of course they were alone, he thought. It's pretty plain what they were doing there. According to intelligence, the closest village was two miles inland. But maybe he was a sentry and she had come to see him. No. They both looked too young for that. They looked too young to be doing what they had obviously been doing, Ellis thought, but this was another country, another way of life. They gave no sign of having seen or heard Ellis and stood momentarily wrapped in each other's arms. They're not Adam and Eve, Ellis reasoned. It's unlikely they're going to walk away naked. Perhaps when they start to get dressed things will become clearer. Most Sandinistas wore uniforms, and they certainly carried guns. What would these two reach down and pick up?

He didn't have to wait long to find out. The boy bent over and pulled a white cotton dress from the ground. As the girl held her arms upward, he slipped it over her head and let it fall softly around her. He bent again to retrieve his things, and as he did she rubbed her hand gently across the curve of his back and the round of his buttocks. With a wad of clothes in his hand he stood up straight and kissed her. Then he handed her his shirt as he slipped his legs into a pair of well-worn jeans. She held his shirt open so he could slip his arms into it. It was a short sleeve checkered job he didn't bother to button or tuck in. They both slipped on sandals and arm-in-arm turned and began to walk away from Ellis, deeper into the jungle canopy.

Unarmed, Ellis thought. No uniform, he said to himself. No binoculars to watch the coast with. Two kids who had simply slipped away to make love, and now they had to make their way back before they were discovered. Romantic, but what difference did it make? His orders were straightforward. His mission was unambiguous. Recon the area. Clear it if need be. Clear it if he found *anything* there that wasn't supposed to be there. He was hardwired to follow orders. Complete the mission. It would be easy enough. He could drop them both instantly from this distance. Or he could close quietly and quickly and finish them off silently with the six-inch blade he carried on his waist. Or... he could let them walk away... and wait. Wait to see if the boy returned. One way was swift, sure, absolute. One way was not. There was no doubt in his mind that he should act. But his act was to let them walk away.

Ellis held his position in silence for half of an hour. Then he radioed back to the trawler. Beach uninhabited and secure.

The eleven Nicaraguans were escorted to the beach in small boats. Ellis watched them come ashore and start making their way inland. As each went by him, they either smiled or touched his shoulder or gave him the high sign they had learned in the states. He had risked his life for them. He had cleared the way. They were appreciative. They would now do what they could to get their country back.

It wasn't until two days later, back at his barracks, that Ellis was informed by his commanding officer that all eleven men were dead. They had walked into an ambush somewhere between the beach and the village. Apparently a civilian spotter had relayed their position to a Sandinista unit who set up claymore mines and fifty caliber machine guns and cut them to pieces before they could even return fire. All that training down the latrine, his commander bitched. Hell of a waste of time and equipment he moaned.

Just thought you ought to know, he told Ellis. Fortunes of war, he said. Don't give it a second thought. We completed our mission. We brought them in just the way it was written up. Hey, shit happens.

Ellis didn't answer. He couldn't. The knot in his throat was the size of a baseball. He just kept seeing the faces of those eleven husbands and fathers and patriots who thanked him as they walked by. Eleven good men died because he did what he thought was right instead of doing what he was told. He had decided that his judgment was a more accurate moral compass than his superior's orders.

Should two seemingly innocent people have died? Don't innocents always die in war? Was the boy the spotter? Who decides whether the life of two is better than the death of eleven? He kept turning those questions over and over in his mind. And he kept hearing the voice of the very first squad leader he ever had. The one who said, "You're given a mission, you see it through to the end. You don't ask why. You don't quit before it's over. You don't abort. You do what has to be done."

It had only been a road sign that brought it all back. Ellis hoped they wouldn't see another one any time soon.

Chapter 10

Once west of San Antonio, the quartet turned north. The gently rolling land of the Texas hill country began to stretch out as they made their way past Kerrville, Fredericksburg, and Junction. As they veered west again, conversations would start and stop and start again, with Alison sharing more than her traveling companions wanted to hear about Motif's sexual proclivities. She seemed to have no memory of Ellis walking in on the pair's men's room coitus, and no one in the car felt the need to bring it up. When Tilton wasn't waxing lyrical about the beauty of the Texas countryside he was engaged in a monologue about the comfort of Japanese autos versus the drivability of German makes. Lela would interject from time to time when she felt Tilton had droned on enough. Then she would query her back seat companion about the inner workings of the magazine that employed her. Ellis quietly took it all in, politely answering if he was asked a question, but preferring to gaze out the window at the land that was becoming browner, dustier, more barren.

With less and less civilization between towns that seemed smaller and smaller, they stopped for gas and snacks in Sonora, passed by Ozona, and began the long empty stretch to Fort Stockton. Endless nothing. Occasionally interrupted by a Road Runner scampering across the blacktop.

"So, where's the Fort," Alison piped up.

"What?" Tilton asked.

"The fort. This is Fort Stockton. So there must be a Fort," the redhead went on.

"We can pull off the highway and look for it. I'm sure it's around here somewhere," Tilton volunteered.

"No, don't. It was a rhetorical question."

"Fort Stockton is where the 9th Calvary housed the Buffalo Soldiers," Ellis interjected. "It was a regiment created for black men who enlisted a couple of years after the Civil War. Buffalo Soldiers is what the Comanche called them."

"Well," Tilton said, "that's an interesting bit of trivia from someone not steeped in Texas history."

"I always thought of it as military history. Twenty years in the service gives you plenty of time to read, you know."

"Christ," Alison cut in, "I hate history. I'm sorry I brought it up."

Alpine followed Fort Smith and after that the only thing between the foursome and their destination was more parched earth, scrub brush and black asphalt with a yellow line down the middle of it that pointed the way toward the setting sun. It would be dark before they reached their journey's end, but there would soon be more lights illuminating the darkness than simply those emanating from Tilton's high beams.

"What's that? In the sky. Off to the left," Lela asked.

Heads turned and the eyes in those heads grew wider. Dancing across the sky, in colors that seemed to change intermittently, were shafts of light. Or what appeared to be light. But the dark black earth in the distance gave no sign of a source for the shimmering pink, orange, and yellow streaks that seemed to emerge, move and swirl at will.

"Must be a meteor shower," Alison ventured.

"Not bright enough for that," Ellis said. "Those lights are more translucent."

"Maybe it's some kind of static electricity," Lela added.

"Nope," Tilton cut in. "They're not meteors. Not static electricity. Not swamp gas. Not camp fires."

"Some kind of phosphorescent minerals?" Ellis queried.

"No my friends. Those are the ghost lights of Marfa."

"Ghost lights. Did you sneak a drink or two at that last stop?" Alison asked.

"No, wait. I've heard of those," Lela said.

"Yep," Tilton began, "folks have been reporting sightings of these weird lights outside of Marfa for over a hundred years now. They just appear out of nowhere. Do their weird thing in the night sky with seemingly no rhyme or reason."

Ellis quizzed, "Bet there's been lots of speculation as to the cause, huh?"

"Oh yeah," Tilton went on, "nearly a hundred different folk tales about what they are, or why they're here, or what they mean. Everything from your modern theories of alien encounters to more primitive ideas. The Apaches thought they were stars that were literally falling out of the sky. But most of the different explanations have one thing in common." Three seconds of silence later, it was obvious Tilton was pausing for dramatic effect.

"Okay, okay…so what do they have in common?" Alison asked.

"Almost everyone agrees that a sighting portends evil. Something bad will likely follow," Tilton said.

"Yeah, like me having a bladder malfunction if we don't get there soon," Alison said.

The accompanying trio chuckled, but couldn't help pondering, based on recent events, if the night's strange apparition might not indeed store trouble in its wake. However, the prospect of journey's end, and the faint outline of city lights on the horizon, was enough to steer their thoughts to less ominous concerns.

As they entered the outskirts of town, which proved to be a pretty short skirt, Ellis thought how one small town in the middle of nowhere looked much like another. The gasoline stations, convenience stores and do-it-yourself car washes had a way of bringing familiarity to towns from California to Texas and almost everywhere in-between. Their highway signs reduced your speed from 70 to 55 to 30, and if you were smart, you heeded them. Traffic violations were often a major source of income for towns whose salad days were far behind them. And that's definitely the initial impression Marfa left with Ellis.

It didn't take long for them to reach the four-cornered center of town with a lonely stoplight that gave Tilton time to survey the surrounding intersection and its environs. Spying the prototypical courthouse dome to his right, he turned in that direction when the light changed from red to green. He didn't have to go far before the illumination, along what was obviously the town's center of commerce, helped him spot The Hotel Paisano. Available parking spaces in front of the hotel were already taken and valet parking had yet to intrude upon Marfa. Then Tilton saw there was additional parking on the side street next to the hotel. So he took a left and pulled into one open space that had another beside it. Ellis helped Tilton unhitch the trailer full of paintings they had hauled from Houston and the pair pulled it into the empty space beside Tilton's car.

"You think it will be okay here?" Ellis asked.

Tilton responded, "This is Marfa, Brig, not the big city. She'll be fine for one night."

The Hotel Paisano had been Marfa's finest hotel for the last seventy-five years. In truth, it's only fine hotel. The town, which was founded fifty years previous to the hotel's arrival in 1930, started out as a place to stop for water along the Texas and New Orleans Railroad. Ranching dominated most of its initial century. In fact, it was ranching that brought the biggest thing that ever happened, or ever was likely to happen, to Marfa and the Hotel Paisano. George Steven's selected the land surrounding Marfa as the primary location to film the 1956 movie of Edna Ferber's sweeping saga of cattle and oil and family passions called *GIANT*. The Hotel Paisano was central headquarters for the crew and cast that included Elizabeth Taylor, Rock Hudson, James Dean, Dennis Hopper, Chill Wills, and more. Vestiges of Hollywood's royalty remained a big part of the hotel long after the stars departure and continued to draw curious travelers to the unlikely outpost. But hard times and dry holes took their toll on Marfa, much as they had on many once prosperous hamlets.

Then a strange thing happened. In the late seventies, art once again raised its capricious head in the Big Bend Country. New York's prestigious Dia Art Foundation agreed to fund an art installation located on the former site of Fort D.A. Russell in Marfa. And a few years later the Chinati Foundation opened its publicly funded, independent, nonprofit institution to the public.

All of a sudden, a desert town bare of shade, style, and sustenance, was on its way to being hip. Albeit in a remote sort of way. More artists followed. Writers came. And why not? If Marfa was anything, it was cheap. Tourists started coming back. And with them, the revival of the Hotel Paisano to its former glory. A glory that was about to be inhabited by four tired and hungry travelers from Houston.

Tilton, Ellis, Lela, and Alison walked around the corner and entered through the main entrance on North Highland. Never noticing that their car was parked just outside the hotel's patio, which provided a shorter route to the main lobby. The stucco building with its ornamental Spanish flourishes and arched entryway was a welcome site for the frazzled four. Crossing the earth-toned tiles that lead them through the lobby and toward registration, they couldn't help but notice the displays highlighting original movie posters of *GIANT*. Handmade signs had been added letting guests know they could rent a video recorder and watch the movie in the privacy of their room. For a nominal charge, of course, and provided guests had a little over three hours to kill, which frankly in Marfa, most guests had. Alison, on the other hand, didn't have three seconds to kill. She was hell-bent on finding the ladies room. Spotting it to their right, she veered off without bothering to reiterate her pressing need to her fellow travelers.

The check-in counter itself boasted even more tile. Colorful brown, yellow, and beige geometric patterns that put you in mind of nearby Mexico. There was one of those old fashioned silver bells on the counter and Tilton banged it with gusto. Seconds later a sad-eyed senior citizen with hair the color of bailed hay emerged from a hole-in-the-wall office only steps away. He asked for their names and one by one checked them off a list Wendell James had given him. One room for Tilton and Lela. Another for Ellis. Tilton had made the extra room a condition of his participation. Lela, mindful of her back seat companion of the last number of hours, asked if there were additional rooms available.

"No. We're all full up," the septuagenarian said. "Bunch of arty people here. A lot of 'em are in the restaurant now. I'd keep my distance though, if I were you. Some of 'em are kinda' weird."

"Good advice," Tilton replied satirically, "arty types can definitely be a pain in the butt."

"But what are we going to do about a room for Alison," Lela continued.

"I said I'd bring her here and take her back if need be. What she does while she's here is her problem."

Lela wasn't letting him off the hook that easily though. "Tilton, we need to look into it."

"Well look, we're all hungry anyway," Tilton answered. "Let's see who's in the restaurant. I'm sure we can get with Wendell and work it out." Then turning toward the old timer behind the desk, he said, "If a redheaded lady comes out here looking for us, tell her we've gone in to get something to eat. Okay?"

"I'll tell her," the frail night clerk answered. "But watch out for them artists I mentioned."

"Got my eye peeled, partner," Tilton replied, as the trio turned away from the counter and strode past the fireplace, the cowhide couch with matching rocking chairs, and the roughhewn coffee table holding horseshoe ashtrays and spurs in service as paper weights. No one had to tell them which way to go. The noise spilling from the open glass-and-wood-frame doors made it obvious where the action was.

A semicircular bar stood a few feet from the white tablecloth dining area that made up the bulk of the room. Wendell James sat cross-legged on one of the stools surrounding it. A glass of white wine stood at attention near his resting elbow. Tilton suggested that Lela and Ellis take a table near the boisterous commotion coming from the sextet near the doors that opened onto the patio. He had recognized a couple of the faces in that crowd and felt like joining what he assumed was their merriment. But first he wanted to touch base with the man who had brought them all here.

"Don't forget to ask about a room for Alison," Lela reminded him. Tilton told her he would as he veered toward the bar.

"Wendell, what are you doing here all by yourself? Why aren't you over there with the rest of your retinue?

"Just taking a break," the gallery owner said to Tilton. "A moment of solitude in an evening of revelry."

"Very wise, Wendell. Very wise. Always good to pace yourself. Otherwise those young bucks can run you ragged. Say, what's Reyes doing here? You didn't tell me he was part of this fandango."

"Oh, he's not. He told me he was visiting his parents. Supposedly, they live south of here in Presidio. Said he heard about the exhibition and wanted to stop by. I told him everyone was arriving tonight, so he came over."

Across the room, Lela and Ellis had taken a table for four next to the larger group. A group that consisted of New York figurative painter Brad Aarons and his wife. His character studies of those psychologically damaged by wars and their aftermath had helped make a name for him internationally. Aarons was gaunt with salt and pepper hair that seemed to part naturally in the middle of his head and lay symmetrically on either side. From time to time he'd nervously use his index finger to brush his forelocks to their respective positions. Particularly when his wife, who was seated next to him, commented acerbically on the immaturity of the wine, the appalling lack of Evian, or the delightfully hideous accent of the waitress. Aarons' wife was as ugly as her attitude. Beneath her Prince Valiant hairdo, her face was crimped, pinched and lined. Horn-rimmed glasses straddled her nose and made her dark eyes look like two giant black olives.

Next to her was Wendell James's empty chair. On the other side, Alejandro Reyes commanded one corner. His gangly arms and long legs made him look like a bird of prey hovering selfishly over carrion. Motif was on the other corner with both elbows on the table. He held a half empty glass of champagne and kept blowing into the hair of the young blonde who sat between the two artists. She was subsequently introduced to Lela and Ellis as Justine, an intern at the Chinati Foundation.

After a couple of minutes Tilton and James left the bar and strode over. Another round of introductions followed. Reyes suggested that the others make room for the new arrivals at their table. Tilton demurred; saying there was no reason to crowd everyone and commented that there was another member of their party who would be along shortly.

"Well, take my advice and avoid the Shiraz at all cost, "Aaron's wife volunteered, to her tablemates' obvious chagrin.

"No need for Shiraz, love, this is Texas. And here come those pitchers of Margaritas I just ordered. Put two on their table and one on ours, will you dear," he said to the waitress who arrived gripping the handles of all three pitchers in one hand and balancing a tray of salt-rimmed glasses in the other.

As the tart tequila-laced cocktails started to be consumed, Lela said, "Maybe I should go check on Alison. I'm beginning to worry about her."

"Giver her another minute or so," Tilton suggested. "My guess is she's putting her war paint on and gearing up for a hell of an entrance."

Ellis slowly sipped his Margarita and surveyed the surrounding scene as conversations bounced back and forth between the two tables. Decibel levels grew higher. In a whispered aside, Tilton mentioned to Lela and Ellis that the reason Wendell James was sitting alone when they walked in wasn't due solely to the odious nature of Aaron's wife. Though obviously that contributed to it. He said the impresario of the weekend event confided that he needed a moment to gather his composure after Motif told him that, on further reflection, the paintings the two had selected together no longer seemed appropriate. Not austere enough, the Creole artist said. So he had taken a shotgun and blown holes in them from various distances. A statement about what war does to art, he said. James had yet to see the results and felt the need to brace himself should a third of his planned exhibit be nothing more than tatters.

"Speaking of shotgun blasts," Tilton added, "here comes Alison."

The redhead's stiletto heels clicked across the hardwood floor like the sound of woodpeckers in stereo. But it was her bounteous cleavage, barely covered for maximum effect, which heralded her arrival between the two tables. She had obviously spent time in the ladies room changing clothes, combing her hair, painting her face and steeling her resolve.

"Hello everyone, I'm Alison Wayne. I'll be covering this weekend for *All Things Art.*"

The bug-eyed Mrs. Aarons made the mistake of saying exactly what she was thinking.

"You're a journalist," she questioned sardonically, unable to mask her fascination with the red head's plunging neckline.

"Damn straight four-eyes," sprung Alison's reply. "Just because I've got big tits doesn't mean I can't write my ass off."

Aaron's wife turned away without reply. Aaron smiled and nodded a gracious touché. The rest, at both tables, chuckled somewhat embarrassingly. Alison then picked up the Margarita that had been poured for her at Tilton's table, held it up to the light as if examining it and said, "Oh, looks like something's in my drink. Think I need a fresh one." Then with a no-look flip of her wrist she sent the contents of her glass flying toward the corner of the table Motif was occupying. The green liquid caught him squarely in his Creole grin.

With the smile still wide on his face, he slowly raised his napkin from his lap, dabbed his eyes, licked his lips and said, "Good to see you, babe."

Chin held high, Alison spun around, took her seat at the foursome's table and poured herself another.

"Hell of an ice breaker," Tilton said. "Now this soiree can really get started."

The combined tables went through three more pitchers before the festivities started to wind down. The Mexican elixir seemed to have a calming effect on all present and after a while couples and individuals started to take their leave. The Aarons were the first to go. Once they were out of range, a chorus of "What a bitch", "How does he stand her?" and "Can you believe that broad?" filled the air.

Alison's aggressive antics had orchestrated an abrupt end to Motif's interest in the Chinati intern. So much so that the artist and writer had eventually gotten together and started to nuzzle one another with attendant groping. This led to the embarrassed exit of the young woman in short order.

Lela said she was totally wiped out, and agreeing with Tilton that Alison obviously wouldn't be needing a separate room, said her goodnights and left to go to bed. Tilton said he'd be along later. He had nightcaps, Cohibas and more conversation in mind. So he suggested Wendell James and Alejandro Reyes leave their larger table and join him and Ellis for an after dinner drink and a smoke. Alison and Motif had already retired to the patio for fresh air, stars, and nobody wanted to imagine what else.

Before the drinks could be ordered, Reyes politely said he'd had more than enough and should be on his way. Ellis watched him leave the dining room and noted that, at the counter in the lobby, the painter turned left. Interesting, he thought to himself, remembering that the main entrance to the hotel required a right turn.

When the waitress brought the three brandies to the table, she saw that Tilton was about to light up. "Sorry, sir, you can't do that in here. But you can have your drinks and your cigar on the patio or by the fireplace if you like."

"Better go for the fireplace," Tilton responded, "Alison and Motif are on the patio and we best leave well enough alone."

Retracing the path they had taken into the restaurant, Ellis, Tilton and Wendell James retired to the fireless fireplace. Tilton stretched out on the couch while James and Ellis each dropped into a rocking chair. Ellis couldn't help but notice that the direction he had seen Reyes take led to the stairs rather than any discernible exit. He knew his concern about his employer and Reyes sharing the same elevator bank in Houston had been plausibly explained by Lela, but he had no way of knowing if she had really been telling the truth. There continued to be no definitive reason to doubt her. But he couldn't shake the feeling that there was more to the Mexican's relationship with Lela Mangas than met the eye.

The smoke rose languidly from Tilton's Cohiba as he sipped his brandy and bantered with Wendell James about the vicissitudes of the art world. James, just barely able to keep from slurring, indicated his enterprise was not doing as well as it once had. That gave Tilton the opening to say the owner wasn't taking enough chances with more leading edge artists. James countered that he knew Tilton was talking about himself and he had no intention of rehashing all the reasons he didn't display the Houstonian's work in his Austin gallery.

"You can't steal second without taking your foot off first," Tilton volunteered. The apt analogy, though admittedly somewhat of a non sequitur, breezed right by the inebriated art dealer. Shortly thereafter he bid his comrades adieu.

"Well, looks like it's down to just you and me, hoss," Tilton said, feet now resting on the rustic coffee table. "When are you planning on hitting the hay?"

"I'll go to bed when you go to bed," Ellis answered.

"Jesus, still working, huh? No wonder that brandy snifter in your hand is devoid of lip prints."

"Hey, let me ask you a question, Tilton. What do you think of Alejandro Reyes? How long have you guys known him? Any reason to think he's got a problem with you?"

"I may be a tad tight, my good man, but that sounded like three questions to me. Let me see if I can get 'em in the right order. Reyes is a damn good artist. A little geeky at times. We've known him for a couple of years. Ernie Beeker, back in Houston... you remember Ernie, right?"

"Sure," Ellis answered.

"Well, Ernie was the one who first introduced us. He saw some of the guy's paintings in El Paso and sort of took him under his wing. Got his work noticed around Houston. The only problem Reyes might have with me is probably the same problem he has with lots of other artists. He thinks he's a lot more talented than most of us. And he keeps wondering why he doesn't get as many gigs as some of the rest of us do."

"Why doesn't he?" Ellis asked.

"Ernie wants to bring him along slowly. Doesn't want him to get over-exposed too quickly. Takes the guy a long time to do one of his paintings. If he does it right. Ernie doesn't want him just churning stuff out, you know. Just to make more money. That's shortsighted. There's a fine line in this business between hot, ubiquitous, and yesterday's news. Oh yeah, I almost forgot. He's got a thing for Lela too. Course, a lot of guys do."

Ellis was about to ask Tilton what he meant by that when Alison and Motif waddled into the lobby soaked to the bone and dripping all over the tiled floor.

"I didn't think they had a pool here," Tilton said.

"They don't," Alison replied. "It's raining."

"It never rains in the desert," Tilton came back.

Motif responded, "It fucking does now, man."

Chapter 11

The sun was just beginning to paint the sky pink as Ellis showered, shaved and started down the stairs decorated even more lavishly than the rest of the hotel with ornate Mexican tiles. He had awoken early and decided to stretch his legs before the day began. Stopping at the counter, he gently roused the elderly desk clerk they had met the night before. The old fellow was slumped in a chair, eyes closed, with an open magazine in his lap. He came to quickly though with little consternation, as if this sort of thing happened to him frequently. Ellis asked if he had a Mr. Reyes registered at the Hotel. The man rose, with less effort than Ellis assumed it might have taken, adjusted his glasses, and after asking how the name was spelled, peered into the computer monitor as he two-fingered R E Y E S on the keyboard. His response was negative. No Reyes registered. Ellis then asked him if the hotel happened to have another way in and out other than the main entrance. This time he got positive feedback. The clerk told him that the restaurant led to the patio, which exited onto the street, and there was also a separate, back stairwell available for emergency exits too. Ellis thanked him, wished him well and headed outside.

The rain from the night before had left the sidewalk spotted and damp in places. Must have rained for a long time, Ellis reasoned. He wasn't sure because he had nodded off pretty quickly. Less a function of the alcohol, with which he had only played around the edges, and more a result of the long car ride, he concluded. But the day was beginning on a sunny note, and he could tell by looking at his surroundings that this was a town that could use all the rain it could get.

It didn't take him long to walk to the end of Highland, passing shops and art galleries, budget stores and a small library. Signs that tourism was now the town's main source of income. Once beyond the concrete confines of the meager downtown area however, he began to get a sense of scope for the vastness that surrounded the tiny Texas community. Far off in the distance, the Davis Mountains formed a jagged line from horizon to horizon. And there seemed to be little other than distance. A flat, brown land speckled here and there with green cane cactus, a Pinion Pine or a Live Oak. It was still early enough, and quiet enough he guessed, that on the outskirts of town he was able to watch a small herd of white-tailed deer emerge from a ditch running alongside a two-lane road. They darted across the blacktop, and then as if their legs were spring loaded, bound effortlessly over a barbed wire fence and headed away from any remnant of their human neighbors. Not the sort of thing he'd see on his morning run in San Diego's Balboa Park, he said to himself. Unless of course, he was running through the zoo.

By the time he got back to the hotel he was wondering more than ever how an isolated hamlet like Marfa could change from cow town to oil town to world-renowned art enclave. It just didn't seem to compute. Luckily Tilton and Lela were awake and dressed and raring to take him to breakfast at Consuela's where Tilton would tell him all about it.

According to Tilton, the real reason the Chinati Foundation existed, and the reason they got all that New York money to begin with, was because of an artist named Donald Judd. Judd came to prominence in the sixties and was one of the leading components of minimalism.

"To Judd," Tilton said, while simultaneously making his way through a plate of huevos rancheros, "less really was more. It wasn't just about simplifying. It was about deconstructing everything that everybody thought about art. To him and his ilk, even abstraction wasn't enough. Art's always going through changes. And the thing that changes the most is the whole idea of just what constitutes art. From your realists to your surrealists to your expressionists to your impressionists to your abstractionists to your minimalists to your fucking cartoonists... art is whatever one group of people can convince another group of people that art is. Hell, Judd even thought color was too complicated. He wanted to really boil things down to their essence. Natural. Individual. That's what he was into. So much so, well, you'll find some folks who won't even call him an artist. Some say he was just a savvy designer. But differences of opinion is what makes baseball and it's also what makes art."

"Okay", Ellis responded, "but why here? Why out here in the middle of nowhere?"

There was a momentary pause as Tilton had a mouthful of eggs and was unable to respond. During that silence, Ellis actually came up with his own answer. "Wait, that's it, isn't it? The middle of nowhere. Nothingness. Nothing around to get in the way or hamper people's appreciation of his work. Less is more, right?"

"You're a pretty quick study, lad," Tilton piped in.

"And let's not forget," Lela added, "that the price was right back then too. This is not exactly beach front property, you know."

"Absolutely," Tilton agreed, "the most artistic thing of all is often finance."

The trio finished their breakfast, drove back to the hotel, hooked up the trailer, then headed over to the Chinati Foundation to meet with Wendell James and start setting up. The trip took all of about five minutes. Marfa's a damn small town. Ellis wasn't sure what he was expecting to see. But he had a quick and familiar response. He had been around enough military installations to know one when he saw one. So it was not a complete surprise when Tilton mentioned that the grounds they were on was the site of the former Fort D.A. Russell.

"What are those concrete blocks off to the side there?" Ellis questioned.

"Art," Tilton answered. "That's part of the exhibit." From the look on Ellis's face, the Texan felt the need to add, "No shit."

Fifteen massive concrete squares, open in the center, stood in two columns that narrowed toward the end. Grass, now starting to bend slightly from an embryonic breeze, grew wild around them. The word "junkyard" came to Ellis's mind but remained unspoken. He had never pretended to be an expert and he certainly wasn't going to start now.

The group's destination was a series of wood-framed buildings that Ellis quickly recognized as barracks. One of which had been completely emptied of its normally permanent displays in order to house the wake-for-peace exhibition that Wendell James had championed. Each of the artists had four different paintings they would be hanging. Tilton, who definitely had more energy than most, if not all, of his artistic contemporaries, had arrived first to hang his work. Wendell James had already worked out exactly where each of the twelve different paintings would be. So Tilton, Ellis and Lela set about uncrating the paintings and putting them in their preordained positions.

As Ellis helped carry the frameless works to the spots James pointed out, he couldn't help but be mesmerized by the content between his outstretched arms. The ash-filled canvases had always had a macabre aura about them, but this was as close to them as Ellis had ever been. And if anything, his sense of discomfort was even greater. For these paintings had not only the fine granular texture of the ones he had seen previously, but upon closer inspection also contained the tiniest bits of bone. Small shards like concentrated gravel. The fact that Ellis was carrying what was once a living, breathing, human being gave him pause. Particularly when he thought of the context of this particular exhibition. A wake for peace. How odd, he thought, that one of the people putting these paintings in place was a man who had spent the majority of his life practicing the art of war. Ellis was a man who tried to save the life of his comrades by taking the lives of others who stood in their way. Was this a warrior in his own hands? Or someone who had never known the battlefield? The thoughts swirled in his mind as he stood in the center of the long building and stared intently at what he was holding.

"Brig, are you okay?" Lela's voice registered a moment or two after she had spoken.

"Yes. I'm fine. Where does this one go?"

Once they were up, and standing back at a distance, it was easier for Ellis to put them in perspective. Whether or not it was the proper perspective, who could say. The paintings consisted of symbols. Two symbols intertwined in each painting. In one, the Union and Confederate flags of the Civil War. Another had an oval representing the Japanese rising sun combined with a Christian cross. The third contained a Vietnamese conical hat and a G.I.'s steel helmet. The last, an Apache lance and a U.S. Calvary saber. Each painting, five feet long and three feet wide. Big. Graphic. Varying earth tone colors. Staggering really, Ellis thought to himself. When you realize it's not just symbols you're looking at, but people. People hanging on the wall.

Wendell James had photos of the paintings Brad Aarons would be bringing over later in the day. You could hold the photos in your hand, but simply looking at them gave you the feeling they'd occupy a place in your heart for years to come. He passed them around and let Tilton, Lela and Ellis take a look. Each one was a face. A haunted face. Faces that had seen things people shouldn't see. The young. The old. They were all burningly realistic representations of the same thing. The absence of hope. Ellis had seen such faces before. Not on walls but in suffocating jungles and shells of cities and endless deserts that never entirely vacated his psyche. Jesus, he thought to himself. Wendell James's event was shaping up to be pretty damn depressing.

"Motif should be here soon," Wendell said to the three. He's supposed to set up next."

"I think we'll take Brig over and let him see the boxes," Tilton said. "This is his first time here. We'll circle back in a little while."

The three left the barracks and started across the compound amid the sound of thunderclaps and progressively threatening skies. It had started to rain again while they were hanging Tilton's paintings, and it certainly looked like more was on the way. The wind had picked up too, causing them to sidestep a couple of tumbleweeds the size of medicine balls that bounced across their path.

Reaching the first of two consecutive buildings, both far larger than the barracks they had been in, the trio stepped inside. Tilton spoke first. "We're in what used to be an artillery shed. There's another, exactly like this one, just beyond. This building and the other one house the most famous work here."

Stepping through the atrium, they entered a huge open area. Concrete pillars, right and left, were spaced evenly on both sides of the building. Running down the center of the shed and also flanking the pillars on both sides were immense aluminum boxes. They were all exactly the same size, forty-one by fifty-one by seventy-two inches. And while the initial impression was that they were all precisely the same, as the three walked slowly by and around them, Ellis saw that each was slightly different. One would be open on top. Another would have one side open. Still another would have two sides open. Or the top would drop down at a diagonal slant. Or rise from the bottom similarly. Since the sides of the building were floor-to-ceiling quartered and squared windows, light would pour in from outside making not only each box look different, but so too the shadows that each box cast. And though the weather outside was turning more and more ominous, Ellis couldn't help but feel a sense of peace and tranquility standing among this unique dichotomy of conformity and individualism.

"What is all this called?" Ellis asked.

"It's known simply as one hundred untitled works in mill aluminum," Tilton answered. I guess Judd thought giving it a name would be uncalled for. Another layer that wasn't really needed. The guy was definitely into minimalism."

"Isn't it wonderful how the openness of the building gives you the feeling that all of this is right in the middle of the untouched land," Lela added.

"It's pretty impressive," Ellis said.

"There's a cleanliness to it all." Tilton came back, "Speaking of clean, it's damn sure getting cleaner outside."

It was as if a faucet had been left open. The force of the rain splattered the dirt and sandy ground around the building. Water poured down on the galvanized iron roof and echoed with a rat-a-tat-tat that put Ellis in mind of a fully functioning firing range. The wind was now bending the tall clumps of grass perpendicular to the earth. It was beginning.

Far above them, beyond their or anyone's control, incompatible forces were in motion. Cool, dry air from the Rocky Mountains which had been moving south and down through the central plains, was now on a collision course with warm, moist undercurrents which had come up from the Gulf of Mexico. Each would soon meet in the far southwest corner of Tornado Alley. And neither would be willing to yield.

"Jesus, I'm glad we got in here when we did," Lela said. "Nothing to do but wait it out. Tilton, you did remember to put the windows up on the car, didn't you?"

"Wet car seats may be the least of our worries, babe," he said as lightening cut a gash across the horizon, lit up the brooding firmament and moments later was followed by a crack of thunder that sounded like the building was being cleaved in half.

The already darkening sky became blacker. The rain started to bounce. Because it wasn't rain anymore. It was hail. Hail that began the size of pebbles. Almost charming at first. Little ice balls clopping on the ground like candy spilled on a hardwood floor. Then the charm started to dissipate as the candy grew to the size of jawbreakers and started coming down horizontally, banging against the glass windows that surrounded three apprehensive people and fifty indifferent boxes.

"You get this a lot in Texas, do you?" Ellis asked, trying to lighten what was up to this point, a collective but unspoken concern.

"Frankly," Tilton answered, "I don't like the look of it. When you get big weather out here, you get really big weather."

Back at the barracks, which was considerably smaller and not nearly as sturdy as the former artillery shed Tilton, Lela and Ellis were sharing, Motif and Alison were huddled on the floor, backs against the wall, wishing they were back at the Hotel Paisano. Wendell James was pacing like a caged circus cat and muttering to himself. Not only was he concerned about the storm raging around him, he was also less than delighted with Motif's buckshot-blasted canvases. Incoming critics might view them as genius, or they might view them as excrement, depending on their mood, James thought to himself. And if this damn storm keeps up, he concluded, their mood will be decidedly foul. "That's assuming any of them even show up," he unwittingly said out loud.

The hail and wind and rain continued unabated for at least an hour. The occupants of the different buildings held their positions and kept wondering when it would stop. Slowly, the hail turned back into rain. The rain decreased in ferocity and slowly turned into a drizzle. The wind died down and the sky turned from charcoal to an odd green, almost the color of pond scum.

"Let's go check things out," Tilton said. His two cohorts agreed and followed him outside. From across the divide they could see Alison, Motif, and Wendell James cautiously emerging from their shelter. The two groups of three walked slowly toward one another and met approximately halfway between their respective buildings.

"Hell of a storm, huh Wendell," Tilton began.

"Yes. I just hope it's over," the gallery owner answered.

"I wonder if any of the cars were damaged in all that hail," Lela asked.

"Bet they were," Alison said. "It was coming down hard enough to dent asphalt."

"Hopefully the Aarons had the good sense to wait out the rain before they left the hotel with Brad's paintings," Wendell James said.

"Wendell, they're from New York. Good sense has nothing to do with it," Tilton quipped.

Ellis hadn't joined in the chatter. He was too busy looking around. Looking particularly at the green sky and cumulous clouds that were rolling in from a dark expanse of the heavens in the direction of town.

About a hundred feet south of where the group was huddled, a jackrabbit scampered from behind a patch of choler cactus and headed west at a dead run. "Oh look," Lela said, "bet that poor little guy got soaked."

No sooner had she completed her sentence than a mule deer emerged from behind the barracks housing the artists' paintings. The startled buck took off like a shot; high tailing it in the same direction the rabbit had taken.

"Can you believe that?" Alison said, drawing the others attention to the fleeing deer.

"And look over there," Motif shouted, pointing to a hairy-backed, short-legged, snorting javelin that was also tearing west across the open land.

"What do you think is going on?" Wendell James asked no one in particular.

"They're leaving," Ellis said. "They know something's coming."

The wind seemed to come up immediately, swift and strong, and blowing in the same direction the animals had fled. Fat raindrops started to spot the people standing there and the ground around them.

"We've got to get undercover," Ellis said. "And we've got to do it now."

"No," Alison argued, "Motif and I want to go back to the hotel."

"There's no time," Ellis said sharply. "And anyway, the hotel is that way."

Everyone looked in the direction Ellis was pointing. And none would ever forget what they saw. There are times in life when nature makes it abundantly clear how totally insignificant people are. This was one of those times. Each person standing and staring in the direction of downtown Marfa saw the same thing. And the enormity of what they saw filled them with horror. It was at least a half-mile across. A churning, black cauldron of clouds that seemed to form a monumental anvil across the sky. Lightning was darting from it like electrified serpent tongues. Wispy, curling clouds were beginning to drop from its backside forming a tail that grew longer and longer. Then the tail started to sway and the earth beneath it began to churn.

"Come on, Ellis said, "we've got to get inside the largest building." He knew there was no alternative. The land all around them was too open. He could only hope the structure would be strong enough.

The group all took off for the artillery shed Ellis, Lela, and Tilton had been in before. Rain had turned to hail again and pelted them as they ran. Alison wasn't used to sprinting and almost slipped and fell. Motif grabbed her and held her upright as they continued to run. By the time they reached the shed, all were soaked to the skin. They hurried in and closed the massive doors behind them. Pulling them tightly shut to make sure they'd lock in place. Then, as if hoping they wouldn't see what they knew they'd see, they all went toward the east windows to gape in disbelief at the juggernaut on the horizon.

Hail, now the size of baseballs, thundered down just on the other side of the glass, pummeling the already soaked earth. The immense configuration they had seen before had now taken on an even more massive form. It hovered like a giant mother ship, obliterating all light below it.

"It must be between downtown and here," Wendell James said, "but at least it looks like it's stationary."

"It doesn't look like it's moving because it's coming straight at us," Ellis responded.

Lela gave voice to what everyone was thinking. "Oh God!"

"Quick, come away from the windows," Ellis ordered. Twenty years of military training instinctively rose to the surface. "We should all get in the center of the building."

The sound came next. Something beyond the shrillness of the wind. A low rumble, almost imperceptible at first. But building. Then all eyes were drawn to the bottom of the funnel which seemed to be shredding the earth as its tip ripped the landscape, flung cars into the air, uprooted trees, snapped telephone poles, leveled houses and barns like they were made of matchsticks. All still in the distance, for now. But the monster's effluence was about to announce its impending arrival.

The debris storm began. Rocks and boulders bounced along as if they were tumbleweed. Slats from fences and ripped-up panels from porches flew by like missiles. Pebbles, gravel, barbed wire and nails started to pelt the reinforced glass windows with the force of a fire hose. Then, all of a sudden, from the very sky itself, something came tumbling and turning and slamming against the window with an enormous thud. A collective gasp, like wind escaping from an upper cut to the stomach, rose from all present. The force of the gusts was holding something tight against the glass, and the something was staring at them. It was a face. A child's hopeless stare captured on canvass. One of Brad Aarons paintings.

"Everyone, now," Ellis shouted, tearing their attention from the oil painting plastered to the window, "we've got to get inside these boxes. These boxes running down the center of the building. Find an opening and get inside, quickly."

"We can't do that," Wendell James blurted reflexively. "This is priceless art."

"You better hope its damned strong art," Tilton interjected, inherently understanding Ellis's command. "Those windows may not hold. These boxes are bolted to the floor."

Motif hurriedly jumped into one of the open top boxes and helped lift Alison in with him. Tilton took Lela by the hand and scurried down the row until he found one that opened from the opposite direction of the approaching maelstrom. He helped Lela in and then got in behind her. Ellis took Wendell James by the arm and rushed him along the row until he found another open top. "In you go," he said as he helped the frightened gallery owner over the top. "And stay down," he said to him. Then he shouted for all to hear, "Stay down. No matter what happens. Stay down!"

They only heard part of what he said. By now the low rumble had turned into a pounding, pulsating freight train of sound. Ellis looked up to see darkness virtually encircling them. Then he saw the barracks they had been in earlier come apart like a house of cards. Roof, walls, and everything inside collapsing, then being instantaneously catapulted across the Texas countryside. The sound was deafening now. It was roaring all around them. The building itself began to tremble. The funnel was almost upon them. Ellis knew he had to enclose himself like the others. But he was transfixed by the whirling majesty of the awesome power just yards away. Now the rumble turned into a quake as the building began to shake violently. And Ellis was yanked out of his momentary trance by what he saw. Amid the twisting, spinning, revolving funnel that connected to the evil anvil above it, a body was spinning like an ice skater in mid twirl. It seemed to be caught in the vortex, unable to be released. Then, as if shot from a canon, it was hurled headlong into and through the upper window of the building itself. The disintegration of one pane precipitated the collapse of all, as the entire wall shattered like crystal. The force of the oncoming gale blew Ellis toward the building's far wall like graffiti in the wind. He knew his last chance was the row of boxes lining that side of the structure. If he blew by them, there was only the other glass wall between him and a lone star eternity. Then his midsection felt like the edge of a two by four had swung into it as he was slammed into the side of one of Donald Judd's milled aluminum boxes. The pain in his gut pulled a trigger that fired a thought directly to his brain. This box was open topped. He threw his head forward and flipped himself over and into the confines of the square as what sounded like a jet engine roared over him. Balled up, his feet braced against the sides of the box, he closed his eyes and awaited his fate. As the whirlwind screamed around him, his box, firmly anchored to the cement floor, creaked and rattled and shook, but held its ground.

Ellis had been under attack before. Not by nature but by man. And just as there had always come a time when he sensed the incoming artillery or the unfriendly fire was not going to find him, he soon sensed the dragon was going to pass him by. Enough so that he opened his eyes and watched the remainder of the terrible green and black monster disintegrating above him. Deciding it was virtually done, he turned in his box, got to his knees and raised his head just enough to see the tornado, now past, rampage through a line of pinion pines, pulling them up and tearing them away like roots pulled from the earth by the hand of God. But apparently the storm felt a postscript was needed. So the whirling pull of the after-wind began to suck what was left of the carnage behind it. Something, Ellis never knew what, made him turn his head to the right, just in time to see the body that had crashed through the glass wall of windows prior to the storm, being plucked again from a box it had been flattened against during the assault. Like a vacuum cleaner, the gust whisked it up and away toward the border in which it was headed. But as it left the building, the whirling dervish passed closely enough for Ellis to spot the dark black hair, bug eyes, and face forever frozen in fear, of Mrs. Brad Aarons.

Chapter 12

At a bench in Balboa Park, Ellis sat sipping coffee and enjoying the sunshine. His bright, white, tree stump of an English bulldog lounged on the bench with him. Ellis had retrieved his dog, Osgood, from the kennel when he returned to San Diego from El Paso. Osgood wasn't crazy about the kennel, but he was resigned to the fact that his master was often gone for certain periods of time. And if he had to be somewhere without him, the kennel seemed as good a place as any. It had individual runs, both inside and outside for each dog. And once a day, playtime was invoked, allowing four or five dogs to romp together. Though frankly, Osgood wasn't much of a romper. He was more of an observer, preferring to let the human, or in this particular instance, canine comedy, unfold before him. While the Dobermans, Dalmatians, Spaniels, and Schnauzers were wildly cavorting like Christian youth camp attendees on steroids, Osgood would take it all in, process it, and in the end choose to simply decline participation.

He much preferred where he was today. In the company of his master, enjoying a quiet respite, awaiting the arrival of an attractive woman with soft hands who would stroke him and babble gibberish. Being a keen spectator and recorder of life's recurring events, Osgood had seen this scenario unfold numerous times before. Ellis would take him to the park, position him prominently on the bench, and before long a sweating female jogger or cleanly-scrubbed feminine stroller would wander by and be unable to keep her hands off him while asking his master all sorts of questions about him. Yes, Osgood was also resigned to being a babe magnet.

But today, Ellis wasn't using Osgood as bait. He had already made arrangements to meet someone at the very bench he and his portly pooch were occupying. Ellis had returned to San Diego from El Paso. But his trip to El Paso from Marfa hadn't followed the prearranged script. As had been discussed, Tilton and Lela were going to drive him to El Paso after the weekend Wake For Peace and then head back to Houston. But nature's wrath had thrown a rather monstrous monkey wrench into virtually everyone's plans who was anywhere near the vicinity of Marfa.

The Wake For Peace never happened. Once the tumultuous Texas twister blew through, there was no longer any place to have it. Not to mention the fact that the paintings that had been gathered for the show were somewhere between Marfa, the Davis Mountains, and the Mexican border. What was left of the Chinati Foundation art installation was basically two sets of fifty milled aluminum boxes affixed to two huge slabs of concrete standing uncovered in the west Texas prairie.

Tilton and Lela's luxurious Lexus was eventually found. Unfortunately the hail had hammered pockmarks into it that put one in mind of Manuel Noreiga's profile. In itself, that would have been bad enough, but the whirlwind had also swept up the Tokyo steel and tossed it about five hundred yards from where it was parked. The word totaled was employed, but somehow it seemed woefully inadequate. So the three wound up renting a car and driving to El Paso. Then each flew back to their respective homes.

The Hotel Paisano and parts of downtown Marfa had been battered but not totally destroyed. You couldn't say as much for Wendell James psyche, however. He had put a lot of his money and what was left of his fraying prestige into what he hoped would be a highly publicized and well-attended event. Neither was obviously going to happen and he headed back to Austin without speaking to anyone.

Motif and Alison bragged about making it in their particular box as the fury raged around them. Nobody really believed them, but then nobody totally discounted it either.

Mrs. Brad Aarons had yet to be found. Several of her husband's friends and associates were heard to comment that although he was, of course, devastated, the artist did seem to be holding up surprisingly well.

Ellis hadn't heard anything more about Alejandro Reyes or what the destruction might have been in surrounding communities. Everyone had been in a hurry to put time and space between them and what they had experienced. It was a normal reaction, Ellis thought.

"So, this is where you prefer to meet for a first date, huh?

Ellis looked up into the dark, brown, smiling eyes of the flight attendant he had shared an attempted hijacking and a few drinks with in Houston. "Rebecca," he said, smiling back.

"And who is this handsome devil?"

Osgood accepted her gleaming grin and gentle petting as if he had been expecting it all along. Which of course, he had.

Ellis, having made note of Rebecca's name and number when he left her asleep in a Houston hotel room, had called her upon his return to San Diego. He suggested they meet in the park, in the morning. Brunch seemed a good way to begin. Confiding that he had jotted down her address and subsequently checked information for her phone number, he wasn't sure how she'd react. But after spending an inordinate amount of time on the phone apologizing for what she called very abnormal behavior, she enthusiastically agreed to meet him for brunch. Ellis didn't really need Osgood for moral support, but he brought him along because he felt bad about having him boarded and then leaving him alone in his apartment again. Plus, he was always curious whether women he personally found attractive would be attracted to Osgood. Most of them were.

The threesome, man, woman, and bulldog, walked lazily through the lush, green gardens and meticulously manicured lawns of Balboa park as they made their way to Prado. Selecting a table outside, in deference to their four-legged companion, but in all honesty, because it was a drop-dead gorgeous day, Ellis and Rebecca got to know each other better over mushroom omelets and Mimosas. The sunshine and the champagne, plus their mutual attraction and the fact that they had gone through a truly life-threatening trauma together, all combined to have them eventually wind up in Ellis's apartment, which was only minutes from the park.

As soon as they were in the door and Ellis stood back up after bending down to release the leash from Osgood's collar, Rebecca slammed him against his front door and slammed her mouth even harder into his. Lips meshed, tongues intertwined, teeth gnawed necks and the race was on to see who could get the other naked fastest.

Such conduct being old hat to Osgood, he simply waddled over to the window seat and took his customary position, which granted him equal access to the pastoral scenery outside or the passionate scene inside.

Animal instincts have a way of rendering shyness and conventional behavior absolutely irrelevant. So it was with the two writhing bodies, one tan, the other chocolate, grasping, groping, and tumbling onto and off of the couch in Ellis's living room. More nimble than Ellis had any idea she'd be, Rebecca scrambled up first, pushed his chest away with a running back's stiff-arm and buried her head in his crotch. Taking him in her mouth, she engulfed his manhood like it was dessert and proceeded to turn skin, tissue and blood into something that could drive roundhead nails into two-by-fours. Adrenaline, ardor and simply unleashed energy made it impossible for Ellis to remain passive. So he crunched his stomach muscles and sat up. Grabbing her head in both hands, he pulled her free of him and crushed his mouth against hers. Then dropping his hands beneath her armpits, he raised her up onto the couch, fell to his knees and wrapped her thighs around his ears. With her approaching the breaking point, moaning and laughing and tears running down her cheeks simultaneously, he got to his feet, pushed her knees on either side of her breasts and entered her. Each thrust was achingly better than the one that preceded it and moments later the two exploded together. Then they pulled each other close in a sweat-soaked embrace. Ellis looked at her, dropped his head slightly to the right and nestled into the softness of her neck. There he rested. Spent. Even Osgood was impressed.

One of the additional benefits of firestorm sex, thought Ellis, as he and Osgood walked Rebecca back to her car in the park, is that you don't have to come up with all the particular reasons or excuses about why it happened. It's patently clear to both parties. So when Ellis leaned down, stuck his head in the window of her car and kissed Rebecca before she pulled away, neither had to say anything about calling. Both knew they'd be getting together again. And soon.

Back in his apartment, Ellis was pulling his shirt off in preparation for a quick shower when the phone rang.

"Ellis here."

"Brig, this is Lela, have you got a minute to talk?"

Ellis flopped down on the couch, reflexively scanning it to make sure there were no remnants of the last hour's activities and said, "Sure, how's it going?"

Lela began by telling him everything was fine and that they had gotten back to Houston okay. She asked about him and he replied that everything was copacetic. Then she got into the real reason for her call.

"Brig, Tilton's gone to Cuba."

"Cuba. What the hell's he doing there?"

Lela went on to explain that on their return to Houston, Ernie Beeker had called and asked Tilton to accompany him to Havana. He had apparently agreed to provide art and an artist for a cultural exchange seminar and he wanted Tilton to join him representing avant-garde work in the American Southwest.

"I wasn't aware our government has gotten that friendly yet with the Cuban regime," Ellis quipped.

"Our government's not really involved. It's not a U.S. sanctioned event. Ernie and Tilton have gone down to Mexico and will be going to Cuba from there. Ernie has contacts that can apparently get them in and out of the country through what he calls back door channels."

Ellis responded, "Well, I just hope it's a door that swings both ways."

"Ernie knows what he's doing. He's been down there before. And Tilton didn't feel like he could pass up the opportunity for some international recognition, you know? It will really be a high-profile thing in world art circles. In fact, some of the crowd you know are pretty jealous of Tilton for getting the invitation. I know Alejandro was badgering Ernie for the longest time to get in on it. Motif too. But Ernie said he could only take one artist and he opted for Tilton."

Ellis flashed back to the argument he had seen Alejandro and Beeker having in the Galleria. *Maybe that was the cause of it,* he thought to himself.

Lela went on to explain that she had wanted Tilton to ask Ellis to accompany him, but that her husband said he didn't need a baby sitter so far away from those who might have a bone to pick with his particular artwork. Ellis didn't mention that he had been keeping a tally on who was around during the two possible attempts on Tilton's life and that Beeker was definitely on the list. No point he thought. They've already gone off together now.

"So is that why you called," Ellis asked. "I'm not sure I can do anything about it now."

"Actually, I was just filling you in," Lela answered. "The real reason I rang you is because of the second call we got."

She went on to explain that before Tilton left for Havana, Benny DeMarco, the diminutive jazz violinist had telephoned. He said he was being given a gala tribute in his native Chicago in honor of his life and work. "The people putting the evening together are holding it in an art gallery and they told Benny he could fill the space with any artist's work he wanted. So he asked Tilton to provide all the paintings. It was Benny's way of using Tilton's work to thank the different audiences he's played to all his life. As he said, the nameless, faceless, people who never receive any recognition at all.

"Quite a guy," Ellis said, "He's getting honored and he's thinking about how he can honor others. One of a kind, I guess."

"Yep. That's the kind of man he is. And he didn't say it, but he knew it would be good for Tilton too. To have his work displayed like that in Chicago. Benny's a good friend. Anyway, Tilton was really thrilled and there was no way he could turn him down. So the last couple of days before he left for Havana, he worked around the clock to get a new painting finished that could be part of the night's festivities. It's called *Desert Sunset*. That's also the title of the last album Benny did before he stopped recording. I think Tilton actually used the ashes from that individual you two picked up at Fontana's. You know, before we all took off for Marfa."

"Well, look Lela, this all sounds great, but where do I come in?"

"Tilton and I want you to come to Chicago, Brig. He won't have time to come back through Houston. He and Ernie will only get there a few hours before the night's festivities. We were hoping you could help me put things together at the gallery and then sort of watch over things at the event itself."

"Lela, we were going to look into getting someone to help you guys in Houston, remember, and —"

"I know it's an imposition, Brig, but it's really crucial. So many things have gone wrong recently and the night is so important... especially for Benny. He wanted you there too. He did. He said to be sure and bring that guy who talks so loud."

Ellis chuckled, "Okay, okay. But after this, we work something else out, all right?"

"Absolutely, Brig. We will. Listen, I'll get back to you on the details. We'll probably need to get to Chicago in a couple of days. I'll arrange all the flights and the hotel and that stuff. Then I'll call you. The event is on the seventh. We should be there a couple days ahead of time. Just to make sure the paintings arrive okay, and then to set up the day before."

"Listen, when you call back, give me the name of the gallery owner, okay? I want to see what their normal security operations are. We've got a chance to get in front of this one, so let's do it. I'll also want a list of everyone who's being invited and how many are expected to show up."

"You're a doll, Brig. I knew I could count on you. Tilton will be so pleased."

"Right. Listen, are you sure everything's going to be okay in Cuba?"

"Ernie's in control, Brig. He knows what he's doing. Gotta' run. I'll call you tomorrow. Bye."

She hung up before Ellis could respond. He looked down at Osgood and said, "Well my friend, in the last few days yours truly has had to deal with not one, but two skyjackers, a bodacious bull, a pissed-off preacher, a rampaging sport utility vehicle, and a storm that made me wonder if the

Almighty himself wasn't calling in his markers. I sure as hell hope somebody's in control."

Osgood cocked his head and stared questioningly into Ellis's eyes. "Okay, you're right," Ellis said. "There was also that little fracas that recently transpired here in the living room. Maybe there's something to be said for reckless abandon. But only when you're sure who you're being reckless with, right?" He reached down and gave the shorthaired sandbag a rub across its king-sized head. "Let's go grab a shower."

Chapter 13

That morning, the two men got up early and went to the Havana harbor to explore the stone encasements of El Morro Fortress. After climbing to the top of the lighthouse that has stood sentinel for over four hundred years, they stared out at the city's rooftops and down at the waves lapping on the sandy shore below.

"The Spanish built this fort," Ernie Beeker said to Tilton, "to give their canons more range. More range meant better protection for the fleet getting repairs, supplies, and whatever else it might need to cross the Atlantic and take its... some would say... ill-gotten gains back to Spain. See right down there," he said pointing. "They'd even hang a huge chain across the entrance, from El Morro on this side to La Punta on the other. More security, you know."

"Funny, isn't it," Tilton began, "back then they were doing all they could to keep people out. Today they're doing all they can to bring people in."

"Apples and oranges," Beeker replied. "It was the Spanish trying to keep people away from their ships and their cargo. Now it's the Cubans themselves who need more cargo to come in."

Looking out at the sun-splashed morning and the colonial buildings in multiple ice cream colors, Tilton was reminded of the country's own particular population sundae.

"Spanish, Africans, indigenous Indians... you mix all that with colonialism, feudalism, American gangsterism, communism, and Catholicism... no wonder this place looks great from a distance but pretty grimy when you get up close, huh?"

"That's what most of the world looks like, Tilton," Beeker responded. "Some places just hide it better than others."

An hour later they were walking down Calle Hamel in the heart of Havana. All around them giant, abstract murals covered the sides of buildings and towered above the streets. Vibrant colors of blue, yellow, red, and green, proudly shouted their African heritage for all passersby to see. As Tilton and Beeker scanned the public art that encircled them, iconic eyes peered back from one painting after another. Eyes that seemed to follow them as they strolled and looked and talked.

On the way back to their hotel, down a street, up an alley, or around a corner, they would continuously come upon Detroit sheet metal. Some of it parked. Some rolling. A 58 Chevy. A 62 Ford Falcon. A 74 Plymouth Duster. Even an old 55 Buick Roadster. They weren't the beauties they once were. They hadn't been restored to their original luster. They were simply painted and tarted-up like old women trying to look young. And hanging from their open windows, both front and back, were actual painted and tarted-up young women trying to look old enough as they plied the trade that economic stagnation, lack of work, chronic shortages of food and essentials always breeds. Tilton wondered as he walked whether it was the repressive system itself, the collapse of capital infusion from formerly well-heeled benefactors like the Soviet Union, or the long-time American embargo that continued to make prostitution the most economically rewarding option for these girls who couldn't be more than sixteen or seventeen. Probably even younger.

"Hey, meester... want a date? Want to buy me deener? Come on, meester. Two for one... yes? Or one for both of you?"

"Just smile, shake your head no and keep walking," Beeker advised. "There's much better at the hotel."

Crossing the broad Arms Square, the two reached their destination, the Hotel San Isabel. It was a three-story colonnaded structure that started life as the palace of the Count of Santovenia. Since countries other than the U.S. had started to make Cuba a tourist destination of some renown, the hotel had been brought back to life and retrofitted to an appearance more befitting its historic colonial splendor than the practical proletariat state it now found itself part of.

Tilton and Beeker strode beneath the shaded columns, through the cream-colored, ornate lobby, past the plush red velvet chairs flanked by decorative iron end tables with inlaid tiled tops, and into the dark mahogany and mirrored bar. The revolution had long since reached both a philosophical and working compromise with imperialist luxury where hard currency was concerned.

"Dos mojitos," Beeker said to the bartender as they entered and took a table against the wall. While their butts eased into chairs, both sets of their eyes were drawn immediately to the girl at the bar.

If ennui had a face, hers was it. A countenance at once beautiful and sad. Her pencil thin eyebrows arched upward and long. Dusty, eye-shadowed lids fell low, half covering brown eyes so dark they looked black. A short, Roman nose led to lips painted the color of purple satin. Thick, curly black hair, cut short, covered her crown and surrounded her tiny ears whose white studs gave the appearance of pearls in dark seaweed. She stared into the polished wooden bar as if she'd just told it the secrets of her despair. A dark bottle of beer and a half-filled glass stood in front of her but she never reached for them and she never took her gaze from her own distorted reflection in the bars sweeping grain.

"What did I tell you," Beeker said to Tilton as the bartender dropped off two glasses of rum, soda water, and lime juice with mint sprigs clinging lazily to the ice floating in them.

"Her? Looks like she's lost her last friend."

"All part of the show," Beeker went on. "She's a drama queen. Got her sob story all prepared to help run up the price on some naive tourist."

"You're not thinking of looking into that, are you Ernie? Mrs. Beeker wouldn't be too thrilled if the little gift you brought her back from Cuba was a dose of the clap."

"Mrs. Beeker doesn't round out the top of a bar stool like that one does, my friend. Mrs. Beeker doesn't have skin the color of caramel and Mrs. Beeker sure won't let me do whatever I want to do to her for thirty bucks or so."

"You think that's all it would take?"

"Oh, she'll ask for more. But once she realizes this is not my first rodeo... she'll settle for thirty. Fifty, tops."

"Well, I assume you've got some protection with you," Tilton quizzed. "I mean, besides me."

"Don't need it," Beeker replied. "She'll have more condoms in that little purse of hers than she has pesos."

"Well, just don't forget, we need to leave for the Ministry of Art by six, right?"

"Right. We'll meet in the lobby at six. After you finish your drink, you go on up first, okay? I'll sidle over to the bar and have another, I think. Unless you'd like first dibs, Tilton."

"No, the mojito's all I need. I'm gonna grab a nice long nap before the symposium tonight."

Draining the last liquid from his glass, Beeker turned to Tilton and said, "Yeah, well I'm gonna grab me some of that. So don't get concerned if you hear a lot of thumping and moaning coming from my room okay?"

"No, I won't get concerned," Tilton said. "I'll just assume that's you having a heart attack. Later, man."

"Yeah, later. Much later," Beeker responded, never taking his eyes away from the bar as Tilton left and made his way upstairs.

Beeker then took the seat beside the girl at the bar and hoping she spoke at least some English, motioned to her glass and said, "Would you like another?"

"I won't say no," she replied, without looking at him.

"Well, that's just the kind of woman I find intriguing... one who won't say no. Bartender, a mojito for me and a refill for the young lady," he said, feeling more sure of himself.

Despite his bravado with Tilton, Beeker was less confident than he let on. He seldom doubted his ability to fix things that needed fixing. But that consisted mostly of reacting or responding. Initiating was another thing entirely. Especially when it involved such lovely potential.

As they waited for the bartender to bring the drinks, the woman continued to stare into the wood grain in the bar and circle the top of her glass with a thin, manicured index finger. Sensing she was in no hurry to make this easy for him, Beeker broke the silence.

"Do you come here often?" It had barely left his lips before he realized how pathetically banal the question was.

"More often than you, I suspect, senor."

The bartender sat the drinks in front of them and walked to the far end of the bar. He knew such negotiations were best left to the potential business partners. Discretion, he had learned early on, was frequently rewarded with a generous tip at the close of such proceedings.

"Yes, I'm just a visitor to Havana, but I take it you're a native?"

"A prisoner, senor." she said, taking a sip of her beer and then continuing, "A prisoner of fate."

"Well, I'm a great believer in fate," Beeker replied, now spurred on by his second mojito. "I think it's probably fate that has brought us together. Here in this bar. At this time."

For the first time, she slowly raised her head and looked into the eyes of the man she had been conversing with. "Can fate take you places, senor? Does fate have such powers?"

"I believe it does. I mean, it brought us together, right? But what did you mean about being a prisoner of fate?"

"You are Americano. I can tell by your accent. I am... how did you put it... a native. Americanos do not feel imprisoned by fate. You go where you want, do what you want, buy what you want. Fate does not keep you imprisoned on an island you cannot leave."

"It may be fate that you were born on this island," Beeker began, "but it's the government that keeps you here. Your glorious leader. He's the one keeping you chained up here."

"Would you like to see me in chains, senor?" She said with a low guttural voice as she reached across the bar stool and rested her hand on Beeker's thigh.

"I'd like to see you get what you want," he replied slowly.

"I want to go to America, senor. The land of the free. The home of the brave ones. I want to know what it is like to do anything you want... to become anything you want. I would like you to take me to America, senor. You are rich. You stay in this fancy hotel. Surely you can take one poor Cubano girl to America?"

Beeker was momentarily taken aback. Was this part of the pitch? Or was she serious? Unsure, he sought to nip such a crazy notion in the bud.

"I'm not rich. I'm only here for a short while. And I certainly can't take you to America."

"Of course you can, senor," she said as she slid her hand up the inside of his leg until she found what she knew she would find. "You are *muy* macho. You can do whatever you want. You have everything and I have nothing. I never will have anything. But perhaps I can have America. Si, senor? Perhaps I can have America this afternoon in your room. You can do that. You can take me there. Can you not, senor?"

His sense of relief was exceeded only by his stiffening resolve as he sought to quantify what had just been suggested. "How much?" He asked inelegantly.

She removed her hand from his leg and picked up her glass to take with her — a glass now decorated with a bottom lip print the color purple. Then she said, "You decide, senor. You decide how much fate is worth."

Sunshine has a way of masking finality. Certainly the afternoon sun spilling into Beeker's window and caressing the naked form of the girl standing beside it gave no clue of what was to come. To the aging art dealer, she was even more alluring nude than she had been on display in her tight, working wardrobe in the hotel bar. He sat on his bed staring at the sweeping curve of her bottom, the dark protruding nipple and aureole of the breast closest to him, her thin arm and slender fingers that were spread and resting on her rump. The more he looked at her, the more his desire grew. He told her to walk around the room. She did. Strolling from the window to the wardrobe, to the desk, then the door. He told her to lock and chain the door, which she did. Then she didn't wait for instructions, she simply leaned back on the doorknob and surrounded it with her bottom. His heart caught in his throat as she slowly moved on and off the knob. He bade her come to him. The Viagra he had taken before he joined her at the bar was working its spell and her touch made him feel like he could do anything. She slid in bed, spread her legs and guided him into her.

Beeker could have looked over at the mirror to marvel at his performance. It was exceeding anything he had achieved in years. But he would have had to notice his balding pate with the silly comb-over falling askew, the varicose-veined legs, hairless and skinny, the sunken chest and flabby paunch hanging like a child's life preserver that's lost its air.

Rather, he closed his eyes and saw himself as he once was. A virile young man with more life in front of him than behind. The kind of man who was used to pushing deeper and deeper into pretty women. The kind of man who could grind and thrust and use his pelvis like a jack hammer to make women beg for him and not his money. As he saw this image of what he once was, or what he imagined he once was, he pushed deeper and harder. Not just with his loins, but with his arms and hands too. Arms and hands that had worked their way from her chest to her mouth, and then to her throat. His eyes were clamped shut. All of his being was laser focused on recharging his life in the center of this woman who was pounding and pulling and clawing at him with her nails until blood began to run down his forearms. Convinced he was driving her to unbelievable carnal ecstasy, he carried on impervious to her choking and gurgling and gasping for air. For those weren't the sounds that Beeker was hearing. Beeker was hearing the sighs and desire and love screams of a woman under his spell. So he pushed deeper and harder and faster and more intensely until finally he shuddered with spasmodic joy. It was at least ten seconds later that he opened his eyes, looked down, and realized he had just forced the last breaths of life from the girl's crushed windpipe.

Chapter 14

There was a message waiting for Tilton when he came down to the lobby at six. The hotel clerk recognized him because he had been told the American would have a beard on his face and a hat on his head. Tilton read the message from Ernie Beeker. It apologized for his absence and gave the street address of the Ministry of Art where the symposium was to be held. It also contained the name of Santo Madera who would be awaiting Tilton's arrival and who would be serving as moderator for the evening. Beeker ended the note by saying he'd join the discussion in progress.

A crowd of at least three hundred filled the hall in folding chairs that had been set up for the evening's gathering. At the front of the large room was a slightly raised platform. It held three folding tables with seating for the nine participants which consisted of the moderator, a Cuban surrealist and his government sponsor, a German abstract artist and her exhibitor, a Mexican painter famed for his bleak landscapes, a Chilean sculptor renowned as a rock carver, Tilton, and an empty chair for Ernie Beeker. A large screen was positioned behind the dais so slides of the artists' works could be projected on it as they spoke.

One by one the practitioners of their particular specialty rose and discussed what they did, why they did it, and in keeping with the international aspects of the event, the importance of art as a great unifier. About halfway through the German's diatribe, Ernie Beeker arrived and silently took his chair beside Tilton. The Texan put his hand over his microphone and asked Beeker why he was so late, but the art dealer simply brushed his question aside with a mumbled "Not now," and turned his chair so that he could see the screen as the artist talked.

When Tilton's turn came, he rose and a murmur began among the audience. Which was followed by a number of individuals making the sign of the cross as he discussed the medium in which he worked. Going into a dissertation about the kinship of shared mortality and everyone's fascination with the mysteries of life and death, he touched upon style, symbol and meaning in his work, but he said he preferred that viewers form their own interpretations about different paintings rather than imposing his upon them.

In a follow-up question and answer session, he got a number of pointed queries about whether or not his work was a polemic against the corrupt American capitalist system that degrades and devalues individuals as well as communities. Refusing to be drawn into what he knew would be used as propaganda, he again fell back to the point that the meaning of his work was more easily found in the eye of the beholder than in the mouth of its creator. A nice sidestep, but ultimately irrelevant. Unbeknownst to him, the damage was already underway. Here was an American artist, who paints with the cremated remains of human beings, standing up before the microphones and cameras of a Communist dictatorship to address the party faithful. At least that's how it would be played on the following day's cable news channels back in the USA.

Ernie Beeker was supposed to follow Tilton. But he advised the moderator, Santo Madera, that since the program had indeed run an hour over its allotted time already, he would forego his public remarks. Then he immediately turned and left the dais, leaving Tilton to relay to Madera their appreciation for inclusion in the event. By the time Tilton had done so, Beeker was nowhere to be seen.

Chapter 15

Ellis's flight from San Diego to Chicago was happily, as far as he was concerned, without incident. He spent the majority of the long arc from the west coast over the Rocky Mountains and across the Great Plains dozing. A second, more traditional date with Rebecca had ensued the evening before he left. And while dinner and wine at a cozy Italian restaurant in the Gas Lamp District had been relaxing enough, the long night of sexual calisthenics that followed had left him a bit red-eyed the following morning. Particularly since he had to get up early and drop Osgood off at the kennel before heading to the airport. Osgood took this latest confinement in transitory lodgings with his customary good humor. He was familiar with these temporary exiles and spent his time in the front seat of Ellis's classic 64 Benz 230 SL with the head-in-the-wind confidence of one who had been around this particular block a number of times before.

When he wasn't slipping in and out of consciousness, Ellis listened to the channel on his headset that featured standards from the forties and fifties. He wondered how many times Benny DeMarco had performed those same tunes in towns and cities all across the country he was flying over. And he couldn't help but wonder what the hell he'd be doing if and when he ever reached the four score years Benny had put in on this planet. But such questions never lingered long in Ellis's mind, answered or unanswered. He saw no point in trying to outline a future he knew no one could really be sure of from one day to the next. He had listened to too many good men's hopes and dreams that had been prematurely and permanently eradicated by a firefight or a sniper or just pure dumb luck. So Ellis didn't put much stock in long-term planning. He let questions of fate flow out of his mind as easily as they flowed in.

The plane touched down at O'Hare just a little past three in the afternoon. Though Ellis had packed light, he still had to go to baggage claim to retrieve his luggage. While pilots were fast approaching the point where they could keep a weapon with them, passengers were not. After retrieving his grip, he decided to walk through the tunnel to the train station in the terminal. A forty minute train ride for two bucks just seemed a lot more reasonable than taking a taxi for forty bucks and rolling the dice on what traffic would be like at that particular moment. Even though he was traveling on someone else's dime, he had a hard time justifying the difference. Puritan work ethic, he guessed. Then he reminded himself he should really try to get over that.

After sliding a five in the ticket vending machine, thereby securing his return trip to the airport as well, he headed down the tall escalators to the boarding platform. The sign above his head indicated that the next train into the city was leaving in less than two minutes. So he went ahead and stepped into the waiting railcar. Moving down the aisle to look for a seat he wouldn't have to share, he paused for an instant as he saw a familiar face peering out the window. It was Wendell James, architect of the unfortunately aborted wake for peace in Marfa. Conveniently, the seat right behind him was unoccupied, so he slid in with his gear while simultaneously saying hello.

"Hello, Wendell. Brig Ellis, Tilton's friend."

"Mr. Ellis... of course. What are you doing here in Chicago?"

"Oh, I'm here to help Lela and Tilton out with some things at the show night after tomorrow."

"Show? I'm sorry, I don't know what you're referring to."

Ellis just naturally assumed James was in town for the same event that had brought him there. He wasn't. The Austin gallery owner said he had a sister in Chicago who was battling a long-term illness and that he made occasional trips to the Windy City to periodically check up on her. Ellis, having already spoken of the event, still didn't feel it was his place to invite anyone, so he said he wasn't sure about the time and place and suggested that James contact Lela at The Drake Hotel so she could give him specifics.

The rest of the ride into the city was taken up with talk of the tragic events that transpired in Marfa. James indicated he had been so shaken by the whole thing that he had retreated into a cocoon of his own making since then and was only recently lured out of it because he received word that his sister's condition was worsening. He confided in Ellis that he had lost a considerable amount of money with the implosion of his west Texas wake and that his Austin business seemed to be in a protracted free fall as well. Seemingly happy to have someone who would listen, he went on to add a number of details Ellis had just as soon wished he hadn't about his sister's disease and the potential ramifications of it. So that by the time the train pulled into the Clark & Lake connector, Ellis was relieved to be able to separate himself from Wendell James's tales of woe.

Unsure of the precise number of blocks from his train stop to his destination, Ellis hailed a taxi and five minutes later pulled up in front of Chicago's famous Drake Hotel. From the view-challenged back seat of a cab, it's hard to get a perspective of the things that tower above you, so Ellis, like most first time guests at The Drake, missed entirely the stately gray stone edifice that fronts Walton Place in the heart of the city's Gold Coast neighborhood. After paying his fare, he stepped out onto the sidewalk and was pointed toward the revolving doors that would lead him into the hotel. Wood and brass handrails pointed the way up a wide staircase to the ornate lobby. A gigantic crystal chandelier was centered over an exploding yellow, green, white and rose floral arrangement that sat on top of an Italian marble table and greeted him as he scanned the wide expanse looking for guest check-in. A long, dazzlingly polished dark wood counter with gold filigree and inlaid lighting beneath it announced its presence to his right. Checking with the desk clerk he found that Mrs. Mangas had already checked in and had taken care of his room as well. After securing a key, he walked back across the magnificent Oriental rug in the center of the lobby and up another set of stairs to the Palm Court bar area. Ellis was in the habit of reconnoitering new surroundings he found himself in. It wasn't just to take in the fabulous atmosphere and environment that he now was suddenly part of, it was also to get a feel for entrances and exits. History had taught him the hard way never to be in any place very long that he didn't know how to get out of in a hurry. But taking in the luxury that was surrounding him, luxury that someone else was picking up the bill for, made him doubt both the need and the desire for a quick getaway any time soon.

After taking the elevator up to his room on the sixth floor and opening his door, he was greeted with what years of training had instilled in the hotel staff. The room had been arranged so that the incoming occupant could see completely across the room to the meticulously drawn and tied drapes that framed the glitteringly azure water stretching out endlessly beyond his window. The staff must have been drilled with *you never get a second chance at a first impression,* Ellis told himself, as he was sucked across the room anyway to gaze out at the three hundred mile long, one hundred and twenty mile wide body of water audaciously classified as *Lake* Michigan. The ringing phone interrupted the experience.

"Hello."

"Brig, this is Lela. I asked the front desk to give me a call when you checked in."

"Well, they're pretty responsive, I see."

"Just wanted to remind you that we're having dinner here with Benny tonight in the Cape Cod room. If you like, let's meet for a drink in the Palm

Court at seven-thirty, then we'll walk down to meet Benny in the restaurant at eight."

"Sure. Sounds good. By the way, I need to fill you in on something."

Ellis went on to explain how he had run into Wendell James on the train and inadvertently mentioned the upcoming tribute. Lela suggested that it was no problem and that she'd call James and tell him to feel free to attend. This was supposed to make Ellis feel better, and it would have, had Lela not gone on to say that the event was getting a lot bigger than they thought anyway and a few more people weren't going to make any real difference. Great, Ellis thought. So much for nailing down a guest list in advance.

"Grab a nap, if you like," she suggested. "I'll see you downstairs to-night."

Ellis decided to take her advice and was asleep in short order.

Chapter 16

The waitress glided effortlessly between palm fronds, players on the prowl, businessmen on the make, and tourists who wanted to be able to tell their envious neighbors they had shared a cocktail with the hoity-toity at The Drake. Delivering the two Jack-black-on-the-rocks, she bent over at the waist giving Ellis a generous eyeful of cleavage while simultaneously eliciting exaggerated guttural noises from the salesmen tabled behind her in direct eye-line with her thigh-high mini skirt.

"Now there's a girl who knows how to increase the size of a tip," Lela quipped as she raised her short, rounded crystal and clinked it against Ellis's.

"Just doing her job," Ellis said. "Practice makes perfect."

The chilled whiskey was both tasty and calming as the two began to discuss the bizarre events of the last couple of weeks. Then Lela asked what he had been doing in California the few days he was back there. Never being one to kiss and tell, he avoided mention of his encounters with Rebecca and simply said he had been hanging out with his dog and taking things as they came. Then they moved from the recent past to the present.

"Talk to Tilton today?" Ellis asked.

"Yes. He said the symposium went well and they're still on schedule to get here... day after tomorrow."

There was something in the way she paused mid-sentence that made Ellis say, "But?"

"But Tilton said Ernie's really been acting strange."

"Strange?"

"Quiet. Aloof, you know? Tilton says he's really been keeping to himself. He said he was fine at first. Enjoying the trip. But since the night of the symposium he's just been acting differently. Tilton doesn't know what to make of it."

"Well, I don't know enough about the guy to venture an opinion. But if he had asked me before he left, I'd have suggested not going. Or at least taking me or someone else along with them."

"Yeah, that's why he didn't ask. But he figured the farther he was from all the recent controversy, the better off he'd be. At least that's what he said."

Ellis figured this was as good a time as any to broach some things he hadn't spoken to Lela about. "Let's talk hypothetically for a minute, okay?"

"Sure. Why not? Hypothetical was one of my majors in school."

Ellis began slowly, wanting to make sure he phrased everything just right. "Lela, you asked for my help because you thought Tilton might be in danger. And three times over the last couple of weeks he's come close to getting hurt pretty badly. Maybe even killed. Now, the tornado can obviously be chalked up to fate. But the other two incidents, well, I'm not so sure about those."

"That's why I asked you to help, Brig. The bigger the venues, the bigger the crowds. The more nut-jobs get involved. People who might do something crazy."

"That's true," Ellis responded. "But that's only part of the possible equation."

"What's the other part?" Lela asked.

"Well, there are wackos you don't know. That's for sure. But there could be some you *do know* too."

"Brig... you don't think anyone we're close to is involved... do you?"

"I'm not making any accusations. I'm just bringing up the fact that at both Flashpoint and Gloria Preston's party, some of the same people were present."

"Well, sure. But it's people like Ernie... and me... and Alejandro, I guess. And come to think of it, Motif and Alison. And, well... that Baptist preacher, that Reverend Tompkins."

Ellis added, "Wendell James was at both gatherings too."

"Yes, but Wendell. For goodness sake, Brig, he's as harmless as they come."

"This is all hypothetical, remember?"

"Okay, Sherlock," she said kidding, "go ahead and hypothesize."

"Look, when anyone's in harm's way, you always have to ask yourself, why? And it may not be as simple as you initially think. Sure, there are people out there who don't like what Tilton does. But there are also people who might be jealous that he's becoming a lot more well-known than they are."

"You mean other artists?"

"There are also people who might stand to make more money from Tilton if he weren't around. Doesn't the work of dead artists frequently sell for more than live ones?"

"You mean Ernie... or Wendell?"

"There could be some who feel a handsome young widow with a number of cashable paintings might be lonely and vulnerable?"

"You mean... well... just who the hell do you mean?"

Ellis figured since he had wandered this far out on the limb, he might as well go a bit farther. "There are even those who might say that some men's wives might consider themselves better off with a wad of insurance money and the rights to all of an artist's paintings."

"You mean me? You bastard!"

"Now calm down. I don't mean any of it. I'm just trying to help you see that there could be more in play here than simply people who get extremely pissed off about the fact that Tilton paints with human ashes."

Lela had to admit to herself that he had a point. But she wasn't crazy about the way he had made it. "How do you know whether we have life insurance or not?"

"I don't know. Remember please, I'm speaking hypothetically."

"Hmm," she said, her composure returning as she straightened herself in her chair. "Well, I guess I got my money's worth when I hired you, huh? You certainly look at things from a lot of angles."

"A lot of these angles I'm sure you can rule out. I just didn't want you to fixate on one at the exclusion of the others."

"And what about the possibility that no one's made any attempt on Tilton's life? That it's all been just weird, accidental stuff."

"That's definitely something I'm considering," Ellis said. "But it's not the only thing."

Holding her glass now in both hands and looking Ellis directly in the eye, Lela said, "Come on then. Let's finish what's left of these drinks and go meet Benny before you try to convince me that sweet little guy's got it in for Tilton too."

"Nope. There's no way Benny could have been playing the violin in Gloria Preston's music room and trying to run an SUV over Tilton and me at the same time. I think he's safe to have dinner with. Bottoms up."

"Is that a reference to our waitress?" Lela joked.

Ellis grinned. Then drained his glass.

After Lela signed for the drinks, the pair left the Palm Court, crossed the lobby and went downstairs to the corridors that wound around the base of the hotel. Along the way they passed clothing shops, art galleries, and jewelry stores that paid dearly to be located in The Drake. Of course their customers paid even more dearly. Passing one window filled with cowboy boots, an embroidered and fringed leather jacket and silver studded belts, Ellis commented, "Looks like they knew you were coming."

"I can get all this in Houston for a lot less," Lela responded. "But I'm glad to see that some western style has made its way to Chicago."

When they got to the side of the hotel that faced Lake Michigan and Lake Shore Drive, the entrance to the Cape Cod Room appeared on their right. Stepping inside they were immediately aware of a change in atmosphere. Unlike the sleek modernity of the Palm Court bar, or the gilded opulence of the lobby and shops, the Cape Cod entrance was smaller, darker, warmer, and more confined. A completely bald, older man in a white shirt, club tie, and blue blazer, greeted them at the host's desk. Lela gave him her name and was told that the third of their party of three had already been seated at their table. They followed the gentleman with the slightly eastern European accent past the semicircle oyster bar and into the multilevel dining room. Passing the red-checked tablecloths, exposed wooden beams, stuffed sailfish and hanging copper pots, Ellis's reaction was just what the designers of the restaurant had hoped for. He felt as if he were about to have dinner at a cozy inn in New England rather than in the middle of a bustling Midwestern city.

Benny DeMarco was ensconced in the center of a high, wooden-backed corner booth that gave him full view of the room and its occupants. He was dressed in a tweed jacket and his signature black turtleneck. Directly in front of him was a glass of white wine that had yet to be touched. As Ellis and Lela arrived to join him, the ancient musician looked at Lela and said,

"Forgive me for not standing... my joy at seeing you would embarrass us both."

Lela grinned, bent over and kissed him on the cheek then slid into the side of the booth facing him. "You're incorrigible," she said. And followed with "You remember Brig."

Ellis shook his hand then slid in beside her as Benny replied, "Of course, it's the fellow who likes to shout at old people. I thought you'd be rid of him by now."

Ellis and Lela were glad to see the little man's dry sense of humor was as tart as usual. The waiter asked what they'd like to drink and both agreed to have a glass of whatever was sitting in front of Benny. As they waited for their drinks and scanned the menus, the talk turned to Tilton and his impending arrival, as well as Benny's upcoming evening. Lela thanked him once again for inviting Tilton to share his work. Ellis asked if there was anything in particular that DeMarco would recommend and Benny responded with "Anything but the fish." Lela chuckled again implying this too was not to be taken seriously, and Ellis reconciled himself to being the evening's straight man.

After the initial glasses of wine and the first course, Ellis finally got the diminutive jokester to replace the comedy routine with actual conversation. He did so with questions about the violinist's early career and his particular interest in art. Benny confided that he had always been somewhat of an artist himself, finding painting a calming way to unwind after a big show. Or a way to keep himself busy on tour when he'd have lots of time to kill in one hotel room after another.

"What kinds of things would you paint?" Ellis asked.

"Birds mostly," Benny answered.

"Why birds, particularly?" Lela questioned.

"When I was a kid growing up on the south side," Benny began, "we never really had enough to eat. The depression, you know. So my mother would always send me out to get sparrows. I'd take my air rifle... we called it a BB-gun back then, and I'd shoot these little sparrows that flew around the houses and the buildings. It would take two or three to make any kind of meal. But anyway, I had to do that a lot. So when I started painting, I'd draw these birds. And paint them all sorts of colors. Kind of made me feel like I was putting some back, you know."

"Oh, Benny... that's so sweet," Lela said.

"Yeah, we had to do it to survive. I mean that's how a lot of people ate back then. But once I was grown up and on the road and on my own... and I could buy my meals, I never ordered foul once. No chicken. No turkey. No duck. No birds. Just couldn't bring myself to do it. Still don't eat 'em to this day."

Luckily, everyone was having fish for a main course, but to redirect the conversation a bit anyway, Ellis said, "Must have been difficult, carrying painting gear around with you plus your instruments and everything."

"No," Benny said, "we had to travel light in those days. Couldn't really bring any extra luggage. So I'd roll up some sketch sheets and keep them and my chalk inside my instrument case. Always liked to work with colored chalk. Course' it did tend to get on things. Couldn't afford to mess up my clothes, had to wear 'em for the gigs, you know. So I'd paint in my underwear."

"What!" Lela said. "You're having us on again, aren't you?"

"Nope," Benny replied. "That's how I'd do it. I'd get in my underwear and step into the bathtub. Then I'd tape a sketch sheet to the tile wall and go to it. That way the pastel dust would fall into the bathtub or on my underwear. And I could wash either."

"Now that's a mental image I can easily conjure up," Lela said.

"Sure, you think of me standing in the bathtub in my skivvies and you have a laugh. I think of you standing in the bathtub in your underwear and I have a heart attack."

"You just can't stop being a flirt, can you?" Lela asked.

"Can a tiger change its stripes? Can a leopard change its spots? I am what I am," Benny sighed. "And I'm too far gone to change."

After dinner and over coffee the conversation wound itself back to the upcoming event,

Ellis asked Benny if he had any idea of the number of people who would be attending and before he could answer Lela jumped in with, "Oh yeah, I forgot to mention it earlier, but I heard from some of the gang in Houston today. They're coming up too."

"The gang?" Ellis said.

"Yeah, you know, Motif and Alison... and Alejandro Reyes."

"I didn't realize they were such fans of Benny's," Ellis said.

"I didn't really realize it either," Lela said. "And truth be known, they probably want to mix and mingle with some of the art crowd as well as music aficionados who will be there. You don't mind, do you Benny?"

"The more the merrier," Benny replied. "I'm not paying for the eats."

"Not then and not tonight," Lela said. "Waiter, check please."

Both Ellis and Lela walked Benny to the front of the hotel and made sure he was safely inside the taxi before bidding him goodnight. As the cab sped away the two looked at each other for an uneasy moment before Lela spoke first.

"Want a nightcap? Or has it been a long enough day for you?"

"I think I'll pass if you don't mind. I was thinking of taking just a bit of a walk before turning in. Care to join me?"

"A bit too chilly for me," Lela said, bringing her hands up to her forearms. "Why don't we head over to the gallery tomorrow morning about ten, okay?"

"Sure thing," Ellis responded. "In the lobby at ten. Goodnight."

Later, as he was taking a turn down Michigan Avenue, walking past the showcase stores of major retailers that make up Chicago's Magnificent Mile, Ellis paid little attention to the glass front offerings of Nike or Apple or Burberry or the rest. He was preoccupied with why Lela hadn't remembered to mention the other Texas attendees when the two had been discussing that same cadre of people earlier in the evening. Had her surprise at his suggestion that Tilton might be in more danger from people he knew, than people he didn't know, make her blank it out? Or did the entire discussion give her pause about mentioning it at all?

Waiting for the light to change at Ohio and Michigan streets, his contemplation was interrupted as his eyes happened to meet and lock with those of the passenger in the back seat of the taxi turning the corner right in front of him. Eyes he suddenly remembered seeing in front of Tilton's painting at Flashpoint. Eyes he saw again the following night staring into the glaring lights of television cameras in front of Gloria Preston's home. They were the eyes of the Reverend Barry Tompkins. And as far as Ellis was concerned, that was the final nail in the coffin of multiple coincidences.

Chapter 17

The sun sliced cleanly down the middle of Superior, leaving one side of the street in charcoal and the other in bright light. The sunny side happened to house the Liz Randall gallery, which was hosting Benny's soiree. It was in the middle of the block. A block full of red brick warehouse conversions that now sported huge ground floor windows whose purpose was to lure passersby with wide angle views of the art on display. Six foot by two foot rectangular flags in graphic black and white adorned the outside of each particular gallery giving the intended impression of a bona fide art district. The unapologetic opulence of Chicago's magnificent mile was replaced here with a degree of understatement befitting those who sell their wares for the same outlandish prices, but without the benefit of massive television and magazine advertising budgets.

In fact, in this River North district of Chicago where a thirty-five thousand dollar painting shared it's corner with the elevated train which carried people all over the city for a dollar seventy-five, the melting pot mingled with the swells marvelously, as long as the panhandlers didn't have the audacity to loiter in front of one of the countless shops catering to the art crowd. Certainly everyone was encouraged to stroll down the streets and take in the sites. That's why there was a Starbucks on every fourth corner. But if the Brazilian coffee was affordable and the bronze cherubs weren't, the owners preferred that you restricted your ramblings to the sidewalk as opposed to the bleached hardwood of the gallery floors. A practiced attitude of sales staff indifference generally managed to redirect any yahoos who might wander in with the sole goal of simply killing time.

Ellis and Lela had decided to walk from The Drake to the gallery. The beginning of the day was crisp and cool and a morning stroll was a little something different for both of them. Ellis generally spent most mornings running through Balboa park, and while Lela kept herself in shape by working out at the gym or sometimes running around Memorial Park in Houston, neither of their hometowns or states for that matter, had what you'd call, hard core, committed pedestrians. So, after getting directions from the concierge at the hotel, they struck out on foot. It took them between fifteen and twenty minutes with the occasional wrong turn and a bit of window-shopping along the way.

Ellis made note of the entrance as they arrived. There were glass doors that led into a small vestibule with a short flight of five stairs that took you up to two more glass doors that opened into the gallery itself. Stepping inside they were greeted by a tall, young man with dark, short hair who introduced himself as Bernard. Lela let him know who they were and asked if the paintings had arrived yet. Bernard told her that they had and walked them back past the main square-shaped gallery, which had an enclosed counter area in one corner. As they walked, the employee told them that Liz Randall had not come in yet. He went on to say that she had left instructions for Mr. Mangus's representatives to simply lean the paintings against the particular areas on the wall where they would like them, and once she had arrived and agreed with their placement, they would be mounted appropriately.

As was his habit, Ellis made mental notes of the interior as he followed Bernard and Lela to the back of the gallery where the paintings had been held upon their arrival. Directly off the large, open front of the gallery, which could easily be seen from the street, a narrower walkway jutted off to the right. There was room along that walkway to display at least a couple of paintings as well. It opened into a smaller rectangular area that provided more wall space for more art. On the left side of that rectangle there was a door with a white plastic sign just above it. The sign read RESTROOM and had both a male and female icon beneath it. Continuing toward the rear of the gallery, the trio passed through two doors that opened from the center inward revealing a storage area filled with giant bins that held canvas after canvas.

"This is where we keep everything that's not currently being displayed," Bernard said. "As well as all the art that's either arriving or leaving."

Ellis spotted two large doors in the rear of the storage room. Pointing toward them he said, "Where do those lead?"

"They open into the alley behind the building," the young man answered.

"Would you mind if we have a look?" Ellis asked.

Though Bernard wasn't sure why someone would want to take a look at the alley behind their building, he kept that thought to himself as he said, "Certainly."

Walking over and releasing the lock that opened the doors, he took no note of Ellis paying close attention to what was involved in the locking procedure. There were apparently no electronics. Bernard simply lifted out a large two by four metal rail that was in the center where the two doors met. Then he pulled the lever down that slid the bolt from its encasement. Reaching out with his foot, he used the toe of his shoe to release another latch that held the doors in place at the bottom. Then he shoved open the right door and the trio walked out into the alley.

"Yes. Looks like an alley to me," Lela said jokingly.

"Deliveries and pickups happen back here," Bernard said. "That way the streets are not being constantly blocked by trucks loading and unloading."

"Wish they'd do more of that in New York," Lela said. "Every time Tilton and I go there it's such a hassle to get across town because there are so many trucks clogging the streets, slowing everything down. Doesn't seem that way here at all."

"If Mayor Emanuel was there instead of Chicago," Bernard replied, "you can bet it would be easier to get around. Seen enough?"

"Yes. Thanks." Ellis answered.

"So, where are the paintings from Texas?" Lela asked.

"Right inside. Come back in. I'll show you."

After re-locking the doors, Bernard took them over to the west wall of the storage room where a number of paintings, still in their crates, were leaning against the bins.

"These arrived yesterday from Houston. I'm sure they're the ones you're here for. I'd help you with them myself, but I need to keep an eye on things out front until Ms. Randall arrives."

"Oh, it's no problem," Lela said. "We dressed for the occasion." Then she held her jacket open revealing she had on jeans and a sweatshirt.

Ellis was slipping off his jacket as he said, "Got anything to help get these crates open?"

Bernard showed him where he kept the crowbar and other tools in the back room, then he went back up front as Ellis and Lela went to work.

Chapter 18

The Reverend Barry Tompkins sat in the corner booth of Claire's Coffee Shop on Lake Street. Since it was after the morning rush and before lunch, he had the place virtually to himself. In the quarter hour he had been there, two men had come in separately. Tompkins had determined quickly that neither was the man he was waiting for. The first was tall, thin, well-dressed, and black. The second was older, heavier, a laborer of some sort, Tompkins assumed from his khakis, work boots, and waist length windbreaker. The Reverend was waiting for a smaller man, younger, more intelligent looking. He would be short, Tomkins thought. Though he hadn't described himself that way. Short people never do. He had simply said he'll be wearing dark slacks, a plaid shirt, blue tie, and corduroy jacket. Tompkins bet he'd also have glasses. After the laborer left and the minister had ordered a second cup of coffee, he won his bet.

"Mr. — I mean, Reverend Tompkins... I'm Joshua Steiner... with the *Tribune*. You are Barry Tompkins, right? The Reverend Barry Tompkins."

The Reverend looked at the younger man standing beside the booth, waiting for an answer. Right shirt, right slacks, right tie, and jacket... and he was at best five foot six. "Yes, Mr. Steiner. I'm Barry Tompkins. Thank you for coming."

The reporter slid into the booth. Sitting opposite the preacher, he pulled a small notepad from his shirt pocket and was about to say something when Tompkins spoke first.

"Would you like a coffee, or something else? Bit early for lunch, I guess, but if —"

"Nothing for me, I'm fine. In fact, I've only got a few minutes, then I have to get back to the paper. If you don't mind, we should probably get right into it." Steiner wasn't sure there was really a story here, but since he had been assigned to the arts and entertainment section the opportunities for anything beyond cultural events and celebrity sightings were rare. So he was willing to take a flyer in hopes of finding something with a little more weight to it.

"Did you check the wire services and cable news, I was traveling last night and didn't get a chance to see anything?"

Steiner responded, "There was a little piece on the international report about the art symposium in Havana. And it did mention there was an American artist there. A painter who uses cremated remains. But it wasn't the lead or anything and I'm not sure there's a lot to follow up on. Art enthusiasts keep their eyes and ears open for these things but the general public tends to glaze over when it comes to anything they think is too highbrow."

"That's why I wanted to see you," Tompkins replied. "This isn't an art story. This is a human-interest story. A story that needs to be told. The evil sacrilege that man is involved in is coming right here to Chicago. And now his blasphemy has reached even new heights of depravity. He must be stopped."

The reporter could feel the sincerity behind the vitriol. But he wasn't sure he shared it.

"Look, Reverend, I know you're from the South and all, but you need to understand. Chicago is a very liberal town. A town that's not really into censorship or putting the clamps on artistic freedom. We don't have to like or agree with every artist that comes along, but that doesn't mean we should try to keep them from expressing what they want to express."

"It's not about artistic freedom," Tompkins angrily retorted, banging his half-filled coffee cup on the table between them. "It's about profiting from the misery of others. Not just individuals, but groups of people. Groups who have a lot of influence. Groups whom I would have thought, mean a lot to you, Mr. Steiner."

The emphasis placed on the reporter's last name made it more than obvious what group the red-faced Reverend was referring too. And while Steiner was far from being the kind of religious zealot he was obviously talking to, the comment made him want to know more. So he gestured to a passing waitress, and decided he'd stay for at least as long as it took to get through a black coffee with two sugars.

Chapter 19

The two Americans stood in the boarding line that would take them from Havana to Mexico City. One wore a hat, the other a sweat-soaked brow and an air of palpable nervousness.

"What's the matter, man?" Tilton asked. "You got the trots or something?"

Beeker looked around as he said, "I'm just ready to get out of here. A little of this place goes a long way."

"Well, we've got a three hour layover in Mexico City before we get the connection to Chicago. You gonna be able to handle that? You look pretty grisly, you know."

"I'll be fine once we're airborne."

Stuck between perspiring German tourists and mumbling Mexican businessmen as their line shuffled along, Tilton's thoughts were on Chicago, Lela and Benny's big night. Beeker's mind was locked in the recent past. Had he covered all the bases? Paid off all the right people? Done all the things he needed to do? It seemed so. But it would seem a lot better once he was off Cuban ground and headed back to the states.

How had it happened? What had possessed him? The sun knew, but it wasn't talking. The same sunlight that poured through the window and lit up her exquisite skin was just on the other side of the airport glass. Soon they would be walking under its burning warmth when they made their way across the tarmac and onto the plane that stood waiting for them. She would be going by plane too, he thought. But in a different aircraft and in a very different way. Yes, Beeker ruminated, the sun sees all. And surely it has seen worse. It wasn't as if it was premeditated. It just happened. Once it was done it couldn't be undone. What was the point of ruining his life and the life of those around him? It was just something that happened. Something that happened to one person. Why turn it into something that would affect a lot more people? They had said no one would miss her. That her loved ones had long since lost track of her when she came to the city. That's the way it was with so many of those girls. There were ways to take care of things. Ways that would erase moments that shouldn't happen but do. Costly ways, to be sure. But what was the greater cost? He couldn't reverse what had happened. He could only lessen its impact on others. Surely that was the best thing to do. Surely it was. But the more he chewed on it, the more it seemed to bite back, tearing at him and making him bleed.

Chapter 20

Liz Randall had shown up, given her blessing to where Lela had suggested the paintings should go, and instructed Bernard to help Ellis and Lela hang them. By mid-afternoon they were on their way back to the hotel. Walking east, then slightly north from the art district, Ellis said, "So, if you're free tonight Mrs. Mangas, I'd love to take you to dinner. My treat this time. And I won't even bill you back the expense."

It would be their last night before Tilton, Beeker, and the others arrived for Benny's salute. Lela rather liked the idea of spending it alone with Ellis. "Dinner? You mean like a dinner date? Now wouldn't that be something? My God, Brig, when's the last time we had an actual date?"

"I think it was two nights before I headed off to boot camp. I didn't want to make it the night before I left because I knew I'd feel like hell the next morning."

"You did enjoy a drink or two back then, " Lela said.

"Well, I guess some things don't change, huh?"

"So, where shall we go?"

"My treat. My surprise," Brig answered. "I've been talking with the concierge."

They agreed on a time to meet in the lobby and both went to their rooms. Lela drew a deep, hot bath, slipped out of her jeans and sweatshirt and took a long look at her naked form in the mirror. Sure, there were spots she was less than satisfied with, but all things considered, she liked what she saw. She had both grown up and held up well since the last time she and Ellis had been alone together. She thought of herself then as a skinny, frightened kid who was smitten with a tough, good-looking guy, who for some reason, seemed to think she was pretty. She never saw herself that way. And as she ran her hands over her body, she tried to remember what it was like when Brig touched her then. She remembered he always did it slowly. Giving her plenty of time to stop him if she wanted to. She thought of how he would cup her calf and slide his hand upward and around the inside of her thigh on its way to her center. And always gently, lovingly, but passionately too. She remembered when his palm pressed against her and his fingers dipped lower touching her where she had never been touched by anyone other than herself. How warm and safe she felt. Yet she remembered the tears in the corner of her eyes as she softly asked him to stop. Had she really been that young? She guessed everyone had. And like many others with the gift of hindsight, she wished perhaps that she had not said no to Brig. At least that's what she thought, as she slid down in the tub and let the warm water come up to her chin.

Ellis turned on his shower and let the hot steaming spray spill down. As he rubbed the soap over his stomach and his scars, he thought about how odd it was that he found himself preparing to take out the love of his youth. Had it really been eighteen years since he held that pretty girl in his arms and wished to feel himself inside her. Wished that she wanted it too. How many had there been since then? In how many places in parts of the world that most people don't even know exist. How many lifetimes had been lived in the jungles and mountains and deserts that followed those years? How many people get the opportunity to circle back on their lives, he wondered. To see what might have been. He couldn't help but think about her. And he couldn't help but remind himself that he was here because she asked for him. She asked him to help keep her husband safe. That was the only reason she was back in his life. That was the only reason he was here. He would keep telling himself that as the crystal clear water cascaded over him.

Though there was a chill in the air, they chose to walk to the restaurant. It only took them a few minutes to cross Michigan and make their way past a glittering array of Gold Coast department stores, boutiques, and high-rise condominiums. Turning a corner into the heart of the Rush Street nightlife quadrant, Ellis scanned the surrounding signs until he spotted Jake's in white relief on a blue square overlooking a covered awning. He led Lela through the glass front doors and was met at the podium by a tuxedoed man with glasses, dyed black hair, and a smile he had been perfecting for the past two decades. Ellis gave his name and they were escorted to a red-leather booth that could easily seat four. They slid into the horseshoe-shaped semicircle and gave themselves both a view of the restaurant and the small bandstand just across the parquet dance floor that fronted the tables.

"Now, this is what I think of when I think of Chicago," Lela said.

"I hope you're in the mood for martinis and red meat," Ellis came back.

"Isn't everyone?" Lela joked.

"I just thought it would be fun," Ellis said. "I heard they had great steaks here and when the guy at the hotel told me they also have a band that plays music from the forties, with a singer who does the standards... well, I just couldn't pass it up."

"Now, let me get this straight," Lela smiled, "are you almost forty or almost eighty?"

"Does it matter?" Ellis asked.

Lela answered quickly. "Not tonight, Mr. Ellis. Tonight it doesn't matter."

While the band was running through *Perdido*, *Tuxedo Junction*, and *Take the A Train*, Ellis and Lela each managed to make their way through a vodka martini up, then mustered the nerve to wander onto the dance floor for an attempt at something approaching a jitterbug. But just as they got there, the band segued into a very slow and languid *Moonlight in Vermont*. Ellis mimed an exaggerated bow. Lela slipped her hand in his and let his arm come around her waist. At first they moved haltingly around the floor. But once Lela realized that the man holding her knew how to lead, she leaned closer into him and let her head rest in the soft of his shoulder. As the trombone solo wound its way through the melody, the two slid and twirled as one. The years fell away and each with eyes closed, saw the other as they looked nearly twenty years ago in a high school gymnasium with a slow tune lilting over the loud speaker. As the song ended, they both opened their eyes and looked, a bit embarrassed, at each other.

"Man, am I hungry," Ellis said.

"Well, by all means," Lela volunteered, "let's eat."

The filet that Ellis had was charred to perfection. Near black on the outside, red on the inside and filled with flavor. Lela made her way through most of a New York strip and kept up her end of the consumption of a bottle of Jordan cabernet that lasted through dessert. They ordered after dinner Amaretto's but made their way back onto the dance floor before the drinks were delivered.

Ellis, doing his best to keep things in perspective, said, "So, what time does Tilton get in tomorrow?"

"Just shut up and dance, okay?" Lela asked sweetly as she melted into her partner's arms and the brown-eyed beauty behind the microphone began the opening verse of *Fools Rush In.*

"Are they playing that song for us,?" Lela asked.

"I didn't request it, if that's what you meant?"

"No, that's not really what I meant?"

By now, it was as if the past eighteen years had never really happened. She was a moonstruck teenager again, in the arms of a handsome upper classman. He was holding the most beautiful girl in school. Maybe it was possible to turn back time after all.

When the ballad reached its end, the band went into the opening of another up-tempo number, but Lela and Ellis chose to return to the table where their drinks were waiting for them. Slowly sipping the amber liquid, the pair tried hard to find something mundane to say.

"I guess I'm a real sucker for that old music," Ellis began.

"Yeah," Lela answered. "Me too." Then she stopped trying. "Can we get the check and go?"

There were cabs waiting outside Jake's, so they decided to slip into one rather than walking back. Lela got in first but she didn't slide very far across the seat. When Ellis got in he felt the weight of her pressing against him. She put her head on his shoulder as the taxi took them the few blocks back to The Drake.

Going up in the elevator, Lela fumbled inside her purse, looking for her key. "Oh, God," she said, "I think I may need a little assistance. One drink too many... know what I mean?"

"Here, let me help you," Ellis said, as he took her purse and found the key inside. At her door, he opened it with Lela hanging on his arm. They both stepped inside.

"Are you going to be okay?" Ellis asked as Lela let go of his arm and walked forward.

She moved toward the far side of the room, past the bed that had already been turned down, and toward the drapes that had already been closed. Stopping for an instant, she slipped the shoulder straps from her dress and let it fall to the floor. Then she turned to face Ellis. Standing there in nothing but her high heels and thong, she said, "Brig, I'm so sorry we never really made love. Are you?"

He stood for a moment, not speaking. Then it was him moving slowly across the room. On the way he picked up a throw that was draped across the foot of the bed. When he reached her, he lovingly wrapped it around her shoulders and looked directly into her eyes, which were starting to moisten.

"Yes, Lela. I'm sorry too." Keeping her at arm's length, he bent forward and kissed her on the cheek. The scent of lilac from her perfume mixed with the taste of salt from the tear that had run down her face. Ellis felt her quiver slightly beneath his touch. Then he let her go, walked to the door, stepped outside and closed it behind him, without looking back.

Chapter 21

The headline on the front page of the entertainment section elicited a one-word review from Ellis. "Shit." Normally, he never paid much attention to that part of the paper. But this morning, the morning after he left his unclad ex-high school sweetheart standing alone in her hotel room, he was covering every page of every section of the *Chicago Tribune*. Ellis hoped that losing himself in the city's minutia would keep him from thinking about whether he had done the right thing or not. He was pretty certain he had. Yes, it would have been wonderful. Of that, he had no doubt. True, it was only one night in a lifetime. One moment that would probably never come again. But at what price? There would have to be apologies and explanations and rationalizations afterward. There would be a secret he and Lela would have to share from then on. There would be the inevitable guilt he knew he'd feel as soon as he saw Tilton again. And there'd be himself he'd have to answer to. The breaking of his own code. It wasn't written down anywhere. He didn't keep it printed on the back of his business card. But it was there none-the-less. The Brig Ellis code of conduct. The one he had learned the hard way. You take a job. You see it through to the end. You don't abort the mission prematurely. You do what has to be done. And you certainly don't screw the person that's paying you or that person's wife. So Ellis wasn't really wrestling with his decision from the night before, he was just trying to keep the memory of how beautiful she looked somewhere beyond his every waking thought. And the headlines of the day were one way to do that. Until he saw the headline that generated his involuntary expletive. It read:

MUSICIAN TO BE HONORED
AMID CONTROVERSIAL CANVASES
OF CREMATED HUMAN REMAINS

The article went on to say some nice things about Benny DeMarco's career. But then it leapt into an exposition on Tilton and the kind of paintings he was doing. While it couldn't be called an attack, neither could it be said that any restraint was shown when mentioning that organized opposition from civic and religious groups had been extremely vociferous in Houston. Even to the point of police having to be called to restore order. Then it went on to point out that Tilton, who would be attending the event, was coming to Chicago straight from a personal appearance in what the author referred to as Castro's Cuba. It ended by naming the gallery where the event would be taking place and mentioning that it was in the heart of Chicago's River North art district.

This was more than enough to take his mind off Lela. In fact, as he read about the fracas that had occurred in Houston, his mind flashed back to the face he saw in the back seat of the taxicab the night before last. Was Reverend Barry Tompkins stirring things up in preparation for another media event? Or did the impetus for the article originate from the Liz Randall Gallery? Or even from Lela. Maybe it was all part of that any-publicity-is-good-publicity mantra that the artists Ellis had come in contact with lately seemed to believe in. Well, wherever it got its start, he worried that it was going to make his job a hell of a lot harder. Flinging the paper aside, he decided to get on the phone to the gallery to see if he could get ahead of the game.

***

Tilton and Beeker arrived at The Drake in the middle of the afternoon. As Beeker was checking in, Tilton found a house phone and put in a call to Lela's room. After two rings she picked it up.

"Hello."

"Hey, babe this is me. We're here."

"Here in Chicago?"

"No, here in the hotel. I'm downstairs in the lobby. Give me the room number and I'll come on up."

"Well, actually, I was just on my way down. Motif and Alison and Alejandro arrived and they're having a drink in the Palm Court Bar. I was going to join them for a quick one."

"Oh, okay. Well, look, I'll just wait by the elevator bank and meet you when you come down. Then I'll take the key and go on up to the room. I need a shower and a nap before tonight. Everything going okay? Is Brig here?"

"He left a message and said he was going over to the gallery early. Said he wanted to go over some things with Bernard."

"Who the hell's Bernard?"

"He works for Liz Randall. The woman who owns the gallery. And yes, everything's fine. The paintings look great. It's all ready. Should be a big night for Benny... and you."

"I'll see you when you come down," Tilton said. Then he hung up.

Ernie Beeker was waiting at the elevator bank when Tilton walked over. The artist said, "Hey, Lela says some of the gang from Houston are in the bar. Want to catch a drink with them before you go up?"

"No." Beeker responded, then continuing immediately as if Tilton's question had never even been asked, "Listen, a package is going to be arriving. It will come addressed to Lela. I wasn't sure when we'd actually get here so I had it sent to her."

"You had it sent? From where?

"From Cuba. I didn't want to bring it back through Mexico. Be on the lookout for it."

"Okay," said Tilton, "but what is it?"

Beeker stepped in the elevator, pressed the button, then stood with his back to the wall. He had heard Tilton's question, but he paused for a second before answering. As the doors were closing he looked over at Tilton and the artist felt for a moment that his friend was looking right through him when Beeker finally said, "It's either fate, or retribution. I'm not sure which."

Chapter 22

Eight o'clock was the designated hour for the event to begin. That meant no one would really begin to show up until eight-thirty or nine. But Lela had convinced the Texas contingent to go over with her and Tilton. She preferred to have folks around that she knew when the main throng of Chicagoans started to arrive.

Lela hadn't actually seen Ellis all day or talked to him for that matter. He had simply left a message on her phone that he was going over early and would see everyone at the gallery. There was nothing said about the night before. He was too much of a gentleman for that. And there was no indication in his voice that there would ever be anything said. Had it really happened? Had she made a fool of herself? Did she wish those last few seconds in her room had never happened at all? Or did she really want him to know what he was missing. What he had never had. Not really. She told herself she was pretty drunk on both wine and memories. And she was. But it would have been too easy to simply chalk it up to the booze. She had sought him out. She had convinced him to come. There were other alternatives. But she asked him to help. Had she known last night's moment was destined to happen from the start? Had she thought it would turn out that way? All questions for another time, she told herself. Or questions to be stored way and never thought of again. Time would tell.

Ellis was in the main part of the gallery, talking with Liz Randall when Tilton, Lela and the others arrived. After introductions were made all around, the gallery owner said, "Please, see Oscar for something to drink." She pointed to the counter, which had been transformed into a bar for the night's festivities. An older black man with curly hair the color of concrete in the sun smiled and beckoned them over. Behind him was row after row of scotch, bourbon, vodka, gin, all the usual suspects designed to appeal to a thirsty crowd. Ernie Beeker, Alison, Motif, and Alejandro Reyes didn't wait for a second invitation. Tilton and Lela stood for a moment as the others walked away.

Liz Randall continued, "Your friend, Mr. Ellis here, convinced me to put that hideous sign on the door." She was referring to an eleven-inch by fourteen-inch black art board rectangle that had been affixed to the glass doors on the street. In script, the words *Private Function* had been written in white chalk. "Luckily, Bernard's handwriting is not without some degree of style."

"Yes, I met Bernard when we came in," Tilton said.

"It seems Bernard will be serving as unofficial doorman tonight," the gallery owner went on in a reserved, yet still notably perturbed, voice. "Another of Mr. Ellis's *suggestions*."

"I just felt there was no harm in making sure no one wandered in who really wasn't supposed to be here," Ellis added.

Tilton, picking up on Randall's discomfort with Ellis's attempts to employ even the most rudimentary security measures, took her by the arm and turned on all his Texas charm. "Yes, Mr. Ellis is as cautious as he is good looking, but let's talk about something much more fascinating... me and my paintings." Then he guided her toward the nearest one, leaving Ellis and Lela standing alone together.

Lela said, "Brig, about last night..."

"I had a wonderful time, last night, Lela. I hope you did too. It was great to be able to spend some time together."

"I probably had a little too much to drink," she began.

"I know I did," he cut in. "But I'll be sticking to the sparkling water tonight. Back on the clock, you know."

It was obvious to Lela that he wasn't going to say anything about their parting. Just as she was preparing to move on to another subject, she heard Bernard's voice.

"This gentleman mentioned Mr. Mangus's name. He said you invited him."

Both Lela and Ellis turned and saw Wendell James at the same time. The Austin art dealer said, "Oh sorry, looks like I've committed the unpardonable sin of arriving on time."

"Yes. One of those terrible Texas traits," Lela joked. "Come on in and let's get something to drink."

Ellis took the opportunity to observe the known attendees before the unknowns started to arrive. Tilton still had Liz Randall buttonholed in front of the painting he had done just for this evening, *Desert Sunset*. It had a giant saguaro cactus in the foreground with the sun going down over the dry, craggy landscape in back. No doubt Tilton was telling her more than she wanted to know about desert fauna and southwestern weather patterns, Ellis guessed. Lela and Wendell James were giving their drink orders to Oscar. Motif and Alison were ambling down the little hallway, which led to the viewing area in the rear of the gallery. Had there been anyone in front of them, it would have appeared that Motif was gently guiding the redhead with his hand in the small of her back. But from where Ellis was standing it was unavoidably clear that the Creole's mitt was squeezing her right cheek as they walked. Beeker and Alejandro Reyes had wandered to the front windows. The tall Mexican was obviously ranting about something important to him as he sliced the air with one gesture after another. But Ernie Beeker just stood there, staring out at the street, paying little mind to whatever Reyes was going on about.

The other guests started to arrive about a quarter to nine and the gallery began to fill up fast. The haphazard nature of how the event had been put together made it virtually impossible to do any sort of real screening at the door, but Ellis had stationed Bernard there anyway and told the employee to let him know if anyone seemed the least bit suspicious. By nine fifteen there were close to a hundred and fifty people there and what was normally a spacious environment for strolling and viewing was fast becoming a shoulder-to-shoulder gathering. Oscar, the gravel-haired black man who started out as the titular bar tender, had long since abandoned his post and now wandered amid the crowd leaving the event-goers to fend for themselves. None seemed to have trouble doing so and before long the counter that had begun as straight rows of liquor and wine bottles was now a mishmash of tall and short glasses, half-empty decanters and do-it-yourself inebriation.

Benny DeMarco, the night's honoree, had arrived around nine accompanied by family members who did their best to navigate their way through the swelling throng and guide him to his appointed stool. There, beneath Tilton's *Desert Sunset,* he could sit and accept greetings from all those well-wishers who wanted to tell him personally how much they loved his music. Liz Randall had put a number of Benny's CD's on the sound system before the guests arrived so the melodic twists and turns of his fingers and bow were heard hovering just below the surf-like rumble of the crowd. It seemed as if every individual there wanted to say something personal to the little man who had been filling ears with music since long before their parents were born. So the appointed time for a more formal toast to Benny and his legendary career was delayed, but no one seemed to notice.

Ellis had been following Tilton around, much as he had done in previous gatherings. Sometimes he would stand close enough to pick up the entire conversation the artist was involved in, sometimes he'd be just out of earshot. But he was never more than a few feet away constantly scanning those in Tilton's immediate circle.

The Texas crowd had long since co-mingled with the windy city inhabitants, cocktails and accents being excellent icebreakers. And for all, there was the common bond of respect for the tiny man atop the stool in the corner. Wendell James had tried to spend some time with Ernie Beeker earlier, but found the Houston man's inattention to whatever he said so off-putting that he quickly excused himself. Reyes managed to get Lela alone in a corner and occupied a quarter of an hour of her time with a subject Ellis had no way of ascertaining from his position across the room. Motif and Alison had actually separated long enough to wade into the crowd for a bit, each on their own.

By ten o'clock, the organizers knew that Benny was getting pretty tired, so they decided to try to bring some order to the proceedings. Liz Randall had Bernard go to the light switch to bring the lights up and down to get everyone's attention. Ellis stuck close by Tilton's side as the two apologized their way past body after body and snaked a path to the area where Benny was to be lauded. As they were weaving through the crowd, Ellis glanced toward the glass windows at the front of the gallery. Due to the number of those assembled, he couldn't see outside as clearly as he would have preferred. But what he did see, he didn't like.

Just on the other side of the glass, there seemed to be as many people in the street as there were inside. There were all moving, but their flow seemed a lot more uniform and a lot less random than people merely strolling along the sidewalk. Ellis turned and waved at Bernard who was still standing near the light switch. He motioned for the gallery employee to head back toward his position at the door. Bernard understood and started walking. Then Ellis heard a voice from the direction he and Tilton had been heading. He didn't recognize the man's voice, but quickly assumed it was someone who had helped organize the event.

"Attention. Attention everyone. Can I get everyone's attention, please? Thank you all so much for coming." He was a tall, slim, older man with silver hair trimmed neatly. The cut of his suit and the ease with which he addressed the crowd made it obvious he had done this sort of thing before. He continued. "I think the number of people here tonight is testament in itself to the individual we've come to honor. Mr. Benny DeMarco."

The manner in which the tall man said Benny's name invited a round of applause. And the crowd responded enthusiastically. Benny, dwarfed by the lean, sophisticated man addressing the crowd, raised his right hand, acknowledging the audience's gesture and nodded his head appreciatively. Then he went on.

"Benny's career has brought an enormous amount of pleasure to untold thousands of individuals — those who were lucky enough to hear his music in person, and those who listened to him hour after hour in the privacy of their homes through the many recordings Benny has produced. To bring such pleasure to so many is indeed a rare accomplishment."

The attendees again responded with spontaneous applause confirming the speaker's remarks. As they did, Ellis looked outside and saw a crowd that was now much bigger than when he last checked.

"Normally," the tall man went on, "Benny lets his violin do the talking. But he has graciously acquiesced to sharing a few words with us tonight. Ladies and gentlemen, Mr. Benny DeMarco."

Once again the crowd acknowledged Benny with a round of applause as the speaker and a couple of others standing close by, helped the ancient musician onto a small wooden platform that had been put in place just for this occasion. After the applause abated, Benny began to speak.

"And now, it's time for the band to take a short break."

Those who were standing close enough to actually understand what the diminutive one said, started the laughter that rippled halfway through the crowd.

"I want to thank you all for coming tonight. I appreciate Liz Randall hosting this little gathering. And I want to thank my friend, Tilton Mangas, for bringing his friends along. Those who are standing and those who are hanging."

Another wave of laughter started, then died out quickly as a voice rose above it.

"Mr. DeMarco... Mr. DeMarco! A question from the *Chicago Tribune*."

The outstretched arm with the ballpoint pen in it, waved about frantically as the gaggle of bodies parted slightly to allow eye contact between the questioner and the honoree.

"I don't usually do requests," Benny said without missing a beat. "But for our friends at the press, why not. What's your question, Mr. —?"

"Steiner. Joshua Steiner," said the short man in the corduroy jacket.

Ellis's attention, unlike that of the other people in the gallery, was not on the reporter or Benny DeMarco. He was looking back and forth between the front windows where the throng on the sidewalk was wall to wall, and now three or four deep, and the front door where Bernard was leaning against it with one shoulder and using his other arm to motion to those outside, who obviously wanted inside.

The reporter went on, "Mr. DeMarco, are you aware of exactly who you're standing under?"

"Looks like a cactus to me," Benny quipped.

"It's a human being, Mr. DeMarco," Steiner replied, his voice projecting even more. "A human being who deserves more respect than this."

Tilton started making his way toward the front of the crowd so he could be at Benny's side to have a better view of his friend's interrogator. Ellis moved with him.

"I asked the artist, Tilton Mangas, to show his work here tonight, young man. I believe these paintings are symbolic of the many people I've played to over the years. People who sat in clubs and bars and theaters... always in the dark, so the performers could have the limelight. I wanted all those audiences to be honored tonight, Mr. – what did you say your name... oh, yes... Mr. Steiner. I did it out of respect for them. Because I believe art, like music, speaks to and for all people."

By now Tilton and Ellis had managed to elbow their way to the front of the crowd. And had the questioner been just another heckler, both would have begun the process of quieting him. But because he was a member of the press, they held off for the moment.

"That painting on the wall behind you, Mr. DeMarco, does not have a symbol in it. It has a man." Steiner was in full voice now. He wanted everyone there to learn what he had learned earlier. "That man's name was Monroe Greenburg. I don't know how many audiences he may have sat in, Mr. DeMarco, probably not many. You see Greenburg spent the latter years of his life in a bit of a fog. A mental haze from which he was never able to free himself. He was homeless, Mr. DeMarco. One of the many who roam the streets of our cities incapable of coping on their own. But Greenburg had a better excuse than most. His childhood ended rather abruptly. And he didn't really have an adolescence at all. He spent his formative years, from age eleven to age fifteen, in concentration camps. The last being Auschwitz. I doubt that he sat in many audiences there, Mr. DeMarco. Don't you find it a bit ironic that he survived the horror of the Zyklon-B showers, the ovens, and he avoided the fate of becoming a lampshade or an ashtray only to wind up as a saguaro cactus on the wall of a Chicago art gallery?"

A low rumble began to emanate from the crowd. Then, as if on cue, the group gathered outside began to chant. Their shouts were imperceptible at first. Muffled by their methodically pounding fists on the heavy paned glass. Then the closest ones to the windows starting pulling their coats open to reveal they were wearing white t-shirts with big black letters that read JEWS STILL ABUSED. And a few started waving signs. Signs that echoed the words Ellis had seen before in Houston. DEAD DESERVE DIGNITY.

Tilton had taken about all he could of the young reporter giving Benny a hard time. Hat cocked slightly to one side and drink still in hand, he stepped forward and said, "Listen here, four-eyes, get off Mr. DeMarco's case. If you've got a bone to pick about the art here, pick it with me. I'm the son-of-a- bitch who painted it."

Before Steiner could respond, a woman's voice rang out, "Smoke. Hey, there's smoke back here! And the door's locked!"

From beneath the door with the RESTROOM sign atop it, smoke was indeed pouring out and making its way toward the crowded gallery area. A man who had been standing near the shouting woman pounded on the door and yelled, "Is anyone in there? Is anyone in there?" Then he tried to force it open by banging his shoulder against it.

"No... don't do that," came another shout from close by. "There could be a back draft!"

All heads and eyes were turning toward the shouts and smoke now billowing from beneath the locked door. Anxiety began to race through the room with the speed of an electric current. In the corner of his eye, Ellis became aware of an odd shadow streaking overhead. By the time he followed the shadow to what was causing it, the flying object was already on its downward arc. His eyes locked on it milliseconds before it reached its target. "Jesus", he said out loud, as a vodka bottle stuffed with a flaming cloth crashed into the middle of the counter holding the evening's supply of alcohol. The initial fireball threw heat and fear over everyone in the gallery. The delayed explosion that followed sent many tumbling to the floor.

Panic reigned. The wad of people in the middle of the room had one thought and one thought only. Get the hell out. The idea of burning to death or choking on the stifling smoke that was starting to fill the gallery was no way anyone wanted to die. Like a wave rushing toward shore, the mass moved as one toward the glass door entrance. Those closest to the door were overtaken by the more frightened who had been nearer the blast. Pushed and shoved to make way for the swifter and stronger, they began to collapse and fall beneath the onrushing mob. People who hadn't seen them go down, or those too frightened to care, began to run over these squirming, writhing lumps on the floor that couldn't get up but wouldn't give up. High-heeled ankles were turned on soft stomachs that gave way beneath them. Pant cuffs were caught by clutching hands, causing even more people to trip. Soon the human wave was breaking of its own force, spilling people and handbags and hairdos into the vestibule and onto the stairway that led to the main entrance and what they had all thought would be safety. But they had all been wrong.

Seconds before the makeshift Molotov cocktail careened into the assembled alcohol, Bernard had done what he thought was right. He forced himself against the main door leading to the street. Determined not to let the protesters in, he pressed with all his might against the door to lock the rabble-rousers out. But in so doing he locked the attendees in. At the sound of the explosion, he had instinctively turned and started toward the melee. But as he reached the top of the stairs, the flesh and blood tsunami swept over him like a six-foot swell breaking on the beach. Bernard, with the key in his pocket, was now at the bottom of the screaming horde clawing at the locked door.

The initial blast sent shards of glass from whiskey and wine bottles ripping through the room. People sprayed by the flying debris instinctively hit the deck whether the force was enough to knock them over or not. Once down, getting back up amid the dazed and fleeing became a virtually impossible task. The blast knocked Benny DeMarco back against the wall and he slipped from the small platform he had been standing on. Stumbling to the floor, he sat there for a moment trying to unravel what had just happened. Tilton and Ellis, like most of the other people in the gallery, had raised their arms above their heads to shield themselves from any additional explosions that might quickly follow. When that didn't happen, they both started looking around for Lela. Tilton thought he saw her through the smoke, flames, and dust, about fifty feet from where he was standing. "Lela! Lela!" He shouted, and started elbowing his way toward her. Ellis's natural reaction was to stick with him, but something made him turn his head back toward the platform to look for Benny. He pushed his way through the tide of people heading in the other direction and found the dazed and confused octogenarian slumped on the floor.

"Benny... Benny it's me," Ellis shouted. "Come on, we've got to get out of here." Not waiting for a response, he bent down, grabbed the old fellow's right arm with his right hand and hoisted him up and over his shoulder. Then he turned and started off in the direction he had seen Tilton take.

Bodies were banging into one another like bumper cars. Most people remembered the way they came in and struggled to head in that direction, but the pile up at the door and on the stairs had halted all momentum. Now there was only yelling, cries for help and everyone trying to tell everyone else what to do.

Tilton reached Lela who was facing away from him now. He quickly grabbed her by the shoulders and turned her around. In the next instant he felt an open hand slap him across the face and heard a banshee shriek from the woman he had just spun. It wasn't Lela. "Let go of me! Let go! I've got to get out of here," she screamed as she wrestled herself from his grip and broke away.

Smoke was beginning to fill the gallery now and flames were continuing to lap at the area around the counter where the bar had been. Ellis, still with Benny over his shoulder, spied Tilton's signature hat turning this way and looking for Lela in the crunch of bodies. He strong-armed his way forward until he was directly behind the artist and using his free hand, reached out and took the Texan by the shoulder saying, "Tilton, come on, we've got to go this way."

"No, I've got to find Lela!"

"Come away from this mob," Ellis shouted, "there's another way out."

"Not without Lela!" Tilton raged back.

"Look," Ellis came back, his voice just as determined. "Lela knows about the other exit. She may be back there already. Come on."

Taking one last look around the bodies surrounding them, Tilton said, "Okay... let's go see."

Then, turning once more against the tide, the two forced their way down the hall that led to the back of the gallery. On the way, they had to race past flames raging around the counter and near the restroom door that was now glowing black and red from the heat on the other side. Arriving at the wider square near the rear of the building, they found four or five people banging on the doors that led to the storage area. Lela was one of them.

"Lela," Tilton shouted, grabbing and pulling her close to his chest and saying, "Thank God you're all right."

"The doors," Lela screamed, "we can't get these doors open!"

"We'll get 'em open," Ellis said. Then shouting to two men who had been straining away at the doors that closed in the center, he said, "Here, you two take Benny," as he lowered the elderly one off his shoulder. It was only then that he realized that one of the men at the back door was Alejandro Reyes.

"I'll look out for him," Reyes said, cradling Benny under the old man's arms and pulling him away from the door.

"Tilton, grab the end of that table," Ellis shouted, pointing toward an exquisite tile and brushed steel coffee table that was just to the right of them. Tilton moved without a verbal response and the two men felt the weight and sturdiness as they lifted it. With each on either side of the table, they smashed it into the doors separating the gallery from the storeroom. The doors buckled, but didn't open.

"Again," Ellis said.

With all the force they could generate, they thrust the table squarely into the center of the doors. Once again they buckled, but this time they continued to separate and swung open into the storeroom.

"Tilton, help Reyes with Benny," Ellis said as he raced into the storage area and directly to the rear of the room where the back doors lead to the alley. Remembering what he had watched Bernard do, he quickly lifted the two-by-four metal bar that ran across the center of the doors. Then he pulled the lever that slid the bolt from its encasement. Reaching out with his foot, he released the latch on the floor holding the doors in place. Then he pushed the right door open and let in the cool night air. The group was right behind him and moved swiftly out of the building and into the alley.

"Put Benny down against that wall," Ellis said, "and stay with him. I'm going back and let them know there's another way out." Then he disappeared back into the room filled with bins, frames, boxes, crates and now smoke that had followed them into and out of the building.

As Reyes and Tilton gingerly put Benny on the pavement and rested his back against the brick wall of the building opposite the gallery, Tilton asked, "Benny... Benny... are you okay?"

Looking up at the high brick walls, the telephone wires crossing from building to building, and the deep black of the night sky above the glare of the solitary street lamp, Benny mumbled softly, "I never ordered birds. Not once."

Then he closed his eyes and silently slipped away.

Chapter 23

Benny wasn't the only one who didn't see the next day's sunrise. The newspaper and broadcast accounts listed the number of deaths at four. Benny DeMarco got the most ink. He was lauded as a musician's musician. An exceptional interpreter of melodies whose career encompassed big bands, swing groups, jazz bars, recording studios, and concert halls. He was hailed as a virtuoso who cut his own path through decade after decade of changing musical tastes yet still found employment as a working musician into his eighties. One report even went so far as to sentimentalize that he was small in stature but larger than life. The kind of compliment often paid to someone no longer around to hear it; perhaps one of nature's ways of keeping egos in check. But in Benny's case, hardly necessary. Some articles added that Mr. DeMarco's death was not a result of the fire itself. His demise was attributed to a heart condition. No doubt exacerbated by the evening's tragic events.

There was a woman on the list of the dead whose name was being withheld until her relatives could be located and informed. Apparently she had succumbed to smoke inhalation and had been unable to find her way to an exit.

Bernard Karpaski, referred to as an employee of the Liz Randall gallery, was also among the deceased. According to reports, Mr. Karpaski had been knocked down the stairs and subsequently trampled to death when the surging crowd rushed out of the main gallery and came in contact with the doors he had just locked to keep out unruly street demonstrators.

Another victim was also having his name withheld pending notification of next of kin. A dreadful task that fell to Tilton Mangas. Tilton knew Mrs. Ernie Beeker and made the call as soon as he felt the unknowing widow would be awake. He didn't want her to see or hear reports of the incident or get word from someone she did not know. Shattering news can never be delivered well. But Tilton did his best. Rather than telling her that her husband's skull had been cracked as if it was raku pottery untimely placed beneath the heels of a marauding mob of frightened and selfish people, he simply said that in the confusion Ernie had fallen and hit his head. A blow that killed him instantly, Tilton added, determined to ease the pain as much as possible. The artist went on to say that Beeker had actually stopped to help an elderly lady in danger of being trampled. And just after giving her aid, the force of the crowd caused him to lose his footing. All total fabrication, of course. Constructed out of a vibrant imagination and a desire to make a distraught woman feel less devastated.

The truth was Tilton had actually been outside trying to bring Benny back from heaven's orchestra pit when Ernie Beeker spent the final moments of his life being swept along like silt in a fast flowing river. He was caught in the middle of such a jam-packed wad of people, wedged in so tightly that he couldn't even bring his hands up to his face to try to refit his glasses, which had been pushed askew and were barely clinging to his head. Without the aid of his bifocals, all he saw around him was a sea of unfocused fog. Heads without faces bobbing and weaving and moving him inexorably toward the entrance stairs. Stairs that he had no way of knowing were there. So when the level floor beneath his feet suddenly fell away, Ernie fell with it. Unlike Tilton's tall tale of a swift and painless demise, the crumbling Beeker's body was twisted like a contortionist's on its journey from upright to horizontal. First his ankles were stepped on with wing tips and loafers. Then his knees felt the knife of the stair edge. His chest caught the brunt of his collapse as he fell forward and stuck to the stairs like a rumpled carpet remnant. Fleeing feet began moving atop and over him like the pounding hooves of stampeding cattle. Shoved as he was stomped on, he continued his downward descent to the base of the stairs where he joined the hapless, but thankfully already dead, Bernard. Thankful because the Chicago gallery employee was immune to the pain that was to follow when the escaping mob crashed through the glass doors at the street. Unfortunately, the Houston art impresario was still conscious when the glass began to rain down on top of him and was ground into his neck and face by the panicked patrons. One particularly large shard was stamped into his throat by a morbidly obese woman, screaming as she ran. The glass sliced through his carotid artery about as aggressively as if he were being chewed by sharks. Red rain spurted and sprayed ankles and thighs as they continued to clomp over him. Ernie Beeker's lights went out slowly. He knew he wouldn't be getting up. And just before the end, he once again saw a sad girl's black body silhouetted against the white light of a hot Havana afternoon. Then all was darkness.

After the debacle had ended, Ellis managed to find the other people he knew. Motif and Alison had banged their way out the front entrance with the rest of the anxious audience. Wendell James was there too, milling about among the survivors like someone simply looking for a place to sit and rest. The reporter, Joshua Steiner, who had been in full assault before the chaos, was actually trying to help some of the injured on Superior Street. But there was another face Ellis didn't find. A face he assumed would be there looking for air time. The Reverend Barry Tompkins was nowhere to be seen. Not in the immediate vicinity anyway. The vicinity Ellis was surveying once everyone was safely out of the gallery.

Later that night, Benny's relatives joined the medical attendees who took him silently away. Lela and Tilton, Motif, Alison, and Alejandro returned to the hotel. Wendell James said his goodbyes and left as well. Ellis said he was going to stay to see if he could find out anything from the police, fire department, or the arson investigators who were starting to arrive on the scene. If nothing else, he felt he could at least spend some time with Liz Randall who came out of the entire incident looking virtually unscathed. Physically, at least.

It was almost dawn before Ellis returned to The Drake. What he had picked up from the investigators on the scene wouldn't be in the paper the next morning with the body count and the replay of the night's terrible events. Official reports don't go out of their way to divulge too much too soon. But after all the clamor, confusion, concern and excitement, Ellis was pleased to know he hadn't hallucinated that Molotov cocktail beneath the track lights. The experts were sure that the fire had help getting started.

It was the middle of the morning before Ellis arose. He almost never slept that long but getting back to the hotel as late as he did caused him to abandon his early-to-rise schedule. He called for breakfast to be sent up and managed to get in a quick shower and shave before it arrived. Looking at himself in the mirror, he couldn't shake the feeling that bad things were going to continue to happen unless he personally found a way to put an end to it all. Friends or no friends, ex-loves or not, if toes needed to be stepped on to find out what was really going on, today was as good a day as any to start stepping on them.

He called Tilton and Lela's room.

"Hello."

Ellis recognized her voice. "Are you up? Are you guys awake?"

"Sure, Lela said, "it's almost eleven." I'm just —"

"Can you meet me downstairs in the lobby?" Ellis asked. "I'd like to talk to you."

Ten minutes later Ellis was sitting in a fan-backed, thickly cushioned easy chair watching Lela stride across the lobby and take a seat on the corner of the couch next to him. Her bottom had barely settled softly into the plush sofa when Ellis said, "Are you and Alejandro Reyes having an affair?"

"What?"

"It's a simple question. Are you and Reyes having an affair?"

"After everything that happened last night... and that's the first thing you ask me," Lela replied indignantly.

Ellis didn't back off. "Look, Benny's dead, I hate that. Beeker's dead. He shouldn't be. Neither should Bernard or the other woman who couldn't get out last night. But none of that can be chalked up to fate. Someone started that fire. Whether they meant to kill anyone or not is irrelevant. That was the result. In spades."

"How can you be sure the fire didn't get started accidentally," Lela asked. "I didn't see anything about arson in the paper this morning."

"No, and you didn't stick around and talk to the investigators last night, either. I did. I knew that was the case before they told me. It will get to the papers soon enough. Now let's get back to my original question."

"Why would you even ask me such a question? You don't think Alejandro had anything to do with it? Do you?"

"I ask such a question because ever since you first introduced me to the guy, I've noticed that he can't keep his eyes off you. That first night at Flashpoint, he was definitely bending your ear about something he didn't want others to hear. A few days later I happened to see him and you taking the same elevator bank in the middle of the afternoon."

Lela cut in, "Are you talking about the Galleria? I told you what I was doing there."

"Don't stop me, Lela, I'm on a roll," Ellis said, not playfully. "To reiterate. There was Flashpoint. There was the Galleria. There was the first night we spent in Marfa. Reyes left Tilton, Wendell, and me, talking downstairs. But I noticed he didn't go straight out of the hotel. He headed to the stairs that lead to the rooms. One of which you had already retired to. Then he shows up here in Chicago. Even though I've never actually seen him pay much attention to Benny's music when he's had the opportunity to hear him. And he spent a lot of last night jawing with you about something. Now I haven't accused anyone of anything yet, but it wouldn't be the first time in my life I've run into guys who were in love with someone else's wife. Guys who would do just about anything to get that someone else out of the way."

Lela could tell by the way that he ended his sentence he was through for the moment. And while she certainly didn't like the accusatory nature of his question, she could understand now why he was asking it. So she began to reply.

"Look Brig, here's the straight, honest answer to your question. Alejandro and I are not having an affair." She looked at his eyes for a second before continuing. They didn't blink. She glanced away momentarily, then looked back at him as she continued. "But it's not because he hasn't wanted to. I'm the one who hasn't let it happen."

Ellis found nothing calculating in her tone. So he gave her the benefit of the doubt to keep her talking. "Okay, you're not lovers. But it's pretty obvious he's in love with you. Generally there's a reason for that."

Lela began slowly. "Brig, there is something that Alejandro and I have kept from Tilton. And up until now, everyone else for that matter. I think Alejandro's a wonderful painter. I know Tilton does too. I asked him to do a portrait of me. It was to be a surprise for Tilton's birthday. It all started out casual enough. I would come over. He had me sit for him in his studio. The more I came over, the more natural I felt around him. I really wanted this painting to be something Tilton would treasure. Alejandro kept talking about how beautiful I was. I liked hearing that. Believe me, all women like hearing that. I guess I started to believe it as well. He would talk about how Tilton would love seeing me the way I looked best... you know. He said men really love that."

Ellis cut through the double-talk. "So before long you had your clothes off."

"Not all of them," Lela came back quickly. "But some of them. And as the portrait progressed, I could tell Alejandro was having a difficult time with his feelings. He never tried anything. Not physically anyway. But one day he broke down. He actually wept and said he had fallen in love with me. I tried to tell him it was silly. It was merely infatuation. I told him he was just caught up in the painting he was doing. But he would go on and on. Finally, I said I had to stop coming over and stop posing. I let him know that the whole painting was probably a bad idea... that we should just forget it. That's what you saw us arguing about that first night at Flashpoint. But he said it was going to be one of the best things that he had ever done and that he had to finish it, and that I must come back and help him finish. He did come up to my room in Marfa. I told him I was much too tired to talk about it and shooed him away. It's also what we were arguing about last night before everything got crazy. But that day at the Galleria... when I told you I was in the hotel to see an old friend... that was true. I have no idea why he was in the hotel or what he was doing there. It's a big hotel, Brig. There are different reasons for people going there other than afternoon quickies, you know."

She smiled as she finished. And Ellis smiled back. "Thanks for telling me the truth. Then and now. But that doesn't necessarily let Reyes off the hook. In fact, if anything, it just adds real jealously to the professional jealousy he may have been feeling with Tilton's recent notoriety."

"I can't believe Alejandro would try to harm anyone, Brig. He's just not like that."

"Nobody's ever like that. Until we find out they are. The fact is someone's trying to put a stop to Tilton, his work, his success, or all three. And whoever's behind it doesn't show any signs of stopping."

"Signs! That's right," Lela began hurriedly, as if she had forgotten something. "I meant to tell you. When we were leaving last night, I saw some of the signs those protesters were carrying. They were just like the ones the people had at Gloria Preston's party in Houston. That's odd, isn't it... that they'd be exactly the same?"

"Not as odd as you might think. Two nights ago I saw that preacher from Houston here in Chicago. That Reverend Tompkins."

"Tompkins? The same one who organized the Houston demonstration? He's here in Chicago?"

"He was two nights ago," Ellis said. "And those signs seem to indicate he was here last night too. I looked around for him after everything happened. But I never actually saw him at or around the gallery."

Lela was quick to provide an opinion. "Brig, that guy's a bona fide religious nut. He's much more likely than Alejandro to want to do Tilton harm."

"I'm not ruling him out. He could have done something. Or he could have had one of his believers do something. But right now I'm focusing on the people who I know for certain were there. Do you know where Reyes was right before the fireball?"

Lela brought her hand up to her temple as she spoke. "Oh God, things are so hazy and confusing about last night. I'm pretty sure Alejandro was close by me. We had been arguing about the portrait again. But I'm pretty sure we had broken it off before all the panic started." She inched forward on the couch as she spoke. And quickly became more animated. "Yes, yes... now I'm sure of it. We had stopped speaking to one another. I remember because I had turned and stood beside Liz Randall when Benny began to speak. Poor Benny. At least he didn't suffer... like the others... like Ernie." Her voice broke and she brought her hand to her mouth.

Ellis pulled a handkerchief from his jacket pocket and handed it to her. He watched her dab the tears from her eyes as he said, "What about Motif... or Alison? Do you know where they were?"

"Lord, Brig, I have no idea. After what you told us they were doing that night at Flashpoint, I've not gone out of my way to look for them at gatherings."

"How about Wendell James? Notice where he was?"

"I'm not sure, Brig. I know I saw him earlier in the evening. And I think I saw him later, talking to Ernie, but I have no idea where he was when the fire started."

"Speaking of Ernie, didn't you tell me that Tilton said he had been acting strange... even before they left Cuba?"

"Oh Brig, Ernie's gone. And so horribly. He can't have had anything to do with this. Tilton's work made money for Ernie, anyhow."

Ellis came forward in his chair now, "I know. But we also talked once about the fact that dead artists often get a lot more for their paintings than live ones, right?"

The gears suddenly switched in Lela's mind. "Oh my, the paintings. I forgot about the paintings. Were they all... destroyed?"

Ellis, who had stayed behind to talk with the fire and police investigators, was able to answer her quickly. "Three were badly burned. The others were fine. Including the latest one, *Desert Sunset*. In fact, the fire itself did a lot less damage than the panic. That's often the case when too many people are jammed into too small a space. Listen, I'd like to talk to Tilton this morning too, is he upstairs?"

"No. He's not here. He got a call from that reporter's secretary. You know... the reporter who was at the gallery last night. Apparently he felt bad about everything that happened and wanted to interview Tilton. Sort of give him a chance to tell why he does the work he does."

Even before he spoke, Lela could tell by the look on his face that Ellis was concerned about what she had just said. "Where were they supposed to meet?"

"Navy Pier. By the Ferris Wheel, I think. Tilton left a little while ago."

Ellis was already out of his chair and almost past her when Lela grabbed his arm and asked, "What's the matter? Where are you going?"

Ellis looked down at her and said, "I'm going to Navy Pier. It's been my experience that reporters don't have secretaries."

Chapter 24

Tilton took a taxi from The Drake. The cabbie dropped him right outside the main gates. Navy Pier had become one of Chicago's biggest family attractions. Tourists from all over the Midwest came to stroll down the three thousand foot long, almost three hundred foot wide, collection of restaurants, shops, exhibit halls, and theaters. The structure had come full circle since opening to the public as both shipping facility and pleasure pier in 1916. Two world wars had seen it converted to a military training facility, and after those conflicts it had a short-lived revival, then fell into disrepair. But Chicagoans, being both civic minded and acutely aware of how to make a buck, chipped in and restored the historic pier to something far beyond what its builders envisioned. Now, surrounded by fifty acres of promenades, parks, gardens, and family friendly attractions, it reaches into the pockets of tourists, suburbanites, and city dwellers without prejudice. No charge to get in, but few if any ever get away without leaving lots of hard-earned dollars behind.

Tilton wound his way past the peanut and popcorn vendors, the kiosks manned with garrulous guides selling boat excursions onto Lake Michigan, the school groups, vacationers, strolling lotharios looking for widows from Des Moines, and the merely curious. Even though he had never been there, he knew where he was going. All he had to do was look up. Tilton was supposed to meet Joshua Steiner at the entrance to the Ferris Wheel. And since the colossal structure could be seen from as far away as his hotel room window, he figured it certainly wouldn't be hard to find once he got there. He was right.

Looking skyward and walking east along the pier to the midway point, he stopped and craned his neck to see the top of the hundred and fifty foot behemoth that was on a raised embankment with stairs leading up to it. Steel girders and spokes painted bright white shone against the deep blue sky looking for all the world like God's unicycle, Tilton thought. Of course, this unicycle also had forty red gondolas giving lovers, loners, and anyone who had the price of a ticket, a view of the lake, the shore, and certainly the most striking skyline Middle America had to offer.

Tilton traversed the steps slowly, looking as he went for the reporter he was sure he would have come to blows with the night before had fire, fear, and death not intervened. He saw a bench only a few feet from the base of the giant wheel. It appeared as good a place as any to wait for Steiner. So he wandered over and took a seat. He hadn't been there long when he heard a voice behind him say, "Mr. Mangas."

Twisting slightly, but not rising, Tilton expected to see the short, bespectacled reporter. Instead, he found himself staring up into the stern countenance of the man he had crossed verbal swords with in Houston – the Reverend Barry Tompkins.

"Well, well... look who's here," Tilton said. "Long way from home, aren't you, padre?"

"Not nearly as far as you, Mangas," came the reply. "And unlike you, I know the way back."

Tilton stood before he answered, so he'd be eye to eye. "Now don't get all philosophical on me, Reverend. I don't really have time to interpret your voodoo linguistics. I'm supposed to be meeting someone here."

"You need not wait for Mr. Steiner. He never had any intention of seeing you. I had the call made to your hotel. The deception was warranted, I believe. You wouldn't have seen me otherwise. Correct?"

"Deceptions are kinda' like lies, aren't they, brother?" Tilton's ironic tone was unmistakable. "I figured a man of the cloth, like you, would be against such things. And you're right, I would not have gone out of my way to see you." Then something clicked in Tilton's mind. "But wait a minute. How do you know Steiner, anyway? I didn't see you there last night. Though, come to think of it, I did see some of your handiwork. Your street gang's signs were the same as those you used in Houston."

"Those people who were demonstrating are not a gang, Mangas. They are sincere individuals who abhor what you are doing."

"Yeah, well, those sincere individuals helped cause the deaths of some good people last night," Tilton fired back.

"They had nothing to do with the fire, Mangas. No one could know something like that was going to happen."

"All I know is... they were causing a ruckus outside. That's why the door got locked in the first place. No ruckus, no locked door. No locked door, maybe no deaths. Actions have consequences, padre. Intended or unintended... actions have consequences."

Reverend Tompkins became more conciliatory. "Indeed they do, Mr. Mangas. Indeed they do. Look, I just want a few minutes of your time. We're both a long way from our homes. Just give me a few minutes to tell you some things. Things you may not realize." Gesturing toward the Ferris Wheel, he said, "Come, let's take in the beauty while we talk. It might make my words more meaningful."

"You want to go up in that thing? Jesus, padre — oh, sorry. I mean heck, padre, you're an odd one. But you've obviously gone to a lot of trouble to say your piece. So I'll hear you out. But don't expect any miraculous conversions."

The two men turned and walked the few feet to the ticket booth. Tompkins paid the man behind the counter, then they went around to the spot where people were exiting the gondolas on one side as new riders entered the metal pods from the other. Once they were seated, their slow ascent began.

Chapter 25

The taxi was close to the main gates but stalled in a long line of similar transportation vehicles depositing their passengers and concluding their economic transactions. Ellis, plus Lela, who had insisted upon accompanying him, could see the entrance from where they sat.

"Take this," Ellis said, reaching over and handing the cabbie a ten-dollar bill. "And keep the change. We'll get out here."

Slipping out of the car beside the curb, Ellis took Lela by the arm and they both walked briskly past the trail of taxis they had just been stuck behind. Like Tilton before them, they had no trouble spotting the Ferris Wheel. The pair weaved in and out of the foot traffic as they made their way down the pier toward the massive wheel named after the bridge builder from Pittsburgh who designed the first one mankind had ever seen for the 1893 World's Fair, held, oddly enough, in Chicago.

Reaching the steps leading to the elevated spot where the Ferris Wheel stood, Ellis took them two at a time while Lela's legs pumped like pistons to keep up. Arriving at the area directly below the wheel, both started scanning the area, looking in all directions for Tilton and whomever he might be with.

Then the giant wheel came to a stop. There were people still seated in the roofed, yet open-sided gondolas who seemed content to simply sit and wait out whatever malfunction was keeping the huge ride from making its slow circle.

"You sure Tilton said this is where they were to meet?" Ellis asked Lela.

"Yes. Of course, they might not have stayed here. For all we know they could have gone inside to one of the restaurants or something."

"And he didn't take a cell phone," Ellis queried.

"Hates them," Lela responded. "Calls them modern manacles."

No one can stand beside something that's a hundred and fifty feet tall without looking up at least once. It was a bright day, so Ellis held his hand just over his brow to shield his eyes from the glare of the sun. When he did, he noticed a black spec that seemed to be floating freely in the wind.

"What's that?" he said.

Lela looked up in the direction Ellis was staring and also saw some sort of oddly shaped design cutting figure eights in the sky as it slowly made its way toward earth. It looked too strange to be a bird. Which was good, Lela thought, because it was definitely on a gravity-induced trip downward. As it headed toward earth, it would occasionally catch an up-draft and rise a bit or be pushed sideways, interrupting its descent. Both Ellis and Lela seemed to be transfixed as they watched the bizarre object continue on its meandering way.

Almost a minute after Ellis had first spotted it, the unusual entity completed its languid journey to the grassy knoll just a few yards from where the two were standing. Moving over to see what had held them spellbound for the last thirty seconds, they both recognized it at the same time.

"Oh God," Lela inhaled.

"Damn," Ellis breathed out.

Resting, near their feet, seemingly unscathed by its trip from the top of the Navy Pier Ferris Wheel to the trimmed and watered grass below, was a short-brimmed, Stetson Open Road Silver Belly. The hat that Tilton never took off without extraordinary reason.

Like synchronized swimmers, Ellis's and Lela's heads turned as one, back toward the sky from whence the hat had come. Now, both sets of eyes were only able to catch the shadow of a missile rocketing to ground zero at a speed neither could track.

The arrival was spectacular. It included the cracking, splintering, and virtual explosion of the bench that was once only feet from the Ferris Wheel. The force of the actual indentation in the ground was of such startling magnitude that a grown man standing nearby wet himself. Screams that had started prior to impact found their release after the projectile splattered on the ground. A woman, waiting in the attraction's line with her two preschool grandchildren, wilted and crumpled to the ground. The kids looked at each other and began to cry.

Ellis grabbed Lela by the shoulders and held her fast. He said nothing, but steadying her with one hand, brought his other to her lips. She immediately understood she was being asked to stand her ground, silently. Paralyzed with fear, and unsure, even if she had wanted to, whether she could move her legs or not, she did as Ellis directed.

Walking slowly towards the imbedded pile that no one else had gathered the courage to approach yet, Ellis kept glancing upward to make sure the heavens were not about to dispense more surprises. When he reached the hole, still filling the air with dust and debris from the grass, dirt, wood, and metal that were all displaced by the incoming bomb of as yet undetermined origin, he stopped, knelt, and peered downward. There he saw the mangled body and flattened head of the Reverend Barry Tompkins.

Chapter 26

The train slithered through the darkness beneath the street like yesterday's dinner racing down the small intestine. There was no room on either side of the tunnel for man or child, Ellis noted. If you were out there, and unlucky enough not to reach an indentation, or too stupid to know why they were carved in the wall every hundred feet or so, you'd wind up being snatched from the side of the tunnel and spun beneath the electric rails like discarded leftovers in a garbage disposal.

Coming into the light of day, the cement walls topped with razor wire put the particular neighborhood he was passing through into the derisive mental category of the wrong side of the tracks. It was only when those walls fell away and the train sped along open track that Ellis registered any real awareness of the houses, parks, and people on either side of him. We are creatures of habit indeed, he thought. Programmed to feel certain ways about what is positive and negative in the world around us. Hard, dark, rough, equal bad. Soft, bright, smooth, equal good. If only it were that easy, Ellis mused.

Chicago's train system, while moving above city streets, cars, and pedestrians, also occasionally dives underground in places, and runs alongside other transport arteries such as freeways. It's an elevated and an underground and a roadside, if you really stop to think about it, Ellis contemplated. And contemplation was why Ellis was riding the train this morning. He had some thinking to do.

The day before, the police had accepted Tilton's explanation of what led to Reverend Tompkins express trip from the top of the Ferris Wheel to the unforgiving earth below. Especially since it was corroborated by not one, but three members of a Pentecostal church group from Joplin, Missouri who witnessed the entire episode from an adjacent gondola. They readily confirmed that the good reverend had proceeded to get extremely agitated. This became apparent to them when they heard a number of shouts regarding eternal damnation coming from the pod next to them. Looking over, they saw a well-dressed middle-aged man apparently attempting to choke the life from a bearded man wearing a hat. A hat that became dislodged and airborne due to the rather violent nature of the throttling that was being administered. The trio of Pentecostals fervently agreed that the bearded man was doing nothing more than trying to break free from the well-dressed man's grip. And that when the hairy-faced fellow was actually able to pull the other man's hands from his throat, he simply twisted away and slid from the bench to the bottom of the gondola. By then, the entire metal apparatus the two men were encased in was shaking so violently that when the throttler's unbalanced momentum sent him reeling backward, the tilt of the pod and the force of his weight on the door's latch caused it to swing open. Thereby depositing the smooth shaven man into the sky above Chicago. Where he didn't stay very long.

Even with this ironclad, Christian-verified, self-defense alibi, the Chicago police were less than happy about the body count that seemed to be piling up at a rapid clip around Tilton Mangas. And their questioning of virtually every person who was invited to Benny's memorial didn't help their demeanor either. No one seemed to have seen, or admitted to seeing, anything that was beneficial to finding out who actually started the conflagration at the art gallery. The fact that Bernard, whose job it was to keep interlopers out, wound up dead, made it virtually impossible to know whether any of the protesters made their way into the building and turned their verbal assault into a flaming one. And while various demonstrators freely admitted that Reverend Barry Tompkins had helped organize, coordinate, and plan the march on the gallery, none could, or would, say for sure whether they actually saw him there that night.

The arson investigators from the fire department were in a foul mood as well. For while it was obvious to them that the bathroom fire and the bar explosion were the result of premeditation, any evidence of who might have instigated either went up in flames with the toilet and the booze and three of Tilton's paintings. A lieutenant, who began with a distastefully macabre comment about Tilton's works now being a bit like twice-baked potatoes, went on to inform Ellis that whatever was used as the makeshift fuse for the Molotov cocktail disintegrated among the heat and flames.

Two separate instances involving deaths in two consecutive days at two of Chicago's highly publicized and well-promoted areas definitely had city authorities in a snit. Lela, on the other hand, was happy. Well, as happy as a person can be who's just lost two friends and two acquaintances to the grim reaper. She told Ellis she was absolutely convinced that Barry Tompkins was the cause of everything bad that had been happening to Tilton since the aborted bullfight in Houston. Her reasoning was simple. He had been at Flashpoint and made his displeasure known in no uncertain terms. Then Tilton was almost killed by a prematurely released fighting bull. He had been at Gloria Preston's and Tilton was almost run over by a rampaging sport utility van. While he couldn't have done that himself, being interviewed by local TV at the time, he could certainly have arranged to have one of his followers do it while he had everyone else's attention focused on him. He came to Chicago expressly to disrupt Tilton's show, and as awful as that turned out to be, it still wasn't enough. He tricked Tilton into meeting him and literally tried to strangle him. If there was a God in the heavens, Lela was letting it be known, he did the right thing by sending the good reverend to hell.

Ellis, on the other hand, while glad Tilton escaped yet another close call, was not yet ready to lay everything at the feet, now chilling in the morgue, of Barry Tompkins. So he found himself riding the train, looking for answers to a whole lot of questions. Was Lela too willing, and too vocal in painting the holy man as an absolute devil? Had she been totally truthful in regards to her and Reyes's relationship? Why had Reyes and Ernie Beeker been bickering so in Houston weeks ago? Why was Beeker, to use Tilton's phrase, acting strangely in Cuba? Did Motif and Alison really turn up for Benny's big night just to mingle with the art crowd? Why did the reporter, Joshua Steiner, just appear out of nowhere? And how much financial trouble had the Marfa debacle actually caused Wendell James? Was he genuinely here in Chicago simply to see his ailing sister? Ellis wanted his own answers before he concluded Tilton's troubles were now over. And he was setting out to get them as he stepped off the train onto the platform at the station in downtown Evanston.

Evanston, a suburb just north of Chicago, is home to multimillion-dollar lakeside mansions, tree-lined idyllic neighborhoods, and Northwestern University. Like many small enclaves that butt up against a sprawling metropolis, it's bordered by row upon row of apartment buildings, high-rise condos, hospitals and nursing homes. But Ellis wasn't there to check out the community. He had gotten Wendell James's cell phone number from Lela, telling her he just wanted to talk to Wendell about what he might have seen before the gallery fire. And while he did want to do that, he also wanted something else as well. He wanted to be able to cross Wendell James off his list of people who always seemed to be around when trouble came calling.

Over the phone, James had suggested they meet for lunch at a place that would be easy for Ellis to find. The old train station had been converted into a restaurant and it was only a few blocks from where Ellis arrived. Entering the restaurant and being greeted by the host, a young woman in a starched white blouse and blue skirt, he was told that Mr. James had already arrived and had decided to be seated out back on the patio. Ellis followed the young woman through the restaurant and when he stepped outside into the sunlight, the question of Wendell James motive for being in Chicago was immediately put to rest. There, seated beside him, in a wheelchair that had been rolled up to the table, was the sister he had told Ellis about when they both arrived. The resemblance confirmed their kinship immediately.

Introductions were made, pleasantries were exchanged, lunch was ordered and Ellis lost no time in getting right to the matters at hand. "Wendell, can you tell me where you were right before the fire started the other night?"

"Certainly. It's the same thing I told the police. By the time the first shouts were heard and right before that first big flash of fire, I was pretty much squeezed into the middle of everybody else in the main part of the gallery. Like everyone I guess, I was trying to hear what was going on with that reporter, Benny, and Tilton."

"How about before that, earlier in the evening. Didn't I see you speaking with Ernie Beeker," Ellis asked.

"Yes," James replied, "Ernie and I had been talking. Well... be honest, I was doing most of the talking. Ernie was listening, I guess. The fact is, he barely acknowledged my presence at all. I mean his mind must have really been somewhere else. He definitely seemed distracted. I can't believe what happened to him later. What a shame. What a terrible shame."

"Did Beeker give any indication that something might have been amiss with him and Tilton?"

"No. Not to me. Like I said, he barely spoke. I have no idea what was on the poor guy's mind."

For the first time, James's sister injected herself into the conversation. "You seem to be asking an awful lot of questions, Mr. Ellis. Why are you so interested in what my brother was doing? He was invited by the artist's wife, you know."

James jumped in before Ellis could answer. "Now, now. Don't get excited dear. Mr. Ellis is Tilton and Lela's good friend. I'm sure he's just concerned for their welfare. He certainly helped protect all of us in the Marfa storm. I'm very indebted to you myself, Brig, for sort of taking charge then. I'm not sure how many of us would have made it if you hadn't. But I must admit to being mildly curious too. Didn't I read in the paper that some Houston preacher was killed? And didn't it also say that he was thought to be in charge of the demonstration on Superior Street that night?"

"Yes and yes," Ellis answered. "He was in charge of the demonstration and he was killed yesterday in a fall at Navy Pier. A lot of people seem to think he was behind all the near-death experiences Tilton's had the last few weeks."

"But you don't think so, Brig?" James asked. "You think there's somehow more to it?"

Before Ellis could reply, James's sister said, "Surely you don't think Wendell had anything to do with any of those incidents!"

She may be wheel chair bound, Ellis thought before answering, but there's certainly nothing wrong with her powers of observation. "What I don't think much of is coincidence and hasty conclusions," he responded. "Your brother, like me I might add, is one of a limited number of people who have been present during each of the tragic... or near-tragic events that have occurred. As was the Reverend Barry Tompkins that we were just discussing. Now, based on what he tried to do to Tilton yesterday, before he accidentally fell from that Ferris Wheel, one could easily assume he's been the hand behind everything that's happened. And while it does make sense, it's still a pretty hasty assumption."

"You sound like more than just a friend," James's sister said.

"I am." Ellis responded. "I'm an old friend."

Lunch came and with it a break in the direct give and take about Wendell James, Tilton, and Lela. Though by the time dessert was finished, Ellis had still managed to find out, or at least to hear from James, that he and Ernie Beeker had no business dealings concerning Tilton's work. When asked directly if he thought Tilton would turn to him to represent his work, now that Beeker was no longer alive to do it, James simply said, "No, he wouldn't ask me because he knows I wouldn't do it. It's just not the sort of thing I think I could sell. And frankly, I'm not sure I'd want to."

By two o'clock, Ellis was on the train headed back to Chicago. In his own mind, his questions about Wendell James had been answered. The man had been telling the truth about why he had come to the Chicago area. And though he had to take it on James's word, and his own feelings about him, Ellis now believed the Austin art dealer had no designs on relieving his financial woes by making money from Tilton's paintings. But there were still other people to see, and other questions in need of answers.

Chapter 27

Ellis opened the door and walked back into his hotel room at five minutes past three. His eyes were immediately drawn to the flashing red light on his telephone. The message was from Lela. She confirmed that Benny's funeral was being held the next day and she told him that Tilton had invited Alejandro Reyes, Motif, and Alison for dinner that evening. She said Tilton sincerely hoped he would join them as well. They were all to meet in the lobby at seven, then they'd walk the few short blocks to a French-Vietnamese restaurant called Le Colonial on Rush Street.

Checking his watch, Ellis determined he still had time to try to run down a few more answers. He put in a call to the *Chicago Tribune* and asked for Joshua Steiner. After being put on hold for close to a minute, a voice came on the other end of the line.

"This is Steiner."

"Mr. Steiner, my name is Brig Ellis. I was at the Liz Randall gallery the other night when all the trouble broke out. I was hoping we could get together for a few minutes this afternoon. I wanted to ask you some questions in regard to that night."

"Yeah, well you see in my job, I ask the questions. And I don't really have time to talk to someone I don't know about —"

Ellis cut him off with, "Mr. Steiner, I'm a good friend of Tilton Mangas. Both he and I were wondering why your name was used to lure him to a meeting where he was almost killed. A meeting where another man did lose his life."

The silence on the other end of the phone said the reporter was either really surprised or plotting a response. Either one was okay with Ellis.

"I looked into the event you mentioned, yesterday. The authorities didn't say anything to me about my name being used," Steiner finally replied.

"That's because I asked Tilton not to say anything to them. But it's on the table now, Mr. Steiner, and I'd really like to talk to you about it... today."

"Well, listen," the reporter said, "maybe I can get away for a few minutes around five-thirty. Do you know a place called Claire's Coffee Shop on Lake?"

Ellis said he didn't but wrote down the name and address as Steiner gave it to him.

Then the reporter asked, "How will I know you?"

Ellis replied, "Don't worry. I'll know you."

Hanging up the phone, Ellis realized he'd have time to grab a shower, change and maybe look into a couple of other things before he was to meet with Steiner and later, the group for dinner. Good, he thought. Good to be running things down. If it turned out Tompkins was indeed the nut behind it all, fine. He could live with that. He just wanted to be sure Tilton could live with it, if that wasn't the case.

After showering and changing clothes, Ellis put in a call to Houston in an attempt to scratch an itch he'd had ever since the gallery fire. There was only one place the information about Monroe Greensburg, currently covering Tilton's *Desert Sunset* canvas, could have come from, Fontana Funeral Home. But why would Fontana, who was so intent on keeping his association with Tilton secret, provide the facts about Tilton's latest material? It didn't make sense. And Ellis wasn't fond of things that didn't make sense. His phone call was answered on the fifth ring.

"Fontana Funeral Home. I'm sorry, Mr. Fontana's not in right now. No, he's not on the premises at all. Yes. I expect him back later. Probably much later though. All right. Give me the information and I'll have him return your call. Yes, I have it, Mr. Mangas's friend. That's right, I'll tell him you said no matter how late. Very good."

Ellis got to Claire's Coffee Shop fifteen minutes before he was supposed to meet Steiner. It wasn't punctuality compulsion. He simply wanted to be able to secure a spot where he could see if the reporter was coming alone. So he took a booth by the window and sat facing east. That way he could see the corner of Lake and Michigan. Since the *Tribune* was northeast of Claire's, Ellis figured he'd be coming from that direction. At five thirty-five, a short man with glasses wearing an open collar blue oxford shirt, khakis and a darker blue windbreaker, rounded the corner. The shoulder bag he was carrying banged on his hip as he walked. When he crossed the street against the light and came out of the shadow, Ellis made a positive identification. Joshua Steiner had arrived.

The reporter came through the door and started to look around. Ellis rose and motioned with his hand. Steiner walked over and sat down opposite him.

"I'm Brig Ellis. As I said on the phone, I'm a friend of Tilton Mangas. I saw you at the gallery the other night. I heard your discussion before the fire interrupted everything. I'd like to ask you a few questions about that."

"And I'd like to ask you what you meant when you called me and said that my name had been used to lure Mangas into some sort of trap."

Ellis responded quickly. He thought that was the best way to get the reporter to do the same. "Well, I didn't say trap. But you could certainly call it that. Tilton received a call from someone claiming to be your secretary. He was told that you wanted to meet him at Navy Pier and give him a chance to explain his side of why he paints, what he paints, and also what he paints with."

Steiner responded immediately, "I don't have a secretary. Secretaries at newspapers went out with electric typewriters... hell, even before that, I guess."

"Tilton doesn't keep up with newspaper operations," Ellis said. "He bought the set up."

"Well, it wasn't me, and I can't believe it was anyone at the paper. Our phone records can be checked for that sort of thing, you know."

"I'm not that interested in who made the call, Mr. Steiner. Obviously it was made at the request of Reverend Tompkins. And then everything turned out... well, the way it turned out. What I'm really interested in is how you knew so much about the particular individual in Tilton's painting, *Desert Sunset*."

Just then the waitress came by. "Are you guys going to order something or are you just going to sit here and make eyes at one another."

Neither really wanted anything. And they both let the insult slide. Ellis said, "Coffee." Steiner said, "Coffee." The waitress, sporting a nametag that read Louise, left to go retrieve some.

The interruption had given Steiner time to start turning things over in his mind. Tompkins was dead. It wasn't like he'd be betraying a confidence. The guy never really asked me to keep it a secret anyway, Steiner thought. Maybe if I share some information, he reasoned, I'll learn something that will keep this story going for a while.

"Look, here's the way it happened. Tompkins contacted me. Asked me to meet him here, as a matter of fact. He obviously was appalled by what Mangas was doing, but you wouldn't believe the weird shit that passes for art these days. So I was less than enthusiastic about getting involved."

Ellis jumped in. "But you did get involved. Why?"

Steiner continued. "Tompkins told me that one of the paintings on display at this particular event actually used a holocaust survivor in it. With a name like mine, I guess he figured he'd have a sympathetic ear."

"And apparently he did."

"Look, I'm probably not as Jewish as I ought to be... but I know the beginning of a good story when I hear one. And this had all the earmarks of something that people would care about whether they gave a damn about the arts or not."

The caustic waitress arrived with the coffee. She clanked it down in front of both men, turned and walked away. Neither made an effort to thank her or even look at the cups in front of them.

"What did Tompkins say to convince you he wasn't just another religious kook on some sort of anti-art crusade?" Ellis asked.

"The guy had chapter and verse," Steiner began. "He knew the name of the person in the painting... or on the painting... or the painting itself. I'm still unsure how to actually address it. Anyway, he had the guy's name, a copy of his death certificate, photocopies of medical records from Houston hospitals, plus some documents from a mental institution in a place called Rusk, Texas. He even had immigration records too. Then he showed me the guy's name and some of his family's name from a list he had gotten from the Boniuk Library at the Holocaust Museum in Houston. It all looked authentic enough for me to look into it. I checked with the Holocaust Memorial Foundation of Illinois, and when their archives seemed to confirm what he had shown me... well, I thought it was at least worthy of a one-on-one confrontation. I didn't mean to hassle the old musician they were honoring, but I couldn't pass up the opportunity to get into it in a public way. Makes the story that much more attractive, you know. Then the place went up in flames and the whole damn thing took a back seat to the fire and deaths. Believe me, nothing boosts street sales like catastrophe. Particularly when it's in a part of town that's not always on the nightly news stab-em-and-slab-em report."

As Ellis listened to Steiner's account, he found that it raised another question in his mind. "All that information you mentioned. Seems like an awful lot for a Baptist preacher to come up with on his own."

"Well," Steiner replied, "once you have a name and a social security number, you'd be surprised at the things you can come up with. But the fact is, you're right. I asked Tompkins if he had uncovered all this background himself. He said no. Said there was someone in Houston who provided a lot of the stuff to him."

"Did he mention any names? In case you weren't prepared to put all your trust in him alone?"

"No. He let the documents speak for themselves. Said he needed to protect his source. Said I should understand that. And I do."

The conversation went on a bit longer. Steiner volunteered what Ellis already knew, that the authorities weren't anywhere close to knowing who the actual fire starter was. Then the reporter pressed Ellis about the Reverend Barry Tompkins. What did he know about the preacher? Had he and Tilton had trouble before? Had he really wigged out and tried to kill the artist or was he just trying to scare him into seeing the light? Ellis played dumb. He said he really didn't know. The reporter didn't buy it.

"Why do I think, Mr. Ellis, that you got a lot more out of our little sit-down than I did?"

"You did okay," Ellis said. "You avoided a long, drawn out question and answer session with Chicago's finest."

"So you and Mangas intend to keep the Reverend's subterfuge to yourself, huh?"

"Yes. I believe you weren't involved. Tompkins knew that using your name was simply a good way to get Tilton to meet him."

"You believed that all along, didn't you," Steiner said. "You just wanted to find out more about how I got my information. And you did. But look, Ellis, Tompkins is dead. He's no longer a threat to Mangas. Why pursue it?"

"Just tying up loose ends, Mr. Steiner. I'm kind of obsessive that way."

Chapter 28

The six walked west from The Drake, crossed Michigan Avenue, then turned left at Rush. Their mood was quiet, subdued, not punctuated with the raucous laughter that generally accompanied their outings. Reaching their destination, they stepped under the glass and iron fluted awning and into Indochina, circa nineteen twenty. The air was not as thick and damp as Saigon's but everything else in the restaurant did its best to evoke the atmosphere of that city's enigmatic past. Moving amid the palm and banana trees, passing by the fringed lampshades and sepia photographs, the group made its way up the stairs to the open terrace overlooking the street. There, they settled into rattan chairs beneath slowly turning ceiling fans. Unbeknownst to them, this would be their last night together.

While some picked up water glasses and others fidgeted with chopsticks, Tilton took the wine list and said, "Friends, enough of this self-enforced solemnity. Time enough for that at the ceremonies where such things are called for."

"He means the funerals," Lela chipped in. A meager attempt at mirth. But one that produced a few smiles.

Tilton continued. "Now you all know that neither Benny or Ernie would want us sitting here, moping like orphans on Mother's Day. Tonight should be about the good times we had with them. And as I recall, most of those good times started with a drink." He turned to the young Asian man standing beside the table. "So waiter, why don't you bring us a bottle... no, make that two bottles of this Batard-Montrachet Grand Cur. We might as well do this up right."

"I didn't know you had such a command of French," Alison said.

Tilton responded, "I remember as a child, staying up late and watching old movies on TV with my father. Our favorite was *Beau Geste* with Gary Cooper. I thought if he could become a French Foreign Legionnaire, the least I could do was figure out how to order a bottle of wine." Then Tilton added, "Therein lies the beginning and the end of my Gallic education."

"And who played his brothers... John and Digby," Ellis asked.

Alejandro, Motif, Alison, and Lela obviously had not a clue. Tilton spoke up though.

"Ah, a fellow movie buff, eh? The answer, of course, is Ray Milland and Robert Preston."

Ellis acknowledged the correctness of Tilton's answer as heads turned and eyebrows were raised among the others sitting at the table. This was obviously a competition they were unable to take part in.

"And can you tell me, good sir," Tilton said, addressing Ellis who was sitting across from him, who played the evil Markov?"

"Brian Donlevy," Ellis answered without hesitation.

"Please," Lela said, "somebody change the subject. This could go on all night." But secretly, she was glad for any conversation that would take their minds off recent events.

After the wine arrived and the golden tint of the white burgundy put a warm glow in their glasses and their moods, minds quickly turned to the allure of oxtail soup, spring rolls, grilled shrimp around sugar cane and wok-seared monkfish with chili, lemon grass, and peanuts. Somewhere near the ordering of another round of wine and the main course, talk turned back to Benny DeMarco and Ernie Beeker. But now the remembrances were about the good times, the successes, the things they genuinely seemed to want to relive.

Ellis listened as they talked and laughed and told stories. Outwardly, he was there at the table. But inwardly, he was keeping his distance. He couldn't get out of his mind what Steiner had said about Tompkins. The Reverend had someone in Houston who helped track down and supply information about Monroe Greenburg. He had someone who helped convince Tilton he was going to meet with a reporter when he was actually going to meet with an arguably unstable religious zealot. And maybe that wasn't all that someone did. Maybe that someone played the reverend just like he or she had been playing everyone else. Maybe that someone was actually sitting at the table right now, biding time and waiting for another opportunity. And why, Ellis wondered, hadn't he received that call back from funeral director, Frank Fontana in Houston.

Suddenly, his mind was whipped back to what was being said at the table, when Alejandro Reyes, head down looking at his lap, hands moving beneath the table, burst into the middle of a conversation that was already in progress.

"I was a selfish pig," he exclaimed. "I could only think of myself. My appetites. I harassed him. I whined to him like a spoiled child."

It was as if the gangly Mexican was immersed in a monologue with himself. By now everyone was listening. But no one was joining in. Ellis didn't like the way the artist's arms and hands kept moving below his sight line.

"The last times I saw him, I only interrogated him. I made him angry with all my questions. Or I made him sad. All because I wanted more. I wanted to show more work. I wanted to do the Cuban symposium. I wanted all the things he was doing for you, Tilton. I wanted all the things you had. I made Ernie angry. I made him avoid me. The man who helped me. The man who did so much for me. The man who would never harm another living soul. And now he's gone. I cannot tell him how sorry I am. I cannot tell him how much I appreciate what he did for me. So I will tell you, Tilton. I will tell you and your lovely wife that I am humbled and I am grateful for all that you have done to help me. I do not want you to be gone like Ernie, without me having the chance to tell you what I sincerely feel."

Reyes pushed back in his chair slightly, and his hands started to come up from below the table. Ellis pushed his chair back quickly and was almost on his feet when the Mexican revealed what he had been feverishly completing. With a pen in his right hand, holding one corner, and his left hand holding the other, he displayed his white linen napkin now gray and black with the stunning likeness of Lela's face, pensive, penetrating, beautiful.

"I want to do a real painting of Lela," Reyes said, staring directly at Tilton. "A portrait that both of you can keep and share forever. Like you share each other's love."

Ellis couldn't help but notice the pronounced line of sweat atop Lela's upper lip. And the way she was blinking her eyes as if to keep the tears at bay. He doubted that anyone else saw it though. They were too busy looking at the teetering Mexican who had obviously over-imbibed.

The pregnant pause was broken by Motif who grabbed the pen from Reyes hand.

"Here," he shouted, "I'll do a portrait of Alison."

Flipping his napkin on the table, he made two wide swirls and accented both swiftly with two large, concentric circles. His entire maneuver took less than five seconds. Then he showed not only the table of Texans, but also everyone else in the restaurant that cared to look, his doodle of two enormous breasts. The Creole was even drunker than the Mexican.

Just then, Ellis's cell phone rang.

Chapter 29

Rain watered the streets of Chicago as if angels were expecting the pavement to grow. It spattered and splashed as puddles collected in potholes and gutters. Spring rain it was. Not overbearing, just constant. The kind of rain you don't mind being out in if you have a hat or an umbrella or maybe even if you don't. It seemed appropriate, Ellis thought. A classically gray, funereal day to say goodbye to a classy guy.

Benny DeMarco, like many of his advanced age, had apparently made his plans in advance. He was to be buried in Oak Park, just west of downtown Chicago. Oak Park was where Frank Lloyd Wright built houses, where Edgar Rice Burroughs created Tarzan, where Ernest Hemingway was born. Benny always liked to run with the chic crowd.

Tilton had hired a car and driver to take Lela, Ellis and him to the cemetery. There was to be only a graveside service. No long, weepy event in a stuffy funeral home with canned music and hard-backed chairs. Benny said his life was exceedingly long so he'd make sure his leaving of it would be mercifully short.

None of the three said much in the car on the way. They all watched the rain spot the windows and thought their separate thoughts. Tilton contemplated the flight back to Houston later in the day. A flight that would have Ernie Beeker on board. But not in first-class or economy. Lela reflected on the night, weeks ago, when she first called Ellis and asked him back into her life. How would things be different, she wondered, if she had never made that call. Ellis thought about the call he got the night before from Fontana. Plus the call he made after that. And he thought about his credo. You don't abort the mission. You finish the job.

Arriving at the cemetery, the car turned right onto a paved drive that ran between two massive iron gates. The asphalt path wound its way through Oak trees and past headstones large and small. Here and there an Italian influenced mausoleum, blacked with the toll that age takes on everything, stood motionless against the charcoal sky. Eventually the sedan came to a stop about fifty yards from where a small group was gathering around a shadowy hole with dirt piled high beside it — dirt covered by a tasteful green tarpaulin.

The trio made their way cautiously from the car to the graveside, stepping gingerly to avoid puddles, mud, and though none mentioned it, the resting places of current long-term residents. Two sets of couples arrived a few seconds after Tilton, Lela, and Ellis had taken standing positions near the slate gray casket with the ornate silver handles. Looking around at those assembled, Ellis put the group at about two dozen. Respectful, but not ostentatious, he thought. The way Benny would have liked it.

The ceremony itself lasted no more than fifteen minutes. Then ended with smiles as well as tears when the priest informed everyone that the one thing Benny had requested be interred with him, would be. "He's got his violin with him and he'll be making sweet music in heaven soon," the cleric said. "Come, let us pray."

People walk away from funerals more slowly than they walk toward them. Ellis, Lela, and Tilton proved no exception. And for the first time since they had gotten into the car that morning, their talk turned to something other than Benny.

"Are you sure you want us to drop you at the train station?" Tilton asked.

"That's why I put my bag in the trunk when we left the hotel," Ellis answered.

Beneath Tilton's protective arm that was draped around her shoulder, Lela said, "I wish you were coming to Houston instead of going back to San Diego. But I know you must be anxious to get home."

Ellis replied, "Yes. Have to pick up Osgood from the kennel. He's probably giving them a hearty ration of bulldog bad news by now."

"Why a bulldog?" Lela asked.

Tilton jumped in before Ellis could answer. "Easy," he said. "They're relentless. Like Brig here. Once they bite down... they don't let go until they're good and ready."

"Am I that easy to read?" Ellis said.

"In some ways, yes. In some ways, no," Tilton remarked. "And you know... speaking of not always being able to read you... you never did tell me what you really think of my work. I still don't have the faintest idea of how you really feel about my paintings... my technique."

They were just short of the car, but Ellis pulled up anyway, stopping before he answered. "Tilton, I'm fine with planting people... like we just did with Benny. I'm okay with dropping them into the sea. I've got no problem with burning them and spreading their ashes over mountains, valleys, or shorelines. I hear they're even sending some of them off into space these days. I'm okay with that. I can even deal with them being stuffed into an urn sitting on somebody's mantle. But the fact is, I just can't get used to the idea of hanging them on the wall."

Tilton looked Ellis squarely in the eye and said, "Well, that just goes to show, my friend, that you don't know shit from Shineola when it comes to art. I'll have you know that I met with some people from Everyone's Eternal yesterday afternoon. You know, the big nationwide funeral chain. And they agreed to buy *Desert Sunset* for fifty thousand dollars. Plan to put it in the conference room of their corporate headquarters in Phoenix. Didn't want to say anything in front of the others last night. Might have seemed a bit braggadocios, you know."

Ellis shook his head as he rubbed his hand over his close-cropped hair. "Never said I was a critic, or even a connoisseur. But at least I know now why you were buying two hundred dollar bottles of wine last night," he said. All three looked at each other and smiled as they got into the car.

The driver knew the way to the train station, so it didn't take them long to get there. As they were pulling up in front, Ellis, who was sitting beside the driver, turned to Tilton and Lela in the back seat and said, "You've got the name and number of that guy in Houston. Give him a call if you need any security work in the days ahead. I found out from some friends of mine in the business that's he's an honest guy. Ex-cop. Knows his stuff."

Lela said, "We will Brig. Thanks for finding him. But somehow I don't think we'll be needing any more of that kind of help. Since that terrible Reverend Tompkins is no longer around."

Tilton added, "Yeah, that guy was definitely one lug-nut short of a tight wheel. I'm not surprised he snapped. He was certainly my public enemy numero uno. Everything will be fine now"

Ellis thought for a moment, then he looked at both of them and lied. "Yeah, Tompkins has been the source of all your problems. But that's behind you now."

At the station, everyone got out of the car as Ellis retrieved his bag from the trunk. He reached out to shake Tilton's hand but the artist bypassed it and wrapped him in a big bear hug saying, "You're a hell of a guy, Mr. Brig Ellis. Lela must have been nuts to let you get away. But I'm damn glad she did. You take care now." Then the Texan got back into the car leaving Lela and Ellis alone.

"Brig," Lela began, a tear forming in the corner of her eye, "there's just no way I can thank you enough. It's been so wonderful having you back in my life. I can't believe you're walking out of it again."

"It's a different life now, Lela. "We're different people. I'm honored that you called me. And you have my number. Let me know when Tilton's about to have a big showing in Los Angeles or San Diego. I'm sure it will happen. He's a talented guy. And he's got a fabulous woman behind him. You can't stop a combination like that."

Lela looked up into Ellis's eyes, "Kiss me goodbye," she said.

Ellis bent down to kiss her on the cheek. But Lela's hand caught his jaw and moved his lips against hers. She held the kiss long enough for him to feel her tear sliding against his face. Then she turned, and got back in the car without saying a word. Ellis stood there a moment as they drove away.

Chapter 30

Walking into the station, Ellis looked up at the directional signs. He spotted his destination and slipped his train pass into the turnstile. Checking the schedule on the wall, he saw that the next train should be arriving in less than two minutes. So he stood by the platform waiting for it to arrive.

The rain had stopped but Ellis's thoughts hadn't. As he stood on the platform his mind wandered back to seeing Lela in the Houston airport for the first time in nearly twenty years. Where does your life go, he said to himself. But it didn't take him long to come up with an answer. He knew where his had gone. To the jungles of Grenada, the streets of Panama City, the mountains of Belarus, the alleys of Mogadishu, the deserts of Kuwait, Saudi, and Iraq. Plus any number of points in-between. Had that been leading somewhere? Or was it all just random? How can anyone ever know for sure, he thought. Then a train began to pull into the station, and where he had been became less important than where he was going. Which was not the airport, but back into Chicago.

Having checked the colored plate on the approaching train to make sure it was the green line back to the city, Ellis stepped into the car when it stopped. On board there was a young black couple with the look – baseball caps, satin jackets, baggy pants, and sneakers. In front of them, an older white guy dozed. His oily hair leaving a spot on the window where his head leaned against it. Beyond him, a businesswoman sat with a small suitcase. The portable kind with the handle that pulls up and the wheels that roll it along. Ellis watched her lips moving as she held a cell phone to her ear. But the rattle of the train on the tracks kept him from hearing her. No matter. He doubted that he would remember any of them tomorrow. And he hoped they wouldn't remember him.

The train pulled into the Clark and Lake station a little past two. Good, he said to himself. Still on schedule. Ellis had made a point, late the night before, to lay out a precise schedule. Knowing what you have to do is one thing. Knowing exactly how you're going to do it is another, he reflected. And precision leads to control. That's all you can really ask for, Ellis mused. Control. If you control the situation and things still go badly, well, that's just fate. But more often than not, they won't. Not if you're in control, and the other person isn't. And for the first time since he had taken this assignment, Ellis felt in control.

Exiting the train, he walked down the platform and up the stairs leading to the raised crosswalk that would take him to the opposite side of the tracks. He crossed the walkway and came back down. There he waited for the brown line that would take him to Sedgwick Station. It was a few stops from downtown. Not as busy in the middle of the afternoon as the ones in the heart of the loop. That's why he had chosen it. Five minutes later the brown line pulled in and he got on.

After Clark & Lake, there were only two stops before Sedgwick. Not much time to gather his thoughts. But he didn't need time now. He had been putting things together in his mind ever since he got off the phone with Fontana the night before. The funeral director called back just to make sure everything was okay with Tilton. He was in no mood to be forthcoming. But when Ellis threatened to go public with his and Tilton's association, Fontana's reply was the opening Ellis was looking for.

"Jesus Christ," the funeral director said, "you're the second person who's put the squeeze on me about Tilton in the last week or so. Do you people belong to some sort of blackmailer's association, or what?"

"I'm a freelancer," Ellis replied. "And it won't cost you much at all. Just the name of the individual who persuaded you to hand over any information you had about Monroe Greenburg."

"Believe it or not, I don't know the person's name. We never got that formal. I was told that if I'd just say who the last poor soul was that I gave to Tilton... I'd be left alone and left out of it. Then, out of the blue, you call. Look, I swear, I really didn't get a name."

"Well, this is your lucky day, Mr. Fontana. Because all I need is a description."

The recorded voice coming over the speaker system brought Ellis back to the present as it intoned, "This is Sedgwick. Doors open on the right at Sedgwick." He left the train and walked back toward the stairs that would take him down to the little cracker box station and onto the street. Heading down those stairs, he checked his watch. Ten minutes ahead of time.

At ground level, he went through the revolving gates and out onto the sidewalk. Sedgwick Station looked to be in one of those transitional neighborhoods. To his right, row houses, apartments, and storage facilities fronted the street. To his left, about twenty-five yards from where he was standing, North Avenue crossed. It was a busy thoroughfare with both commercial and residential buildings on either side. Foot traffic in front of the station was comparatively light. Now and then someone would walk by, but not very often in the seven or eight minutes he was waiting. Eventually, he saw a white taxi with red letters heading east to west on North Avenue. The red light stopped it at the corner of North and Sedgwick, and when it did, the cab's turn indicator came on.

Even though he couldn't make out the passenger in the back seat from where he was standing, something told Ellis that this was the one. When the light changed and the taxi turned onto Sedgwick, then pulled over to the curb directly in front of the station, Ellis's premonition was confirmed.

It took a second or two for the transaction to be completed between the passenger and the cabbie. Then the back door swung open and Fontana's description stepped out onto the curb. Red hair, big tits, foul mouth.

"Why meet at this shit hole?" Alison barked.

Ignoring her question, Ellis asked one of his own, "What did you tell Motif?"

"I told him I wanted to do some more shopping before I left. He took an earlier flight."

"Come on, let's go upstairs," Ellis said. They headed inside where Ellis used an extra train pass he had purchased to get Alison through the turnstiles. They didn't talk as they walked up the long flight of stairs. Coming out onto the platform Alison was breathing heavily.

"Jesus," she said, "I can't believe some people do this every fucking day."

The south side of the platform they were on was unoccupied. There were two people on the north side. One man was reading a paper. The other had his back turned to them. He was staring out at North Avenue and leaning against the pole that held up one side of the covered waiting area.

"Let's walk over here and talk," Ellis said, pointing to the far end of the platform, a good twenty yards down from the covered waiting area.

"Just a minute," Alison replied. "I'm no idiot, you know."

Then she walked up to Ellis, close enough for him to smell the perfume she had over-indulged in, as well as the liquor on her breath. She reached out and put her hand in the middle of Ellis's chest, between the open lapels of his suit coat. While she was feeling his front side with her right hand, she was using her left to reach around to the small of his back. Ellis had been checked for a wire before so he let her go through her routine without comment. Then they walked slowly toward the east end of the platform.

"Okay, pretty boy," Alison said, "you got my attention with that late phone call last night. Lucky for you, Motif had a little too much to drink and was dead to the world."

"No, I'd say that was lucky for you," Ellis cut in. "One less thing to have to explain, right?"

"Look, anytime someone calls me in the dead of night and tells me they're prepared to give me a load of shit with the company I work for, and the people I know, and maybe even the cops... well okay, I'll give a little listen to whatever it is you *think* you know. But don't be all fucking day about it."

"You really don't seem to have any remorse at all," Ellis said.

"And just what is it that you think I should be remorseful about?"

"Half a dozen people are dead because of you."

"You don't know what you're talking about. And for that matter, I don't know what you're talking about."

"Let me be really specific for you," Ellis began. "At Flashpoint in Houston, you killed the lights and let that bull out in the dark. Maybe you even got Motif to help you with that one. He was so drunk that it probably just sounded like a prank to him. Chances are he doesn't even remember it. But Morello, that's the name of the bullfighter, wound up dying from his wounds, and I had to dispatch the bull to keep him from carving up Tilton, which was what you were really after. The next night at Gloria Preston's party, you took advantage of Tompkins demonstration to try to run Tilton down. You know an opportunity when you see it, but that didn't work either."

Alison was just standing there, feet apart, arms crossed, listening quietly. She was staring into Ellis's eyes, saying nothing for the moment, wanting to hear everything he had to say.

"You saw an ally in Reverend Tompkins. Someone you could use to keep stoking the fires against Tilton's work. That's why you made contact with Frank Fontana. To try to get more info you could use or funnel to Tompkins. Tilton must have let his name slip once, or maybe he just indicated the part of town where he was getting what he needed. You took it from there. You threatened to expose Fontana. And once he gave you Greenburg's name, a journalist like you would know how to run the traps, check the records, find out all there was to find out about this anonymous individual. You must have been thrilled when you discovered he was a holocaust survivor. That made for a built-in cause celeb, didn't it?"

The redhead started to say, "What a crock of —"

But Ellis cut her off. "Don't bother to deny it. I talked to Fontana before I talked to you last night."

"So, that's your whole case, huh? The fact that I had a conversation with some fucking grave digger."

"No, that's about half of it. It gets worse from here. You knew Tilton was going to Cuba, so you checked all the news services and the minute you had anything on the symposium, you funneled it to Tompkins and told him who to contact at the newspaper here in Chicago. You figured the two of them together would definitely paint Tilton's work with a pretty nasty brush. And they started to, didn't they? But even that wasn't enough for you, was it? You decided to help things along by not just destroying Tilton and his work figuratively, but physically as well. You didn't come to Chicago for Benny's tribute, or to mix with the art crowd. You came here to try to finish what you started in Houston. You set that fire in the restroom. Then you turned the latch so it would lock behind you. When everyone's attention was glued on the smoking toilet, you tossed that Molotov cocktail into the bar and sent the whole place up. That led to three more deaths."

"Are you finished? Is that it?" Alison asked abrasively.

"No. That's not it," Ellis replied. "When Tilton walked away unharmed, and only some of his paintings were destroyed, you decided to get him and that wacky preacher together face to face. It doesn't take much to disguise a voice over the phone. A little change of accent... maybe a handkerchief over the speaker. You were hoping the Reverend would lose his cool. And he did. It just didn't turn out the way you hoped it would."

Another brown line train coming from downtown rounded the corner and clattered into the station on the tracks opposite them. The two men who had been waiting on that platform stepped on the train. Three people got off and headed down the stairs Ellis had taken earlier. Alison and Ellis were now alone — the only people on either platform.

Alison unfolded her arms and put her hands on her hips as she said, "Okay, you asked me to meet with you. I've met with you. I've listened to your conjecture, your speculation, and your bullshit. The way I see it, you have one guy in Houston who will say he gave me the name, Monroe Greenburg. As far as facts go, that's it. That's what you've got. The rest is fucking zero... the product of your over-active imagination."

"Why did you do it?" Ellis asked. "Why was Tilton or his work such a threat? You certainly never struck me as a holy roller type."

"Holy roller? Give me a break. I don't give a shit for religion or the people who propagate it. It's just another way to keep people ignorant and medicated."

"Was it jealousy? Was that it? Tilton was getting all the attention, and your boy wasn't. Tilton was getting asked to the dance too often? The Marfa gig. The Cuban trip. A one-man show in Chicago. That must have stung.

And every time Motif actually displayed with Tilton, it was Tilton's work that everybody talked about."

Alison's face started to get as red as her hair. "Tilton's fucking freak show can't hold a candle to Motif's work. Motif is a genius! A genius! His composition, his use of color, his ability to shock, to move, to transcend... it's inspirational. He's a God doing revolutionary work. Work that's going to change art as we know it. And I'm going to help him. Tilton's a fucking hack who's today's trend. He's a son-of-a-bitching *artist du jour* and he's in the fucking way. People can't see Motif's greatness when it's surrounded by Tilton's schlock."

Ellis decided to push a little harder. "Well, that's your opinion. But it didn't seem to be shared by the people who buy and sell art. Like Ernie Beeker and Wendell James."

"Fucking storekeepers," Alison ranted, starting to pace as she talked. "God-damned clerks who couldn't spot a real piece of art if they were locked in Picasso's closet. And what the hell do you know about art anyway? Why am I even talking to you?"

Ellis expected what he was hearing. But he was still having a hard time believing she was that cold. "Six people are gone. You're responsible for those deaths. That doesn't mean anything to you?"

Alison stopped pacing, wheeled back around to face Ellis, and said, "*If* I had anything to do with what you're talking about... and that's an *if* you sure as shit can't prove... no, it wouldn't mean anything to me. Not one of them is worth the sweat off Motif's balls. He's going to make the world sit up and take notice. He'll be bigger than anyone around today."

"Tilton's still around," Ellis said dryly. "He's not only around, he's selling paintings at fifty grand a clip. A little something he neglected to mention at dinner the other night."

Ellis expected her to erupt like Mount St. Helens. But she didn't. Instead, her eyes locked on his. She took a deep breath. And suddenly the gray day grew black.

A quarter of a mile away, a train, eastward bound, snaked around the corner. Ellis could see it headed toward the station. Alison had her back to it. When his eyes left the horizon and settled back on her, she had regained some degree of composure.

The redhead showed no visible signs of rage. She simply looked straight into Ellis's face and said, "You can't prove anything. If you could, we'd be having this conversation with the cops. You don't know anything. You don't know art. There's no way you can even begin to grasp the talent Motif has. The talent that's being overshadowed by Tilton and that little prissy wife of his. And you sure as hell don't know me. Believe me, Ellis, I am not someone you want to fuck with."

The train had finished rounding the curve. It was on the straightaway to Sedgwick Station.

"Let me tell you what I do know," Ellis said. I know six people are dead and you're the reason why. I know that means nothing to you. I know you don't intend to stop until anyone you see as Motif's competition is out of the way. I know you couldn't care less about the collateral damage you'll continue to cause. And I know that your judgment is terribly... one might even say... fatally... flawed."

The train was thirty yards away now, closing fast.

"Oh yeah," Alison barked, "just how so?"

"You've definitely misjudged what I'm prepared to do to stop you."

Their conversation then came to an abrupt conclusion. Precipitated by the bone-rattling clamor of the train blasting by. This was a purple line express. It barreled through Sedgwick Station without stopping.

Chapter 31

The bellman held the box in one hand while he pushed the button with his other. As the elevator doors closed he kept his eyes straight ahead. It wouldn't do to appear overly curious about the package he was delivering to five twenty seven. Other guests might see him and wonder if he was as curious about their deliveries as well. That wouldn't do. That wouldn't do at all. But he had never delivered a package from Cuba before. In fact, he had never delivered a package from anywhere that was as battered and bent as this one. It was a bit nerve wracking, really. The guests in five twenty seven might think that it was the hotel staff that had mangled the package so. He would be sure to explain that was certainly not the case. His captain had told him to be sure to explain that was definitely not the case. Unfortunately, the package arrived in its current state of dishevelment and all the innocent staff could do was deliver it as it was, and possibly incur the wrath of an angry guest. Or what if the opposite happened? What if the guest wasn't angry but disappointed at the unsightly state the package was in. What if it was something the guest had been waiting for, hoping for, longing for. Then it arrives in such a sorry state. Might not the guest break-down right there at the door. There could be tears, heartbreak. The guest could realize that this wonderful thing they had been waiting and praying for, must have surely arrived busted, or broken or damaged beyond all re-pair. If this were the case, one could expect a severe rebuke on the spot, a call of complaint to the hotel manager, an angry dressing down from an embarrassed supervisor, or horror of horrors, there might be no tip.

"Yes," Lela said, after opening the door.

"Here's the package that came for you, madam. I assure you this is the way it arrived at the hotel. The staff would never do anything to –"

"No, certainly. I understand. Thank you very much," Lela said, handing the bellman three folded dollar bills. She then closed the door and didn't see or hear the young man's sigh of relief.

"Tilton," Lela said loudly, wanting to make sure he'd hear her across the large suite and into the bathroom where he stood putting the cap back on the toothpaste. "Did you send me something from Cuba?"

Walking into the room as he spoke, Tilton said, "No I didn't send..." Then as his voice trailed off, his memory kicked in. "Oh, you know what? Ernie mentioned to me that he had sent something to the hotel, here, in your name. He wasn't sure when we were going to get here. I guess we got here a long time before the package did. Looks a bit worse for wear, doesn't it?"

"What do you think it is," Lela began. "Do you think it's something for his wife? With everything that's happened, I'd hate to give her something in this shoddy condition."

"Yeah, and it's kinda' heavy too," Tilton said, taking the package from Lela and shaking it a bit. "Sounds like there's sand or something in there. Whatever it is, I hope it's not broken."

"Yes, but if it's something he got for his wife, it might be really personal, I'm not sure we should open it."

"We can't give her something like this, Lela. It looks like it's been kicked, stomped, smashed, maybe even had something spilled on it. Plus, it's got your name on it. Let's just open it and then we can rewrap it and tell her that Ernie wanted her to have it."

"Okay," Lela said haltingly, "I'll get a wash cloth from the bathroom so we can clean up whatever might be inside."

Tilton sat down on the bed with the pummeled package in his lap. Rather than wait for his wife's return, he went ahead and began pulling what was left of the cardboard covering apart. Inside was another box, rectangular, but of a size and shape and weight that was very familiar to Tilton. Moving it back and forth in his hands, he heard the bumping of something inside the inner box as well. Tipping it on its side so that whatever he heard would be on top, he gingerly opened that corner, making sure not to tear the flaps so it could be re-closed. Looking inside he saw something sitting atop dusty, fine grains that he had come to know well. With two fingers he reached inside and pulled the object out slowly, being careful not to spill the contents that surrounded it. Holding it up in the glow of the bedside lamp, he turned it slowly to make sure he was seeing what he thought he was seeing. The glass itself wasn't what made him study it so. The short tumbler was like many Tilton and Ernie had held in Havana. What made this one worthy of examination was the perfect purple lipstick imprint on the side of the glass.

Walking back into the room, Lela asked, "So, what was inside? Was it something for his wife?"

Tilton answered, "No, it is definitely not for his wife."

"Well, what is it, then?"

"I think… it just might be my next painting."

Chapter 32

The warm San Diego night made the breeze especially welcome as Ellis cruised down Twelfth Avenue on the way to his apartment. Osgood, ever the wind aficionado, sat stoically as his jowls flapped triumphantly in the breeze. A friend at the kennel was used to letting Ellis pick up his pet after hours, especially when he had been out of town for a while and it was obvious to the sympathetic employee that the bulldog was more than ready to go home.

Turning off the street and pulling into the garage under his building, Ellis found a parking spot close to the elevator. "Date night," he said to Osgood, who seemed to grunt in reply. "We're in luck." Leaving the top down on the car, he walked around to the passenger side and let the mighty mutt exit the vehicle on his own. Ellis draped the leash around his own neck as they walked to the elevator. He knew his canine cohort would automatically amble along beside him.

Reaching his apartment door, Ellis opened it and Osgood obliviously trod over the bills, credit card offers, discount flyers, and other unsolicited solicitations that had been dropped through the mail slot while Ellis was gone. Spotting his lookout post in the window seat, the meaty one waddled over and settled in.

In no particular hurry to spend time sorting through junk mail, Ellis left the pile on the floor and walked over to the blinking red light on his answering machine. Pushing the button, he heard the recorded voice say, "You have four new messages. Message one."

There was a simple click. A telemarketer thwarted, Ellis said to himself.

"Message two."

Another click. Persistent fellow, Ellis thought.

"Message three."

"Hi Brig, this is Rebecca. Can't wait to see you. Call me when you get back."

He thought of the last time he had been with her, before he left for Chicago. Better get a good night's sleep first, he mused.

"Message Four."

"Brig, this is Lela. I'm so sorry to have to tell you this on your answering machine, but I wanted you to know. It's unbelievable, really. We just found out a little while ago that Alison was killed. She apparently fell or tripped at one of the train stations. They found one of her high heels stuck between the boards on the platform. It's awful, Brig. Just awful. I guess the only consolation is that the authorities said she definitely died instantly. I'm so glad that Tilton and I are leaving here and going back home. There's just been so much tragedy. But somehow, I get the feeling that it's over. It's finally over. And I believe Tilton and I are really starting a new chapter in our lives. A chapter that's going to lead to the best times ever. Of course, seeing you again was wonderful. I know I told you that before, but I really mean it. I just hope you feel the time you spent with us was worthwhile. Your presence was invaluable. I think you did more for us than you'll ever really know, Brig. We both appreciate it so. Again, I'm so sorry I had to inform you about Alison via this message machine. So, call me, will you? Call me when some time has passed and —"

A shrill sound came on. A sound indicating she had gone over the allotted message time. The recorded voice returned. "You have no more messages." Then it automatically clicked off.

Ellis turned away from the answering machine slowly. He walked over to the window seat, squatted, and ran his hand over Osgood's massive skull. Looking through the window and staring out at the darkness, he whispered to himself, *"You don't ask why. You don't abort the mission prematurely. You see it through to the end. You finish the job."*

BETRAYAL OF A REPUBLIC:
MEMOIRS OF A ROMAN MATRONA

RICHARD M. BANK
THE OAR OF ODYSSEUS

The lost diary of
ANNE FRANK

KENNETH KUENSTER
THE ANNUNCIATIONIST
A NOVEL

ASHBY JONES
THE CROSSING
"When love is trapped in the maelstrom between then and now, the crossing cannot be made"

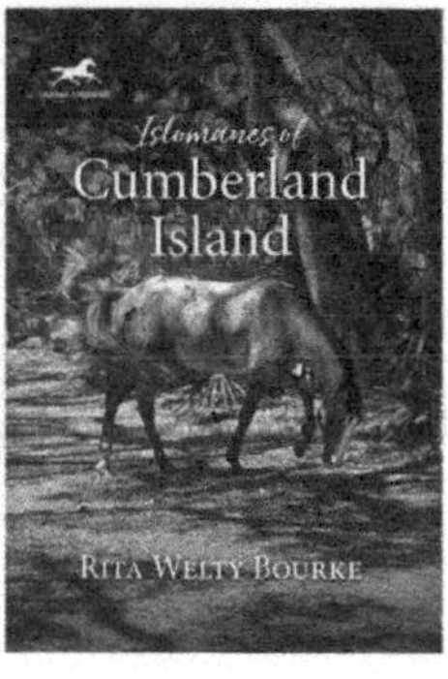
Islomanes of
Cumberland Island
RITA WELTY BOURKE